Finding Me

Judith Keim

BOOKS BY JUDITH KEIM

THE HARTWELL WOMEN SERIES:
The Talking Tree – 1
Sweet Talk – 2
Straight Talk – 3
Baby Talk – 4
The Hartwell Women – Boxed Set

THE BEACH HOUSE HOTEL SERIES:
Breakfast at The Beach House Hotel – 1
Lunch at The Beach House Hotel – 2
Dinner at The Beach House Hotel – 3
Christmas at The Beach House Hotel – 4
Margaritas at The Beach House Hotel – 5 (2021)
Dessert at The Beach House Hotel – 6 (2022)

THE FAT FRIDAYS GROUP:
Fat Fridays – 1
Sassy Saturdays – 2
Secret Sundays – 3

SALTY KEY INN BOOKS:
Finding Me – 1
Finding My Way – 2
Finding Love – 3
Finding Family – 4

CHANDLER HILL INN BOOKS:
Going Home – 1
Coming Home – 2
Home at Last – 3

PRAISE FOR JUDITH KEIM'S NOVELS

THE BEACH HOUSE HOTEL SERIES

"Love the characters in this series. This series was my first introduction to Judith Keim. She is now one of my favorites. Looking forward to reading more of her books."

BREAKFAST AT THE BEACH HOUSE HOTEL is an easy, delightful read that offers romance, family relationships, and strong women learning to be stronger. Real life situations filter through the pages. Enjoy!"

LUNCH AT THE BEACH HOUSE HOTEL – "This series is such a joy to read. You feel you are actually living with them. Can't wait to read the latest one."

DINNER AT THE BEACH HOUSE HOTEL – "A Terrific Read! As usual, Judith Keim did it again. Enjoyed immensely. Continue writing such pleasantly reading books for all of us readers."

CHRISTMAS AT THE BEACH HOUSE HOTEL – "Not Just Another Christmas Novel. This is book number four in the series and my introduction to Judith Keim's writing. I wasn't disappointed. The characters are dimensional and engaging. The plot is well crafted and advances at a pleasing pace. The Florida location is interesting and warming. It was a delight to read a romance novel with mature female protagonists. Ann and Rhoda have life experiences that enrich the story. It's a clever book about friends and extended family. Buy copies for your book group pals and enjoy this seasonal read."

THE HARTWELL WOMEN SERIES – Books 1 – 4

"This was an EXCELLENT series. When I discovered Judith Keim, I read all of her books back to back. I thoroughly enjoyed the women Keim has written about. They are believable and you want to just jump into their lives and be their friends! I can't wait for any upcoming books!"

"I fell into Judith Keim's Hartwell Women series and have read & enjoyed all of her books in every series. Each centers around a strong & interesting woman character and their family interaction. Good reads that leave you wanting more."

THE FAT FRIDAYS GROUP – Books 1 – 3

"Excellent story line for each character, and an insightful representation of situations which deal with some of the contemporary issues women are faced with today."

"I love this author's books. Her characters and their lives are realistic. The power of women's friendships is a common and beautiful theme that is threaded throughout this story."

THE SALTY KEY INN SERIES

<u>FINDING ME</u> – *"I thoroughly enjoyed the first book in this series and cannot wait for the others! The characters are endearing with the same struggles we all encounter. The setting makes me feel like I am a guest at The Salty Key Inn...relaxed, happy & light-hearted! The men are yummy and the women strong. You can't get better than that! Happy Reading!"*

<u>FINDING MY WAY</u>- *"Loved the family dynamics as well as uncertain emotions of dating and falling in love.*

Appreciated the morals and strength of parenting throughout. Just couldn't put this book down."

FINDING LOVE – "I waited for this book because the first two was such good reads. This one didn't disappoint.... Judith Keim always puts substance into her books. This book was no different, I learned about PTSD, accepting oneself, there is always going to be problems but stick it out and make it work. Just the way life is. In some ways a lot like my life. Judith is right, it needs another book and I will definitely be reading it. Hope you choose to read this series, you will get so much out of it."

FINDING FAMILY – "Completing this series is like eating the last chip. Love Judith's writing, and her female characters are always smart, strong, vulnerable to life and love experiences."

"This was a refreshing book. Bringing the heart and soul of the family to us."

CHANDLER HILL INN SERIES

GOING HOME – "I absolutely could not put this book down. Started at night and read late into the middle of the night. As a child of the '60s, the Vietnam war was front and center so this resonated with me. All the characters in the book were so well developed that the reader felt like they were friends of the family."

"I was completely immersed in this book, with the beautiful descriptive writing, and the authors' way of bringing her characters to life. I felt like I was right inside her story."

COMING HOME – "*Coming Home is a winner. The characters are well-developed, nuanced and likable. Enjoyed the vineyard setting, learning about wine growing and seeing the challenges Cami faces in running and growing a business. I look forward to the next book in this series!*"

"*Coming Home was such a wonderful story. The author has a gift for getting the reader right to the heart of things.*"

HOME AT LAST – "*In this wonderful conclusion, to a heartfelt and emotional trilogy set in Oregon's stunning wine country, Judith Keim has tied up the Chandler Hill series with the perfect bow.*"

"*Overall, this is truly a wonderful addition to the Chandler Hill Inn series. Judith Keim definitely knows how to perfectly weave together a beautiful and heartfelt story.*"

"*The storyline has some beautiful scenes along with family drama. Judith Keim has created characters with interactions that are believable and some of the subjects the story deals with are poignant.*"

SEASHELL COTTAGE BOOKS

A CHRISTMAS STAR – "*Love, laughter, sadness, great food, and hope for the future, all in one book. It doesn't get any better than this stunning read.*"

"*A Christmas Star is a heartwarming Christmas story featuring endearing characters. So many Christmas books are set in snowbound places...it was a nice change to read a Christmas story that takes place on a warm sandy beach!*" Susan Peterson

CHANGE OF HEART – "*CHANGE OF HEART is the summer read we've all been waiting for. Judith Keim is a master at creating fascinating characters that are simply irresistible. Her stories leave you with a big smile on your face and a heart bursting with love.*"

~Kellie Coates Gilbert, author of the popular Sun Valley Series

A SUMMER OF SURPRISES – "*The story is filled with a roller coaster of emotions and self-discovery. Finding love again and rebuilding family relationships.*"

"*Ms. Keim uses this book as an amazing platform to show that with hard emotional work, belief in yourself and love, the scars of abuse can be conquered. It in no way preaches, it's a lovely story with a happy ending.*"

"*The character development was excellent. I felt I knew these people my whole life. The story development was very well thought out I was drawn [in] from the beginning.*"

DESERT SAGE INN BOOKS

THE DESERT FLOWERS – ROSE – "*The Desert Flowers - Rose, is the first book in the new series by Judith Keim. I always look forward to new books by Judith Keim, and this one is definitely a wonderful way to begin The Desert Sage Inn Series!*"

"*In this first of a series, we see each woman come into her own and view new beginnings even as they must take this tearful journey as they slowly lose a dear friend. This is a very well written book with well-developed and likable main characters. It was interesting and enlightening as the first portion of this saga unfolded. I very much enjoyed this book and I do recommend it"*

"Judith Keim is one of those authors that you can always depend on to give you a great story with fantastic characters. I'm excited to know that she is writing a new series and after reading book 1 in the series, I can't wait to read the rest of the books."!

Finding Me

A Salty Key Inn Book - 1

Judith Keim

Wild Quail Publishing

Finding Me is a work of fiction. Names, characters, places, public or private institutions, corporations, towns, and incidents are the product of the author's imagination or are used fictitiously. Any resemblance to actual events, locales, or persons, living or dead, is coincidental.

No part of this book may be reproduced or transmitted in any form or by any electronic or mechanical means including information storage and retrieval systems without permission in writing from the author, except by a reviewer who may quote brief passages in a review. This book may not be resold or uploaded for distribution to others. For permissions contact the author directly via electronic mail:

wildquail.pub@gmail.com

www.judithkeim.com,

Published in the United States of America by:

Wild Quail Publishing
PO Box 171332
Boise, ID 83717-1332

ISBN# 978-0-9981950-8-7

Dedication

For all my writing friends, whose support I treasure.

CHAPTER ONE
SHEENA

In early January, Sheena Morelli sat with her two sisters in a conference room of the Boston office of Lowell, Peabody and Wilson, a well-respected law firm, wondering why they'd been ordered to meet to discuss a legal matter with Archibald Wilson himself.

"Do either of you have any idea why we're really here?" said her youngest sister, Regan. "The letter from Mr. Wilson said something about a reading of a will. But that doesn't make sense to me. I didn't even know Gavin Sullivan."

"Me, neither. He's probably some rich uncle leaving us a lot of money," teased Darcy, the typical middle sister, who was always kidding around.

Sheena laughed with her. The three Sullivan sisters had no rich relatives that they knew of in their modest family. They were hard workers who relied on only themselves to make it through life. *Well,* thought Sheena, *maybe Regan wasn't as reliable as she and Darcy.* As the baby of the family, Regan had always been a bit spoiled. At twenty-two and eager to escape her old life in Boston, Regan wasn't about to spend too much time with the family. This time, though, at the formal request of Mr. Wilson, Regan had dutifully left New York City to come to "Bean Town."

As Sheena waited in the conference room for Mr. Wilson to show up, she studied Regan out of the corner of her eye. With her long, black hair, big, violet-blue eyes, and delicate Sullivan features, she was a knockout—a Liz Taylor look-alike.

Darcy sat on the other side of Sheena in a stiff-backed chair. Studying Darcy's blue eyes, red hair, and freckled nose, Sheena thought of her as cute...and funny...and maybe a little annoying, though everyone seemed to love Darcy's sassy attitude. At twenty-six, Darcy claimed she hadn't found her true calling. Whatever that meant.

Sheena had found her calling in a hurry when she got pregnant as she was starting college, where she'd planned to take nursing courses. Ironic as it was, her wanting to become a nurse and getting caught like that, had changed many things for her. Now, at thirty-six and with a sixteen-year-old son and a fourteen-year-old daughter, she still hadn't recovered from losing her dream.

She straightened in her chair as a tall, gray-haired man entered the room carrying a file of papers.

"Good morning, ladies. I'm Archibald Wilson, the lawyer representing Gavin Sullivan. I'm pleased you all could attend this reading of his will," he announced in a bass voice. He looked the three of them over critically. "Which one of you is Sheena Sullivan Morelli?"

She raised her hand. "I'm Sheena. Do you mean the 'Big G' Sullivan?"

Both of her sisters gasped at her. The name "Big G Sullivan" had been mentioned in the family on rare occasions, and only when her father and his two other brothers had had too many beers. And then it was never kindly.

Mr. Wilson nodded with satisfaction. "Yes, that's my client. Sheena, though all three of you are beneficiaries, I will address you on most of the issues, as it pertains to the specific language of the will."

Sheena sat back in her chair, her mind spinning. This scene seemed so surreal. Their father had broken his relationship with this brother years ago.

"He's left something for us?" said Darcy. "I was only teasing about such a thing."

The lawyer frowned at her, took a seat facing them on the other side of the small conference table, and opened the file he had carried in.

He began to speak: "I, Gavin R. Sullivan, of the State of Florida, being of sound and disposing mind and memory, do make, publish, and declare this to be my Last Will and Testament..."

Certain words faded in and out of Sheena's shocked state of mind. Though her sisters might have been too young to remember him, she had a clear image of the big, jovial man who'd captivated her with his smile, his belly laughs, and the way her father grew quiet when they were in the same room together. On one particular visit, Uncle Gavin gave her a stuffed monkey that she'd kept on her bed for years. It wasn't until the fur on the monkey was worn off that she'd noticed a seam was tearing. One day, while she was probing the hole, a gold coin fell out.

Sheena showed the coin to her mother, who snatched it away and whispered, "Don't tell anyone about this. It's very valuable. Someday you'll need it. Until then, I'll keep it safe for you. Uncle Gavin loves you very much." As her father walked through the doorway, her mother held a finger to her lips.

Until now, Sheena had forgotten all about the coin.

Archibald Wilson's voice brought her back to the present. "Sheena, you, Darcy, and Regan are now the legal owners of the Salty Key Inn, but you, Sheena, will be in charge of taking over the small hotel in Florida, as your uncle directed in his will. Is that understood by the three of you?"

Sheena and her sisters dutifully bobbed their heads. The

bewilderment on her sisters' faces matched her own feelings. How on earth were the three of them going to run a hotel?

"Remember," Mr. Wilson warned them, "the hotel may not be sold for a period of one year. And the three of you must live there together for that entire time if you are to have a share in the rest of his sizeable estate, which will remain undisclosed until the end of your year in Florida. You have just two weeks to prepare. In conversations I had with him in setting up the will, I believe Gavin Sullivan intended for this to be a life lesson for each of you."

"Whoa! Wait a minute! What about the lease on the condo I share with two of my friends? I can't just walk away from that," said Darcy.

"And mine?" said Regan.

The lawyer nodded. "Read over the conditions of the will. Any expenses like that will be taken care of by Gavin's estate. All expenses as you settle in will be handled through me. But, beware, there will be hidden tests for you throughout this entire process. Tests that could make a lot of difference to each of you."

Sheena exchanged worried glances with her sisters. She wished she'd asked their mother for more information about the uncle she was never to mention. And now it was too late. Their mother had died a little over a year ago.

"Live together in Florida for a whole year? Was Uncle Gavin crazy when he set up this deal?" exclaimed Darcy. Her indignation was understandable.

Mr. Wilson stood. "I realize you all have a lot to talk about, a lot to think about. And let me know if you need any further clarification of the terms of the will. You are welcome to continue using this conference room, and please feel free to help yourself to any of the refreshments on the side table." His lips curved with a touch of humor in what had been a mostly expressionless face. "Enjoy the challenge."

After Mr. Wilson left them, Sheena sank back into her chair. Her mind raced at the thought of suddenly leaving Boston to go live with her sisters in Florida for an entire year. How could she do that? It would be difficult for her on many levels. They were sisters, after all, and like sisters everywhere, being together for too long sometimes caused battles to erupt. More than that, she had a family. And her husband, Tony, wouldn't like the idea at all. Her children even less.

"What a joke," said Darcy, shaking her head. "Spending every day with the two of you for an entire year? Running a hotel? No way. And, Sheena, Tony would never allow you to do something like this. You're what he calls 'the Mrs'. And what about the kids?"

At Darcy's dismissive tone of voice, Sheena glared at her. "What did you mean by that 'Mrs.' remark?"

"Don't take it the wrong way," urged Regan. "It's just that your family depends on you for everything. Especially Tony."

Deep in thought, Sheena remained quiet. Tony was a good man who prided himself on always doing the right thing. And he expected her to fulfill what he thought was her proper role.

Though their relationship was still new when she got pregnant, Tony had stepped right up and offered to marry her so all her mother's conservative church friends wouldn't count on their fingers how many days it took for their first baby to appear. It helped that their son, Michael Morelli, had started his life in the outside world a little late. Still, Sheena had always appreciated Tony's consideration.

A worried sigh escaped her. She knew Tony wouldn't support her being away from their family for an entire year. That would be going against his idea of her in the proper role of taking care of their family. And yet, with his business doing poorly recently, it might be an answer to their prayers, though

Tony's fragile ego might prevent her from saying so.

"What about you two?" Sheena asked. "You'll have to quit your jobs. What then?"

Regan shrugged. "I don't care. My job is boring—answering phone calls, greeting people and all. They'll just find another receptionist to take my place."

Darcy shook her head. "Receptionist? You were much more than that. More like some kind of hostess with all those special meetings you helped them with. When I visited you in New York, I witnessed how it was—all those guys drooling over you as you served them drinks before they went out to some business dinner."

A blush crept up Regan's cheeks. Her eyes flashed a pretty violet-blue as she stared Darcy down. "It's a decent job, respectable and safe. Those guys can look all they want, but they keep their hands off me. That's the way I set it up, working for this company. Besides they're all old, married men. Why would I want anything to do with men like that?"

"What about you, Darcy?" Sheena asked. "You've got a very good job working in IT."

Darcy grimaced. "Actually, I don't like it very much. Working with numbers and codes all day isn't that exciting. Mom was always so proud of me and my job that I didn't dare tell her I wasn't happy there. But, with her gone, I've been thinking of doing something else." She smiled. "Maybe this whole thing isn't dumb after all. Maybe this will be the beginning of something new for all of us."

Sheena returned her smile. Put this way, it sounded wonderful. If, only ...

Following lunch with her sisters, Sheena took the Red Line on the T to return to Davis Square in Somerville, where Tony, she, and the kids shared a duplex with his parents. When they'd moved into the house as newlyweds, she and Tony had thought they'd live there just long enough to save for a small place of their own. But Rosa and Paul, Tony's parents, were so pleased with the idea of the families living side-by-side that Tony agreed it was best for them to stay there, where everyone was available to help each other out. And with two young babies to take care of, Sheena had thought it was a good idea. Later, after Tony set up his own plumbing business, they decided to keep on renting their unit while they tried to build his business. It was very convenient not to have to worry about a mortgage payment and taxes.

It turned out to be a good decision. A lot of the houses the same size in their neighborhood were now selling in the high six figures—something they couldn't afford. And with Tony being a plumber, they'd added a couple of bathrooms to the building, which made the house even more valuable in this close suburb of Boston. Studying it now, Sheena supposed she was stuck there until the children were grown and gone and Tony's parents gave up the house.

As Sheena walked up to her front door, Sheena's mother-in-law opened the front door on her side to greet her. "Everything all right? You were standing outside looking at the house for a long time."

Sheena smiled. "How are you, Rosa?" If she had just one word to describe Rosa it would be warmth. Short and on the well-fed side, Rosa exuded maternal, protective feelings.

"Fine, fine. Just worried about you," Rosa answered. Her dark eyes were filled with concern.

"No need to," Sheena said cheerfully, though she sometimes felt trapped by the idea that she couldn't do much of anything without her mother-in-law knowing. But she'd never tell that to anyone. Rosa had been sweet to her from the

Judith Keim

time they first met. And when Sheena had produced not one, but two grandchildren to dote on, Rosa became even more of a supporter of hers.

When Sheena walked into the house, Meaghan jumped up from the couch in the living room. "Where were you, Mom? You said you'd go shopping with me for a dress for the Valentine's Dance at school." She narrowed her hazel eyes. "Remember?"

"I had an appointment downtown and was delayed. Honestly, Meaghan, you'd think I was hours late, not just twenty minutes behind schedule."

"I know, but Josie and Lauren have already picked out their dresses. There will be nothing good left for me if we don't get busy." A pout that was becoming familiar spread across her face.

Sheena sighed. "The dance isn't for another five weeks." Her stomach clenched when she remembered she wouldn't be around for the dance. Not if she was in Florida. Two weeks and she'd be gone. Meaghan had been looking forward to this dance all school year—especially after Tommy Whitehouse had invited her to it.

"Well? Are you ready now?" Meaghan said in a demanding tone Sheena found irritating.

Sheena frowned. *When had Meaghan become such a brat?* she thought and immediately felt bad about viewing her teenage daughter this way. She tried to keep things smooth between them.

"Give me a minute to get out of these good clothes and I'll be ready to go," Sheena said and hurried into her bedroom to change. She wanted to be comfortable. Shopping with Meaghan could take hours.

Sheena was emerging from her bedroom when Michael came into the house. "Hey, Mom! I need you to wash my

8

uniform. It has to be ready tomorrow morning. Can I borrow the car? I have to go to B-ball practice."

"Put the uniform in the laundry room and, no, you can't have the car. Meaghan and I are going shopping. Hurry and get ready. I'll drop you off."

"Mom!" wailed Meaghan. "We need to go now!"

Sheena drew a calming breath. "Michael, hurry up. We can't wait forever."

"Geez. Give a guy a break!" he said. "I just got home. Did you get those cookies I wanted?" A taller version of Tony, with his dark eyes and dark, curly hair, his voice even sounded the same.

Exasperated, Sheena shook her head. "No, I haven't had time to go to the grocery store. I've been busy."

Michael rolled his eyes at her.

"Don't go there," Sheena said, a little sharper than she'd intended.

He blinked in surprise. "Gawd! Why is everyone uptight?"

A tense few minutes later, the three of them piled into Sheena's Ford Explorer.

After dropping Michael off at his basketball practice, she and Meaghan headed out to the Natick Mall.

As Sheena drove, she glanced at her daughter. Her fair skin, auburn hair, and Sullivan features had mixed with Tony's darker tones and features to produce a lovely-looking young girl. Though pleased with her daughter's appearance, Sheena was becoming more and more distressed by Meaghan's feeling of entitlement. Tony worked hard, and they lived well, but this idea that everything was all about Meaghan was beginning to wear thin on her.

"Let's see if we can pick up something on sale," Sheena said. "You got a lot of nice clothes at Christmas."

Meaghan's lips thinned. "Mom, this dance is important. I

don't want everyone to think we're poor."

"Meaghan, buying something on sale doesn't mean you're poor," Sheena said evenly. "It means you're being careful with your money. And, in your case, you don't have any money to speak of. You haven't babysat for months."

"How can I babysit if I'm studying for good grades? And if Tommy calls, I want to be available."

"I have no complaints about your grades. You're doing well. But for extra money, you could babysit on the weekends from time to time. Just saying."

Meaghan let out a long sigh. "I don't need to work. Dad's doing okay."

"We'll talk about this another time," Sheena said, telling herself to let Meaghan's attitude go. "Let's just have fun. Okay?"

Meaghan smiled and nodded.

Shopping with Meaghan was fun until Meaghan found the perfect dress—for four hundred dollars. When Sheena told her no, a ferocious creature emerged from the body that used to be her sweet daughter. Meaghan begged and pleaded and threatened her for the dress, but Sheena remained firm.

Tearful and angry, Meaghan followed Sheena out of the mall, stomping her feet like a two-year-old.

Sheena had planned to surprise Meaghan with dinner, but that idea was ruined by Meaghan's behavior. Sheena got behind the wheel of the car and waited for Meaghan to get in and buckle her seatbelt.

Meaghan sulked in her seat, mumbling under her breath when she wasn't staring sullenly out the window. Then, when Sheena continued to ignore her, Meaghan muttered, "I hate you, Mom."

Hurt by her words, Sheena gripped the steering wheel of the car even harder and stared straight ahead. She wasn't about to get caught up in another fight with her daughter. Especially after the day she'd already had.

"Mom? I'm sorry I said that," Meaghan said in a soft voice. "I didn't really mean it."

"Thank you for the apology," Sheena said. "Let's put this shopping day behind us. We'll try again tomorrow."

"Okay. Maybe we can find a dress on sale just like the one I wanted."

Sheena doubted it, but she'd give it a try.

When Sheena walked into the house, Tony looked up at her from the couch where he was watching the news on television. "Where you been?" The dark eyes that had drawn her in from the beginning focused on her.

"Shopping with your daughter," Sheena said. "Did you put the casserole I left for you in the oven like I asked in my note?"

"Yeah. Earlier, Mom knew I was here alone and invited me for dinner, but I told her I'd wait for you." He grinned, lighting his strong features, exposing the small dimples he hated but she loved.

Sheena couldn't help smiling. "Let me get the table set, and then I'll sit with you for a few minutes. Did Michael get a ride from practice?"

"Yeah. He called me, and I went and got him."

"Good," Sheena said. "There's something I need to talk over with you later after the kids have left us alone."

Tony's eyebrows lifted. "Serious stuff?"

"Yes, and very surprising." She turned to go. "Want another beer? I'm going to have a glass of wine. It's been quite a day."

Tony rose and followed her into the kitchen. "You okay, hon?"

Sheena turned to him, too full of turmoil to know how to answer him.

He drew her into his arms. "It can't be that bad, can it?" He rubbed her back in comforting circles.

Sheena rested her head against his broad chest, grateful for his comfort. "It'll be all right. It's got to be." Earning a sizeable sum from Uncle Gavin's estate would help ease the worry of being able to give their children a good education. Tony's attempt to succeed in business was a struggle from time to time.

They'd no sooner sat down to dinner than Tony got an emergency call. He grabbed a few bites of the chicken casserole she'd made, and left.

Sheena hid a groan. So much for telling Tony she was leaving him for a year.

CHAPTER TWO
DARCY

Darcy propped her elbows on top of the marble bar at Clancy's, a bistro close to her condo in Jamaica Plain, still trying to wrap her head around the afternoon's surprising news.

"What do you think about all this stuff with Uncle Gavin's will?" Darcy asked her sister Regan. "It sounds like something out of a bad novel to me. It makes me wonder if Uncle Gavin lost his mind at the end of his life. I don't know much about the guy except he and Dad never got along."

Regan shrugged at her and took another sip of her white wine. "It's weird, this whole challenge of his, but I think it could be great for all of us. Like I told Sheena earlier, I don't care about quitting my job, and you have to admit, it's sort of glamorous to think the three of us now own a hotel."

"Good heavens! We don't even know what it looks like," said Darcy. "When we get to my place, let's look it up online. My search on my phone found nothing."

"The Salty Key Inn sounds classy to me. Where is Salty Key anyway?"

"I've never heard of it," said Darcy, "but then, I've stayed on vacation in Florida only once, and that was in South Beach. My girlfriends and I like to take our winter vacations in Mexico or in the Caribbean."

Regan sighed. "That sounds thrilling. Living in New York City, I can't afford to go anywhere. I can barely afford my share of the apartment I live in."

"Why have you stayed in the city?" asked Darcy. "It sounds pretty dull to me if you can't do anything."

"I thought living there would be glamorous and that I'd meet someone special. But it hasn't happened. Good jobs are hard to find, and the guys I've dated are real jerks interested in only one thing."

Darcy nodded. "Yeah, it's hard to meet good guys. I thought Sean Roberts and I were going to get engaged, but his family objected to our dating. They never liked me coming from Dorchester. Not really. And I sure as hell didn't like them and their snobby ways."

"I guess it's a good thing Sheena's in-laws really love her," Regan said.

"What's not to love? I swear Sheena never does anything to upset anyone. It'll be interesting to find out if she's going to go through with this deal in Florida or not."

Regan gasped. "What if she isn't allowed to go? What will that mean for us?"

"It means I'll go whup Tony's ass," said Darcy, grinning. "Seriously, do you think anyone would give up an inheritance like this? Even Tony will see that Sheena has no choice but to do it."

"Let's finish up here and go back to your condo. I want to see what the Salty Key Inn looks like." Regan sipped the last of her wine and stood.

Hold on," said Darcy. "Let me finish my drink and pay, and then we'll be on our way."

As soon as Darcy and Regan entered the condo, Darcy went into her bedroom and switched on her computer.

Regan followed her into the room and sat on the bed while

Darcy began her search. "There's nothing listed under the Salty Key Inn. I wonder why?"

"Hold on. I'll get the paperwork from the lawyer," said Regan. She withdrew a sheaf of papers from her large, fake Coach bag and handed them to her. "What does it say in there?"

Darcy looked through the paperwork. "Hmmm. The hotel is located at Sunset Beach, north of Indian Rocks Beach just west of St. Petersburg."

Regan turned to her with a worried expression. "Do you think this is some kind of joke? Maybe Uncle Gavin really was as looney as you think."

"We'll have to wait and see. Once we make the decision to do this, Mr. Wilson will give us more information than the broad outline of what Uncle Gavin wanted us to do." At the uneasiness she felt, a shiver crossed Darcy's shoulders. This whole thing was very strange, but she wasn't about to give up the chance for a new adventure. It was time for a change, anyway.

Truth be told, she hated her job. She was and had always been good with numbers, but what she really wanted to do was to write the world's best novel. She'd started one more than once, but each time she got past the first two chapters she became stuck. It was one thing to have ideas; it was another to have them all make sense with well-written words.

At the sound of a commotion at the front door of the condo, Darcy rose from the chair at her desk and walked into the living room just as her two roommates entered.

"Hey, you're here!" said Alex. "I thought you might have been arrested after that weird letter from the lawyer."

Nicole smiled at her. "Seriously, are you okay?"

Darcy's lips curved. "You won't believe it! My sisters and I now own a hotel. My Uncle Gavin left it to us."

Regan stepped up beside Darcy and stood quietly.

"You remember my baby sister, Regan, don't you?" Darcy asked her roommates. "She, my older sister, Sheena, and I will be moving to Florida within two weeks. It's all part of the deal."

Alex frowned. "What about your share of the rent?"

"I'll try to sub-lease the space," Darcy said. "Know of anybody who might be interested?"

"Actually, I do," said Nicole. "An old classmate of mine is moving back to Boston in June. I was just talking to her. She's here for the weekend. As a matter of fact, I was going to ask you if we could make room for her here. But, if she's willing and able to simply take your place, it'll be perfect."

Darcy shook her head. "June? But that's four months away. I don't want to continue paying my share of the rent for that long if I can help it."

"I thought you said you were owners of a hotel. Surely, you can handle that cost," Alex said slyly. "Unless you're lying to us about the hotel. Which hotel is it?"

Darcy bristled at Alex's derisive tone. Regan placed a hand on Darcy's shoulder and said in an undertone, "The lease arrangements are all part of the deal. Remember?"

Darcy brightened. "If your friend wants to move in sometime in June, Nicole, it's fine with me. My share of the rent from now to then will be taken care of by the lawyer. And, Alex, the Salty Key Inn is on the Gulf Coast of Florida."

Alex made a face. "Never heard of the Salty Key Inn, but then, my family's winter home is in Palm Beach."

Darcy rolled her eyes. Alex was such a snob.

Nicole came over to Darcy and gave her a hug. "I'm happy for you. What exciting news!"

"Thanks. I'll tell you all about it when I find out more." Darcy hugged Nicole back. Nicole's warm friendship was the reason she'd agreed to share the three-bedroom condo with her. Alex, on the other hand, was someone she was forced to tolerate.

As Darcy and Regan headed into the kitchen, questions circled in Darcy's head. Why wasn't the hotel on the internet? How could she close down everything in Boston within two weeks in order to make the move to Florida? What kind of life lessons did Uncle Gavin intend for them to face? And why, oh why, did she have to live with her sisters for an entire year?

Darcy still resented the fact that Sheena, who'd been like a mother to her, had abruptly left their house at eighteen to marry Tony. That left Darcy, at just nine years of age, to take care of Regan when their mother was too sick to do it herself. It might seem irrational to others, but Darcy had always felt abandoned by her older sister. And dealing with Regan hadn't been easy. She'd been a whiny, spoiled kid who wanted her mother.

Darcy drew a worried breath. Having to live with her sisters for any length of time was downright scary.

CHAPTER THREE
REGAN

Regan twisted and turned, trying to get comfortable on the pull-out couch in the living room of Darcy's condo. She was both excited and worried about all the changes about to take place in her life. The thought of becoming a new, different person was intriguing. All her life she'd been trapped in the role of beautiful but dumb baby sister. Maybe with the three of them away from their normal routines and in a different setting she could emerge as the person she'd always wanted to be. The person without learning issues. An artist of some kind. The thought was intoxicating.

"Regan, wake up!"

Regan opened her eyes and stared at Darcy blearily. "What do you want? What time is it? Go away."

"Come on, Sleeping Beauty. We've got a lot to do before I take you to the airport to go back to the city."

Regan sat up and yawned. How many hours had she been asleep? She checked her watch. Not many.

"I'm going to meet with Nicole's friend this afternoon about subletting my room," said Darcy. "But, first, I need to find a place to store some of my things."

Regan frowned. "Don't ask Dad. He and that girlfriend of his are planning on selling the house and moving out west to her daughter's town."

"Yeah, I know. I'd be afraid to leave anything with them. How about Sheena's place? She has some room."

Regan nodded. "You could try it. Maybe she'd take some of my things too. I have mostly clothes that aren't suitable for Florida. I thought I'd sell them on craigslist."

Darcy shook her head. "Some of my things are too expensive. I could never..." She stopped and smiled. "I keep forgetting we're rich now. Never mind, I'll sell what I don't need or else I'll give it away."

Regan couldn't restrain herself. She grabbed hold of Darcy's hand and whirled her around. "We're rich! We're rich!"

"Hey, what's going on?" asked Alex, standing in the doorway of her bedroom. "Do you know what time it is?"

"Time for me to move on with my life!" Regan said gleefully, grinning saucily at the girl who'd always given Darcy a bad time about coming from such a modest family.

Alex frowned. "Well, do your silly dancing after ten o'clock. On Saturdays, we sleep in." She went back into her bedroom, slamming the door behind her.

As Darcy lifted her middle finger, Regan and Darcy looked at each other and laughed.

"It's going to be great to move on out of here," said Darcy. "Let's call Sheena."

Regan followed Darcy into her sister's bedroom, eager to learn how Sheena had managed to break the news to her family. Like it or not, Sheena was the key to their success. If Sheena didn't agree to come to Florida, it was over!

CHAPTER FOUR
SHEENA

Sheena was sitting at the kitchen table sipping her second cup of coffee when her cell rang. She checked caller ID. *Darcy*. With a sigh, she clicked onto the call.

"How'd Tony take the news?" Darcy asked without preamble.

"I haven't told him yet," said Sheena with genuine regret. "He came home from a plumbing emergency too late last night and too tired for me to bring it up. And when I planned to tell him this morning, Michael interrupted us, reminding me he needed a clean uniform. And then before I could get him off to his game, another call came in for Tony, a different emergency on a big housing project job they were bidding on. A project that is crucial to the business."

"You've got to tell him right away!" Darcy exploded. "Don't screw this up for us. We have to go ahead with plans for moving. Regan and I are putting everything we won't need up for sale."

"Aren't you going at this a little fast?" said Sheena, unable to hold back a sigh. Darcy could be impulsive. Even as a little girl she'd gleefully head for trouble before thinking about it.

"Regan and I have two-week notices to hand in and other things to take care of. Are you planning to simply walk away from your family?" said Darcy.

Sheena drew a calming breath. "Of course not. I'm just waiting for the right time to tell Tony. In the meantime, I'm trying to put together a list of things that need to be settled before I leave." She felt a sweat break across her brow. No one in her family was going to be supportive. Why would they? Sheena sometimes felt as if she was a slave to them and their constant demands.

"I'm sorry I snapped at you," Darcy said with a note of genuine apology. "It's just that this whole thing is going to take a lot of coordination. And we don't even have a picture of the place. I'll do more research on it and check out the areas around there hoping to get a better idea of what we're in for. But February is a perfect time to make this change. It should be nice in Florida."

"Go ahead with your plans. I'll let you know what my schedule is after I settle things here," said Sheena. "How's Regan doing with all this?"

"She's as excited as I am. Here. I'll give her the phone. You can talk to her yourself."

As the phone was being handed over, Sheena waited anxiously. Of her two sisters, Regan was the one who seemed to drift along without a whole lot of planning. She'd always relied on others in the family to do that for her.

"Hi, Sheena!" Regan said to her. "You're not going to back out of this arrangement, are you?"

"Not at all. I simply haven't had the right moment to talk to Tony about it. He's been really busy. Don't worry. I'll keep in touch. Are you going to be able to take care of making all the necessary arrangements for yourself?"

"Yeah, I don't think it will be a problem—my leaving the apartment. It was pretty crowded. And like Darcy said, I'm not going to even bother to find a place to store my things. I'm going to sell what I don't need. We don't want to store anything with Dad and that woman."

"That woman? Do you mean Regina O'Brien?" Sheena

shook her head. Neither Darcy nor Regan had been happy with the idea that their father was already living with another woman. They didn't understand how lonely he was without their mother. Sheena was pleased that someone else was able and willing to look after him. He could be a handful. Especially after he'd had a couple of beers.

"Whatever," said Regan. "Mom would be shocked if she knew how fast Dad found someone else to take her place. And now they're telling us they're moving out west, away from us, as if we didn't matter."

"Actually, if you think about it, we're about to move away from them. Are you going to have time to see Dad on this trip? I'm sure he'd like it."

"I can't. I've got a flight at eleven. I'll call him later. I promise."

Sheena sighed. Knowing her sisters, they'd leave it up to her to talk to their father about the changes in their lives. It wouldn't be an easy conversation. Their father and Gavin might have been brothers, but they'd always fought bitter battles.

Sheena said goodbye and turned as Meaghan walked into the kitchen.

"I'm ready to go shopping. You promised we'd get my dress today. Right?" The look Meaghan gave Sheena made it plain there would be no negotiation.

"Okay, Michael has the car. We'll take the T into downtown."

"But, Mom ..."

Sheena held up a hand to stop her. "It's that or nothing."

Meaghan grumbled to herself and left the room, smart enough this time not to give her any sass.

Sheena finished a piece of toast she'd been nibbling on and rose. Moving to Florida was looking better and better.

Later, loaded down with bundles, Sheena followed her daughter inside the house and into the kitchen.

Tony was sitting at the kitchen table, eating a sandwich. He looked up at them. "Shopping again?"

Meaghan rushed forward and threw her arms around Tony's neck. "Daddy! Thank you! Mom wasn't going to let me buy this dress, but I knew you'd like it, and I love it!"

Tony chuckled happily when Meaghan gave him not one, but two kisses on the cheek.

Sheena pressed her lips together. Meaghan was Daddy's little girl all right. After another fight had threatened, she'd given in and allowed Meaghan to have the more expensive dress of the two they'd selected as their final choices.

"I've got to go upstairs to call Lauren and tell her about it," said Meaghan. She took a couple of the shopping bags from Sheena before running off.

Sheena set her packages down and sank into a kitchen chair opposite Tony. "Shopping with your daughter is no treat. Especially when we're trying to be careful with money."

"Yeah? What did you get? Something on sale?"

Sheena reached across the table and squeezed Tony's hand. "We have to talk. It's about my meeting with the lawyer yesterday."

Tony gave her a questioning look. "Okay. Let's hear it."

Sheena's mouth felt dry as she searched for the right words. She mentally crossed her fingers and began. "My sisters and I have been left a unique gift from my Uncle Gavin. We each have a one-third share of a hotel in Florida provided we get it up and running. If we do, it could mean a lot of money for the three of us. There are a few twists to it, though. According to his will, my sisters and I have to live there for one year while we see that the hotel is successful."

Before she could continue, Tony's expression changed from curiosity to disbelief. Then a resolute look filled his face—a look Sheena knew all too well.

"There's no way you're going to leave this family for a year," he announced with a firmness that rounded his words.

"Tony, listen to me. You and the kids can visit me, maybe even move there with me."

"Are you crazy?"

"It will be inconvenient for a while, but think what this might mean for our family and to my sisters. We'd have enough money to give the kids a good education and maybe even to set money aside for retirement."

"I'm a good provider," Tony said. "Don't even go there."

Sheena remained silent. Tony's business was not doing well, not since his right-hand guy quit to move out west.

He glared at her. "And what about our children? You can't abandon them."

"I'm not abandoning them or you. We'd be apart for only a few weeks at a time. The kids can come to Florida for school breaks and summer vacation. And I'd want you to come as often as you can. It would, in many ways, be no different than it is for your sister, whose husband is on the road every week for work. Only instead of my coming here, you'd be coming to me."

Tony shook his head. "Go there? Visit you? What about my business?"

Sheena told herself to hold back, but she couldn't. "That's why you have a couple of assistants. Maybe, for once, *they* would have to take weekend duty instead of leaving it up to you. Every. Damn. Weekend!"

Tony leaped up from his chair. "Oh? Now you're telling me I don't run my company properly? What else don't I do properly, Sheena?"

Sheena held up her hands to stop him. "Tony, Tony, let's not fight. Let's give this a chance."

"No, Sheena. If you do this thing, whatever you want to call it, you're as good as telling me our marriage is over."

Sheena's knees wobbled as she got to her feet and faced him. "No, Tony, I'm not. I love you and I love the kids. But this is a chance in a lifetime to help my family. We can make this work. I know we can. And I owe it to my sisters to do this."

He started to sputter. "But...but...

Sheena held up her hand and spoke firmly. "I'm not going to change my mind. I want you behind me on this, but if not, I'll be forced to prove to you on my own that this is an opportunity for all of us."

Tony glared at her, grabbed his truck keys, and stormed out of the kitchen. Moments later, Sheena heard the roar of his truck as he backed out of the driveway and drove away, the tires spinning on the pavement.

Fighting tears, Sheena took her packages upstairs to her bedroom and hid them in her closet. She'd been able to pick up a bathing suit and a pair of pants in the cruise-wear section of one of the department stores downtown. But most of her wardrobe seemed unsuitable for tropical Florida. Maybe, like her sisters, she wouldn't worry about it, but would simply buy all new clothes in Florida. Ordinarily, she'd be excited by such an idea, but her stomach was still in knots from her confrontation with Tony.

She heard a commotion downstairs, and thinking it was Tony, hurried to greet him.

At the bottom of the stairs, her mother-in-law smiled up at her. "Hi. I heard a lot of noise coming from your side and wondered if everything was all right."

Sheena bit back a sour reply about privacy. Rosa Morelli

was the best mother-in-law anyone could have. Through the years, they'd become good friends.

"You'd better come into the kitchen," said Sheena. "We can talk there."

As she tried to form the right words in her mind, she went about fixing a cup of coffee for Rosa—black with a dash of milk—and a cup for herself. They'd often had gab sessions like this, but Sheena knew her mother-in-law would not like what she was about to tell her.

Rosa took a sip of the hot liquid and set her coffee cup down. "What's going on? Tony roared out of the driveway like he was mad."

"Let me tell you what's happened to me and then we'll talk about it," said Sheena, realizing she needed Rosa's perception. Her mother-in-law was honest, sometimes irritatingly so.

After Sheena laid out the odd rules of the agreement, she sat back in her chair, studying Rosa's face carefully. Disapproval was modified by intrigue.

"You wouldn't be able to leave there, but Tony and the kids could visit you?"

"Yes. Uncle Gavin knew very well I have a family. If he'd had any objections about their visiting, his will would have stated something about it."

Rosa shook her head. "It's never a good idea for a woman to leave her husband for any length of time. All kinds of things can happen."

"That's why it's important for Tony and the kids to spend some time with me there," Sheena countered. "Think what this might mean for our family."

"And just what does this hotel look like? Do you have any pictures?"

Sheena shook her head. "Not yet. There's some confusion about it not being on the internet."

Rosa sat back in her chair and gave Sheena a thoughtful look. "What's to say this...this agreement is on the up and up?"

"I don't think..." Sheena stopped. *It all was such a crazy thing, who's to say it wasn't a big joke?*

Rosa gripped Sheena's hand. "I'm just worried you could be searching for treasure like you told me Gavin did, diving for shipwrecked gold, and coming up with nothing."

"But the lawyer is from a well-respected firm. He was very professional. He told us there was a sizeable estate to be had if we took the challenge." Sheena paused and then blurted out something that had been bothering her for months. "More than finding a treasure and helping my family, Rosa, I want to find me. Can you understand that?"

Rosa was quiet, making Sheena wonder if she'd overstepped her friendship with Tony's mother.

"Yes," Rosa said slowly, thoughtfully. "As a woman who raised two children of my own in this family, I understand it all too well."

"I don't know who I am anymore. To Tony, I'm the woman who takes care of him, the house and his children. To Meaghan and Michael? I'm nothing but a slave."

"I'm not sure that's true," Rosa began.

"Well, then, who am I?" Sheena couldn't stop tears from forming in her eyes. She'd been feeling so demeaned, so lonely, so under-appreciated.

Rosa's features softened. "You're a wonderful wife and mother. I love you, Sheena." She patted Sheena's hand. "You go find yourself and your treasure. I'll help at this end as much as I can. But you and Tony have to work out the details yourselves. Remember, I love my son too, and I wouldn't want him to get hurt."

Rosa got to her feet with a sigh and gave Sheena a hug. "I won't say anything to Paul about this until the two of you have it worked out."

Sheena nodded and hugged Rosa back as hard as she dared. It would be their secret for the moment. Her father-in-law wouldn't understand that sometimes a wife and a mother needed to know who she really was.

CHAPTER FIVE
REGAN

Regan walked into the apartment she rented with her roommates, Chelsea and Becca, excited to share her news with them.

"Hello?" she called.

At the silence that followed, she rolled her suitcase into the tiny room that served as her bedroom. Originally, the room had been a storage closet but had since been converted to a bedroom by some enterprising renters before her.

Looking around the space, Regan realized that in the three years she'd lived there, it had never seemed like a real home to her. She'd always used it as a temporary place to exist before she found that special guy who would treat her as if she had a brain. Everyone wanted to be beautiful. But those who weren't would never understand Regan's willingness to trade some of her so-called stunning features for real respect. The idea that she was dumb had started in elementary school. When other kids her age were reading, she was not. It took a couple of years for one nun to finally realize she had a form of dyslexia that made reading problematic but not impossible. But the dumb tag had already been imprinted on Regan's mind and everyone else's.

Regan opened her suitcase. As she replaced her clothes in her closet, she began to sort through all of them, pulling out things she knew she wouldn't keep. Soon, she had a huge pile on her bed.

"What are you doing?" said Chelsea Cochran, peeking into the room.

Regan beamed at her. "I'm getting rid of these clothes. Help yourself! You're never going to guess what's happened to me."

"Are you drunk?" Chelsea said, frowning.

"No, but I might be having a lot of piña coladas in the future." Regan couldn't help doing a little jig. It was such a wonderful thought.

"Okay, seriously, what's going on?" said Chelsea. "This isn't like you at all."

Regan waved her to a seat on the edge of the bed. "Listen to this."

Chelsea's eyes grew bigger and bigger as Regan gave her some of the details.

"You've got to be kidding me!" Chelsea said. "Oh! Think of the vacations I can have there. Remember, you're my best friend in the city!"

Regan sobered. "Yeah, I'm not sure how everything will work out at the hotel. We haven't even seen a picture of it yet. But, Chelsea, I have to be there in two weeks. You've got to help me find someone to take my place here."

Chelsea let out a nervous little laugh. "Actually, Becca and I were wondering what to do. A friend of hers is looking for two roommates in a big, luxurious apartment she wants to rent. But we knew with your salary, you couldn't afford it, so we've done nothing about it." A gleeful expression brightened her face. "Now, maybe we can."

Regan plopped down next to the pile of clothes on the bed. "For me, you were going to give up the chance for a bigger, better place?"

Chelsea placed a hand on Regan's shoulder. "We love you, Regan. Though I have to admit we were pretty disappointed to turn her down."

Regan felt a smile cross her face. "Call her right now. I need to be gone in two weeks. Maybe you can still get in. And like I said, help yourself to any of these clothes on the bed." She gave Chelsea a knowing look. "The ones you like to borrow without asking."

Laughing, Chelsea rose and gave her a hug. "Okay, I'll make the call." She started to walk away and then turned back.

"I'm happy for you, Regan, I really am. Wow! A real heiress!"

A weird feeling filled Regan. Somehow the word "heiress" didn't seem appropriate. But, like she'd originally thought, Uncle Gavin's challenge could be the best thing that ever happened to her.

CHAPTER SIX
SHEENA

*S*ilence can be a terrible thing when it's used as a weapon, Sheena thought, as she set the table for dinner. Tony had returned to the house but had gone right into the den and turned on a football game. When she'd approached him, he'd waved her away.

Now, on a rare night when both children were home without immediate plans, she dreaded the idea of talking to them about her leaving them. But it had to be done.

When she called everyone to supper, there was the usual scramble to get seated.

"Aw, Mom. Lasagna?" said Meaghan. "You know it's fattening."

"It's your father's favorite," said Sheena calmly. Ignoring her daughter's whine, she tried to elicit a smile from Tony. But he was having none of it.

"Eat a lot of salad instead," he said to Meaghan.

"Yeah," said Michael. "Us guys need all the carbs we can get for the hard exercise we do."

"Mom, I've invited a couple of girls to spend the night after the Valentine's Dance," said Meaghan. "You don't mind, do you? You always tell us our friends are welcome anytime."

Sheena drew a deep breath. "Well, this time, you're going to have to ask your father. Not me. I won't be here."

"What do you mean?" The color left Meaghan's face.

"Your mother means she intends to leave us on our own for

a year," said Tony. "We'll have to get along without her."

"Whaat? You can't do that!" said Michael, giving her a look of incredulity.

"Are you guys getting a divorce?" asked Meaghan in a quivery voice.

"No, listen to me. Something wonderful has happened." Sheena told them the details of Uncle Gavin's will, leaving nothing out. "It's important for me to do this for you and your father as much as anything. It could mean a lot of benefits for all of us. And I'm not leaving you for a year. That's silly. We'll see each other in Florida on a regular basis."

"But Dad makes a lot of money. We don't need you to leave us," said Meaghan. Her eyes shone with tears.

Sheena wanted to be truthful without hurting Tony's feelings, but the fact was his business had taken a few hits over the past several months. In the last year, he'd lost out on a couple of bids for big jobs. Jobs they needed. After that, he'd even had to lay off two people.

"It's difficult to run a small business in today's world with so many government regulations and companies trying to outbid one another on the big jobs," said Sheena as diplomatically as she could. "We want you to be able to go to the college of your choice. Michael has just one more year of high school after this, and then he'll be gone. And if I don't participate in the challenge, Darcy and Regan won't be able to inherit the hotel or, later, the rest of Uncle Gavin's estate. It wouldn't be fair to them for me not to do this."

"Why did Uncle Gavin set it up this way?" said Michael. "What's the catch?"

Sheena shook her head. "I wish I knew what he was thinking. The lawyer did say he wanted it to be a life lesson for each of us."

"Whatever that means," said Tony, slamming down his

fork, getting up, and walking away.

Meaghan started to cry.

Michael got to his feet. "Geez, Mom! You're not gonna win either way."

"Thanks, Michael," Sheena said wryly. "That's exactly how I feel."

All evening, Meaghan stayed close to Sheena's side, insisting on sitting beside her while she did online research on the coastal area in which the hotel was located. Though she learned about that part of Florida, like Darcy had told her, the hotel was not listed. That worried Sheena a lot.

Later, after Michael had come home from a friend's house and Meaghan had gone up to her room, Sheena and Michael sat on the living room couch together.

"I need you to be the strong one for Meaghan," Sheena explained. "I'm not going to be gone for a whole year without seeing you like Dad said. It'll just be weeks at a time. You'll come to me instead of me coming to you. You can spend school breaks and the summer in Florida, doing and seeing a lot of new things."

"What about going to the beach in New Hampshire like we do every summer?" said Michael.

"This summer, you'll be coming to Florida instead. I'm pretty sure I can find you a summer job," Sheena said, trying to make a little joke of it.

"If you're going to be rich by doing this, why do I need a summer job?" Michael retorted.

Sheena reached for his hand. "Because, my darling son, it's a matter of learning responsibility and contributing to the common good of the family. Nothing is guaranteed by my going to Florida, but I wouldn't even think of doing this if I wasn't pretty confident that it will be a very good thing for our family."

"If nothing is guaranteed, why in hell are you doing it?" Michael's nostrils flared as he gazed at her.

"Oh, Michael," Sheena said. "It's a chance to take a lot of worry off your father. How could I not do it?

He looked down at the floor and then up at her. "I don't know. I don't know."

She hugged him. "We'll talk more in the morning."

Tony was already in bed when Sheena climbed the stairs for the night. Observing his stiff form in bed, Sheena sighed. She and Tony seldom fought. It hadn't really been necessary because she was content to be his wife and the mother of his children. Now, however, she had to make him understand.

She undressed and took her time preparing for bed before slipping on the nightgown that Tony liked—the short, red one he'd bought her one Valentine's Day. Seeing her reflection in the mirror, eyeing the gown that looked new, she realized that had been several years ago.

Brushing her auburn hair away from her face, she wondered what had happened to the young, innocent girl who thought her life would be devoted to nursing. That girl had wanted an interesting life, a rewarding career, and a good man in her life. Preferably a rich doctor, who would be available only when she wanted him around. Upon entering college, she'd been excited by the idea of being on her own, away from her sisters and parents, and with interesting people who'd traveled and seen a lot.

Still, she could remember the moment she walked into a bar and saw Tony. He was sitting with friends at a table. When he'd looked up at her, it was as if the world around them had melted away. His ridiculously sexy smile and the light in his dark eyes pulled her in, promising her things she'd only read about in books.

Lust was many things to many people. For her, it was a validation of her wish to be someone different from the girl at home who was stuck helping to care for her younger sisters when her mother was ill. It was freedom. And it tasted and felt good!

The face that now stared back at her was still young-looking and pretty. The green eyes that Tony loved sparkled with intelligence and then suddenly filled with worry. She turned away, not liking the change.

As she slid into bed beside Tony, Sheena felt his body tense. She placed a hand on his back. "Tony, please, honey. Let's not fight about this. I'd never leave you. I love you and I always will."

He rolled over and faced her. "But you are leaving me."

She shook her head. "We'll be apart for blocks of time. That's all. You'll come to me. And I'll be there."

His eyes filled. "Without you, Sheena, I don't know what I'll do. You're the anchor that makes our family real. How will we get along without you?"

"You'll do just fine. You and the children. In fact, I think this kind of change will be good for all of us."

"Sounds to me like you're trying to dump the family. What's to say you'll want to come back?"

She laid a hand on his cheek and stared into his dark eyes. "You must know deep inside you that I'd never do that."

"Okay, then, why all these rules that Gavin set up? It could be just a joke. And then where would we be?"

"Right where we are now," she said, hesitating to mention that she truly believed they'd be in a much better financial situation. "Tony, some chances are worth taking."

"You really like the idea of leaving us, don't you?" His gaze rested on her, demanding an honest answer.

"I want this opportunity for our family, but, yes, I've been feeling so lost that it's time to find me."

"But, Sheena, what if finding you means losing me?" Tony gave her a troubled look.

"I don't know. I don't know," Sheena said, suddenly scared.

Sheena climbed the steps of the family home in Dorchester, wishing she could magically exchange places with one of her sisters. Her father would not be happy with the news of her sisters' and her becoming embroiled in one of Uncle Gavin's schemes. She rang the doorbell and waited for her father to answer the door. The cold February wind whipped around her, causing her to hug her down jacket closer. Living near the water had advantages, but winter onshore breezes weren't one of them.

"Well, look who's here," said her father, grinning at her from behind the storm door. "Come in. Come in."

Sheena entered the house. It seemed empty now without her mother's presence. She couldn't blame her sisters for disliking the changes they saw. Her father's girlfriend had a thing for lacy pillows and doilies and things their mother would never have chosen. A stuffed teddy bear, dressed in a frilly dress sat in the corner of the sofa, a reminder of who had replaced their mother.

Sheena's father noticed her distaste and waved away her concern. "Bah! I don't like it much either, but it makes Regina happy. Who am I to complain? She makes a hell of a good meal. That's enough for me."

He grinned at her, and Sheena wondered how happy he'd been with her mother. Patrick Sullivan was a tall, rosy-cheeked, good-looking man who carried too much weight, and recently had retired from the fire department. By anyone's standard, he'd be a good catch for a widowed woman anxious to find a new man in her life.

"When are the two of you moving to California?" Sheena asked him.

"I'm not sure. I told Regina I hate the idea of leaving my girls. Come on into the kitchen. We can talk there. How about a cup of coffee?"

"Sure. I'll take mine black."

Sheena sat at the kitchen table and gazed around, missing her mother so much it actually hurt. Growing up, her mother had been such a kind, reassuring presence in her life. Even when her mother had one of her sick spells, her comforting presence had always filled the house.

Her father handed her a cup of steaming coffee and took a seat opposite her.

Sheena studied him. "You look good, Dad. Are you happy?"

He nodded and smiled. "I still miss your mother, but I'm doing okay. I hate changes in my life, but I'm dealing with it."

"Good," Sheena said, setting down her coffee cup. "Something big has come up, and Darcy, Regan, and I are temporarily moving to Florida for a year."

"Huh? You can't move. You have your family here. What in the hell is going on? You better not tell me you're getting a divorce."

"No, no, nothing like that. It's about Uncle Gavin's will. He's left us a hotel in Florida with a few conditions attached to it." Sheena explained what she meant.

"Don't tell me that son of a bitch is playing games with you from the grave," said her father. "Don't fall for any of his tricks. He's always fooling people with some financial deal or another."

Sheena studied her father's red face, the way his blue eyes snapped with anger. "Why do you dislike him that much?"

"He was always after the golden ring on the carousel. He always had to have the biggest and the best. I found out the hard way that a lot of his talk was just that—talk. He didn't care who he might hurt along the way, including your mother."

"But Mom always liked him."

"*He* always liked *her*," said her father. "Too much, if you ask me."

Sheena hid her shock when she realized a lot of her father's anger had to do with jealousy. She remembered how pleased her mother had always been to see Gavin. And now, she recalled the gold coin.

"Before I leave, I'm wondering if I can take a last look at some of Mom's things I boxed up for storage."

"Yeah, in fact, why don't you take it. You've got your car. I'll help you load it in. It'll be one less thing to pack up when we get ready to move."

"About this move to California ..." Sheena began. "Won't you miss all your friends here?"

Her father shrugged. "Things aren't the same, you know? My best friend, Micky, died just before your mother, and the firehouse is filled with young bucks who don't think much of the guys my age. Time to move on. You girls were the reason I stayed."

He seemed to suddenly age before Sheena's eyes. Filled with compassion, she rose out of her chair and gave her father a hug. "It's hard, isn't it?"

He nodded. "Wicked hard. C'mon, I'll get that box for you. I just hope you're not making a huge mistake, Sheena. You're the most sensible one in the family."

"Thanks, Dad," Sheena said, not sure why she was

thanking him. Being sensible had always meant more responsibility for her than for her sisters.

At home, Sheena carried the box into the kitchen. With Tony at work and the kids in school, Sheena enjoyed the peace in the household. Sheena set the box down on the table. Her mother's jewelry had been distributed to her and her sisters, her clothes given away to charity. The items inside the box were the last of her mother's personal things, taken from drawers in her bureau. At the time, neither Sheena nor her sisters had felt capable of going through them. It would mean losing their mother completely.

Sheena carefully removed the cover from the box. Gingerly, she lifted out the porcelain angel that had sat on her mother's bureau for as long as she could remember. Her mother's favorite rosary lay inside the box nestled in a lace handkerchief with the initial E for Eileen embroidered on it. A few old letters and cards were banded together, along with a couple of photographs her mother had kept tucked away.

Looking at the items in the box now, Sheena hoped to find clues as to the whereabouts of the gold coin. She glanced through the letters and cards. Most were from her and her sisters—old Valentines, birthday cards, and the like. A few notes from Meaghan and Michael were included, which brought a smile to Sheena's lips. Really, they were good kids.

One of the envelopes had her name on it. Sheena lifted it out and stared at the way it was sealed closed and then taped. She pulled a sharp knife from the knife rack and slit the envelope open, careful not to tear anything inside.

The gold coin fell out. Sheena gasped and picked it up. It was as she remembered it, round and dulled with age. Now, she recognized the markings on it as something one might find on a piece of gold from a shipwreck. Maybe all of Gavin's searches for gold hadn't been fruitless. Maybe this is why he had what the lawyer had called a sizeable estate. The thought both scared and thrilled her.

Carefully, Sheena pulled the note out of the envelope that had held the coin. The paper had yellowed and grown brittle with age.

She stared at the words on the note:

"Sheena, this coin was tucked inside the stuffed monkey Uncle Gavin gave you. The coin was given to you to be used at a time in your life when you might most need it. Your Uncle Gavin loved you dearly. Remember that, my darling. Love, Mom."

As she reread the note, a shiver traveled across Sheena's shoulders in waves. She'd been around ten when she last saw him. As the oldest, she supposed Uncle Gavin knew her best. Or maybe, by the time her sisters came along, Gavin knew he was not welcome in his brother's house.

Families are always full of mysteries, Sheena thought, deciding to say nothing about the gold coin to anyone else. She tucked it back inside the envelope and then took it upstairs and hid it among the fancy undergarments she hardly used anymore.

The night before she was to leave for Florida, Sheena decided to make a festive affair of dinner. She was serving chicken piccata, antipasto and what Tony called "Sheena's famous apple pie".

Small, gaily-wrapped gifts sat at each place. She'd spent a lot of time thinking of something special for each of them.

"What's this?" Tony asked as he sat down at the head of the table. He picked up his gift and set it down.

"You'll see." She turned to Meaghan and Michael. "The gifts are reminders that we are a family no matter where we are. The time is fast approaching when you'll both be out on your own. But, like now, nothing makes us less of a family if one of us is missing."

"Wow! You're making it seem like your leaving us is going to be forever," said Michael, giving her a worried look.

Sheena tried to put a good spin on it. "Hey! You all are coming to Florida for spring break. Eight weeks isn't that long. The time will go by fast."

"But, Mom, who is going to fix my hair for the Valentines Dance?" said Meaghan. Her voice held a familiar whine.

"Grandma Rosa has already promised to fix your hair for you," Sheena said quietly. "She'll do a great job of it. Remember, she has a daughter and knows all about those things." Sheena gave them all a smile. "She's promised to be here for each of you no matter the cause."

Meaghan lifted the present in front of her. "Can I open my gift now?"

She carefully pulled away the pink foil wrapping from the small package she held in her hands. Her eyes widened when she saw the velvet-covered box inside. She opened it and grinned. "It's beautiful, Mom! Thanks!"

"Let's see!" said Michael.

Meaghan held up the gold chain and a pendant in the shape of a scallop seashell. A tiny diamond sparkled inside the shell.

"It's a reminder that we're not going to be apart for long."

Meaghan's eyes sparkled. "It'll be perfect for the dance."

"Okay, my turn," said Michael. He ripped the paper off his gift, opened the box, and stared at the contents with surprise. "Wow! Really? The keys to your car?"

Sheena and Tony exchanged amused glances. "Your father and I agreed you can have the use of it while I'm gone. After that? We'll have to see."

"Thanks. It'll be great to have my own set of wheels for a while, at least."

Sheena looked to Tony.

Guess it's my turn," he said. He ripped off the wrapping, lifted the lid of the box, and frowned. "What's this?"

"It's a pocket token. I thought of giving you a watch, but I realized you wouldn't wear it because of the job. This is something you can always carry with you in your pocket."

Sheena had ordered the round, silver, coin-like object engraved with the words: *You, Me, Always.* A simple heart was the only design on the other side.

Tony looked up at her with such a sad smile, Sheena's heart stuttered and then sprinted forward. She knew she'd hurt him by sticking to her resolution to leave, but this was one time her family's demands would not ruin her plans. She'd made the right decision for many reasons.

"Okay," said Michael, jiggling the car keys. "Let's eat! I'm starving! After dinner, I want to take my car for a spin."

"Hold on!" said Tony. "It's your *temporary* car. Got it?"

Michael grimaced. "Aw, Dad. Can't a guy have a little fun?"

Observing their interplay, Sheena wondered how the relationship between father and son might change without her subtle interference. After a while, would they simply go their separate ways? She gazed around at the family she loved and knew the year ahead would be difficult for all of them.

That night, when Sheena came to bed, Tony turned to her. They'd finally agreed that she had no choice but to give the challenge a try. Tony still didn't like the idea of her being gone, but after looking at the financial figures for his business, he'd relented. His business was failing.

Sheena smiled when he drew her to him and pressed her up against him. Aware of his arousal, satisfaction filled Sheena. It had been too long since they'd made love. It was a shame because Tony was a very good lover.

"Take off those pajamas," he growled playfully.

She unbuttoned her top while he tugged the bottoms off. Heart pounding with anticipation at what she knew was coming, she felt his hands on her breasts. Her nipples tightened with pleasure as he stroked them before warming them in the cool air with his lips.

"I've missed you, Tony. Sometimes I think our life together has become so crazy that we've missed out on a lot. We're too young to give up on this and other special moments."

Hey, I'm here." His hands cupped her hips, and soon she was lost in the lust that held them together.

CHAPTER SEVEN
DARCY

Darcy waited impatiently at the curbside of Logan Airport for Sheena to say goodbye to Tony and her children for what seemed like the tenth time. She watched as they hugged and kissed, and then hugged and kissed again. Meaghan, as usual, had dramatic tears streaming down her face. Michael acted like he didn't care, but he went back to his mother for another farewell hug. And Tony? Tony's uncertainty was painful to see. God! He really, really loved Sheena. Darcy sighed. She'd never had a guy look at her the way Tony was looking at her sister.

A pang filled Darcy as she watched Tony clasp Sheena's face in both hands for a long, lingering kiss that would set any woman's insides on fire. Chemistry like that didn't happen often. Knowing how difficult it had been for Sheena to make this trip happen, Darcy had a lot more respect for her older sister. But then, Darcy thought, Sheena was the perfect sister, the perfect daughter in the family.

At last, Tony and the kids rolled away from the curb in Sheena's SUV.

Darcy waved Sheena forward. "C'mon, hurry! It's freezing!"

The cold winter air numbed Darcy's bare hands as she rolled her suitcase into the terminal. The thought of sunny, warm Florida brought a smile to her face. She turned to Sheena. "It's a great time to make this change."

Sheena blinked away the last of her tears and nodded. "Let's hope it turns out to be a good one. Where did you tell me the limo was going to meet us?"

"The email said that a limo would pick us up at the baggage claim area in Tampa. The driver will have a sign marked Sullivan. Regan should already have arrived by the time we get there."

Sheena managed a smile. "And then we'll know what our mystery hotel will look like, huh?"

Darcy grinned. "I can see it in my mind. Tall, beige, stucco building with a red-tiled roof, like the ones you sometimes see in the Caribbean. The beaches along the shoreline look beautiful—St. Pete Beach among them. And, according to the maps, we're not that far away."

"Sounds awesome," said Sheena. "I could go for some lazy days in the sun. These last two weeks have been hectic, to say the least."

"Yeah, I picture myself on the beach with a rum drink, clicking my fingers for service."

Sheena laughed. "I wouldn't get carried away. I'm sure we'll find something that needs to be done."

Aboard the plane, Darcy reveled in the comfort of her first-class seat. Archibald Wilson hadn't protested at all when she'd asked if they could book the upgrade. "By all means, be comfortable," he'd told her.

Thinking about that conversation, Darcy wondered what other privileges awaited her. Until she'd met and roomed with Alex, she'd never been ashamed of her modest upbringing. But Alex had alluded to it so many times, Darcy had finally succumbed to the pressure. Now, she sometimes thought of her family as lower-class people who had no idea how "better" people lived. Not that she'd mention her feelings to Sheena, who would, in her quiet way, rip her head off for being shallow.

Darcy eyed her sister. At thirty-six, Sheena didn't look her age. Actually, she was almost as pretty as Regan. But she dressed as if she were in her fifties, and like the good Catholic schoolgirl she'd once been, she was very modest. Darcy snorted at the idea of Sheena in a bikini.

"What's funny?" Sheena asked her.

"Nothing," said Darcy, and then she couldn't resist. "You said you bought a new bathing suit. What did you get? One of your usual one-piece numbers?"

Sheena glared at her. "What if I did? I'm a mother of two kids. I'm not going to go around in one of those string bikinis you wear."

Just as I thought. Unable to stop mischief from rising inside her, Darcy grinned. "I'm planning on doing lots of things you probably won't approve of."

Shaking her head, Sheena made a face and then leaned back against the seat and closed her eyes.

Darcy stared out the window of the plane. Wisps of clouds blocked her view from time to time, but as she witnessed the wintry landscape below them morph into greener scenes, her excitement grew. But still, she'd miss the comfort of old friends. Her thoughts flew to the impromptu farewell party her co-workers had thrown for her. It had been a total surprise and very pleasing. Oddly, the send-off had made it easier to say goodbye to what had once been her world. She swallowed hard. She hoped she and her sisters hadn't made a horrible mistake. It was too late to turn back now.

CHAPTER EIGHT
REGAN

Regan rolled the smaller of her suitcases through the Tampa airport toward the baggage claim area, feeling as if she was in a dream. Still wearing her knee-high leather boots, she could hardly wait to take them off and exchange them for a pair of flip-flops like she saw on other people's feet. She'd gotten rid of most of her things, but the boots were something she'd saved a long time for and, in the end, she refused to sell them or give them away.

She took off her sweater-coat and rolled it up. All the talk of moving to Florida hadn't seemed real until now. Rather than being elated, worry slowed Regan's steps. She was the dumb one, the one who was last to figure things out. Had she and her sisters made a big mistake by throwing away their lives like their used clothing and coming to Florida? Their future was totally uncertain.

Someone bumped into her, and Regan realized she'd come to an abrupt stop. Gathering courage with her speed, she moved forward, reminding herself that it was too late to change her mind.

Regan grabbed her large suitcase off the revolving baggage belt and found a seat. She had about twenty minutes to wait until Sheena's and Darcy's flight arrived.

She pulled the novel she'd been reading from her purse and opened it up.

A voice interrupted her reading. "Excuse me? Are you by

chance one of the Sullivan sisters?"

Startled, she looked up into the face of a handsome young man holding a sign that said: *Sullivan.*

Regan frowned. "Yes, how did you know?"

His brown eyes sparkled as he studied her. "I was told to look for a beautiful young woman with long black hair and violet eyes. You meet that description very ... well."

A sudden rage filled Regan. *Dammit!* She was not going to start her new life with the same old, grinning, come-on from guys. "Fuck off!"

He looked as startled as she felt.

"I'm...I'm...sorry." She got up and walked away to gather herself. But it had felt good to wipe that smile off his face. It had almost been a leer.

When she returned to her seat, Regan picked up the book, opened it, and stared at the same words over and over again, determined not to look at the guy standing nearby, holding the Sullivan sign.

Soon caught up in the romance, she was surprised to hear her name called.

"Regan! Regan! We're here!"

She looked up to see Darcy running toward her. Wearing a jean skirt, a jersey top, and sandals, Darcy looked right at home in the airport. Behind her, Sheena approached. In black slacks and a beige sweater, she looked like the older sister she was. But her smile was warm and affectionate, and that's what counted with Regan.

She went to her sisters and hugged them.

"Okay, where's the guy with the Sullivan sign?" said Darcy, looking around. "He's supposed to be driving us in a limo to our hotel."

Regan turned and nodded at the guy leaning against the wall.

Giving them a weak smile, he held up the sign.

"Wow! What a piece of eye candy! Check him out," whispered Darcy.

Regan took a serious look at him. Tall, tanned, and well-built, he wore a white T-Shirt that showed off the fact that he worked out. The khaki shorts he wore displayed well-shaped, tanned legs. But it was his fine-featured face that caught her attention. Brown eyes studied her openly. The almost-leer that had ticked her off was gone.

"No drooling," said Sheena. "C'mon, let's get our bags and get going."

"Spoilsport," Darcy said. She signaled the guy to come over to them. "Can you help us with our bags?"

"Sure," he said. "My name is Brian Harwood. I've been assigned to pick you up and take you to the Salty Key Inn. Who is who?"

Darcy did a little curtsy. "I'm Darcy. These are my sisters Sheena and Regan." She indicated each with a wave of her hand.

"Hmmm," he said. "The lovely Sullivan sisters. Just like Gavin said."

"You knew Gavin?" said Sheena.

He nodded. "He and my mother were friends. She owns the bar next door."

"Tell us what the Salty Key Inn looks like," said Sheena. Her eyes sparkled with excitement.

He held up a hand. "Oh, no! You've got to see it for yourself. I'm under strict orders not to give away a thing. C'mon. I'll take you to it."

Regan climbed into the back of the white stretch limo with her sisters. Brian hadn't seemed too happy about keeping the Inn a secret. Her sisters didn't seem to notice his discomfort before he turned away to help with the bags, but she wondered about this guy who brought out so many different feelings in her.

The trip took them across Tampa Bay and then across the peninsula to Clearwater Beach, and along the coastline. Regan stared out the car window at the buildings lining the road and beyond them to white sandy beaches and blue water.

"Roll down the windows," Darcy urged her. "I want to smell the warm, salty air."

Regan dutifully rolled down the windows. The air that swept inside the car smelled of promise to Regan. She couldn't help smiling.

CHAPTER NINE
SHEENA

Sheena stirred restlessly in her seat in the limo as she noted a change in the scenery. The tall condos and hotels she'd enjoyed seeing had disappeared and were replaced by smaller properties. Some of them quite humble.

Before she could remark on it, Brian pulled into a property on the eastern, bay side of the road. Sheena stared in disbelief.

"Oh my Gawd!" said Darcy.

"There must be some mistake," said Regan, her voice high with disbelief. "Uncle Gavin wouldn't do this to us, would he?"

Sheena felt like throwing up. *Would he play a trick like this on us? If what her father had said was true, then he very well might.*

Light-blue paint on the clapboard siding of the long, two-story building sitting beside the road was faded and, in a few spots, had flaked away. What once must have been bright yellow trim was now a color between lemon and egg shell. A gambrel, tin roof topped the building, glinting at them in the sun like a mocking wink.

She studied the sign that read: *Gracie's – best breakfast ever!* The red lettering was bright and clear on what appeared to be a new sign mounted on the exterior. A large patio off that end of the building was filled with tables covered in red-checked, vinyl cloths. A number of umbrellas stood beside the tables.

"Here we are, ladies," said Brian, pulling the limo to a stop in the parking lot lining the front of the building. "We can unload here."

"This is some kind of joke. Right?" said Darcy. Her eyes welled with tears.

"Nope," Brian said. "The sad thing is Gavin died before he could fix it up for you like he wanted. Now, it's up to the three of you. Let me show you around."

He got out of the car and opened the back door for them.

On legs gone weak, Sheena climbed out of the limo onto blacktop that was burning hot from the sun.

Behind her, Darcy and Regan stumbled onto the pavement.

Telling herself to remain calm, Sheena studied her surroundings. The two-story building was larger than she'd first thought. It appeared the parking lot ran the length of it and around the far end.

"The entrance to the restaurant is on the other side," said Brian. "Follow me."

He led them off the parking lot, onto a sidewalk that followed the lines of the circular patio.

A man wearing a white sailor hat, white T-shirt, and khaki pants was swabbing the concrete floor of the patio. He looked up at them and kept working.

Sheena stepped up beside Brian. "Who's that?" she asked softly.

"One of Gavin's people. Don't worry. Clyde's harmless."

"Oh my Gawd! Look at that!" Darcy pointed to a full-sized carved and painted, wooden figure of a pirate standing next to the entrance.

"That's Davy," grinned Brian. "Come on in. Gracie should be here."

Sheena entered the café and stood a moment, assessing it. A breakfast bar with eight stools filled a good portion of one wall that abutted the kitchen. Tables of different sizes, maybe twelve of them, filled the room. The patio, from what she'd seen, held another twelve or more small tables. Dark and on the dingy side, the interior of the restaurant could use some brightening. As her eyes adjusted to the change in light, Sheena saw that the stained walls were made of beadboard. Fishnets, anchors, and seashells were tacked to the walls, adding to the seaside theme.

She heard the clanging of pots and pans in the kitchen and turned to the noise just as a short, heavy-set woman with graying, brown hair strode toward them.

"These those nieces of Gavin's?" she said to Brian. "Look pretty tender to me. Don't know what he was thinking of, turning this place over to them."

"Are you Gracie?" Sheena asked.

"Yeah, sure am," the woman answered. "Guess we might as well get acquainted." She held out her hand, and Sheena took it. "Gracie Rogers."

"I'm Sheena Morelli." She turned to her sisters. "And the red-head is my sister, Darcy Sullivan. And Regan, here, is the youngest."

Gracie shook hands with them and turned back to Sheena. "I understand you're the one who's more or less in charge. We did what we could to fix up the house before you got here, but you'll see it needs more work. Gavin had big plans for this place. Too bad his ticker didn't want to keep going. Gavin was the last of the good guys."

"House?" said Darcy. "I didn't see a house."

Gracie shrugged. "More like a cottage. You can't miss it. It's the building in the back. Brian will take you there on the golf cart."

"A golf cart? Oh, how fun!" said Regan.

"We've got a couple of them for the housekeepers. That is, if we ever need them," said Gracie. "Don't know when that's gonna happen. I serve breakfast and lunch here. You're free to come and eat any time the place isn't crowded."

She gave them a wave of her hand and disappeared into the kitchen.

Regan turned to Sheena. "What are we going to do?" Tears glistened in her eyes.

"We're going to get unpacked and then we'll take a better look around," Sheena said with as much determination as she could muster. She hadn't come this far to fail.

Sheena stepped outside the restaurant and took a good look. A two-story, beige, stucco building ran the length of the lot on the northern side. A smaller, single-story building, matching in style and color, sat across from it. Both needed to be either painted or freshened in some way. In between the two buildings was a smaller, one-story building partially blocking their view of a fenced-in swimming pool shimmering in the middle of a lawn.

The landscaping was a dismal collection of overgrown bushes. Palm trees formed a sub-tropical screen that could be seen in the background, along with thick foliage that she decided must border an inlet of the bay she'd seen. Sheena thought of her neat, trim yard in Somerville and felt her eyes sting.

"Ready?" said Brian. "I'll load the luggage onto one of the carts. You can take the other one." He pointed to the edge of the property. "Behind the one-story building at the edge of the property is a parking lot. A narrow driveway leads off it, down to the house, which sits by the water. Let's get the golf carts. Follow me."

"We might as well see where we're going to live for the next year." Sheena couldn't keep disappointment out of her voice, but she vowed to be strong. Regan and Darcy looked as if they were going to be sick.

Brian led them behind the kitchen, past a fenced area that held a dumpster and several garbage cans, past a doorway marked "office," to a large workshop that held a number of tools, various pieces of maintenance equipment, and two golf carts.

"I get to drive," Darcy hopped onto the front seat of the golf cart Brian indicated for them. Regan climbed up beside her. Sheena slid onto the back seat.

"You go ahead. I'll follow with the luggage," said Brian. "As I said, just follow the driveway off the parking lot behind the single-story building. I'll meet you at the house."

Sheena gripped the seat and held on as Darcy handled the cart as if it was a racing car.

The foliage alongside the drive on either side thickened and then thinned as they approached an open space. A pink-clapboard, two-story house with white trim and bright yellow shutters sat like a tropical parrot on the ground. Beside it, the bay waters sparkled in the sunlight. Shadows from palm trees nearby softened the outline of the house. In front of the entrance to the house, a white picket fence surrounded a rectangular concrete patio.

"Gawd! It looks like some kind of whorehouse," said Darcy. "I suppose we could put a pink light bulb in the front porch light and earn money that way."

"Front porch?" scoffed Regan. "That's not a real front porch; it's just a slab of concrete."

"Yeah? At least it has some chairs," said Darcy. "Ugly, but useful."

"Hold on," said Sheena. "We haven't even seen the inside. It might be nice."

"Or not," said Darcy. "This whole thing is a frickin' mess."

As Sheena studied the narrow house further, she realized the pink paint was fresh. She checked the shutters. The yellow paint on them was fresh too. Was it a joke?

Brian rolled up beside them in the other golf cart.

"It's newly painted?" Sheena asked.

Brian nodded. "Gavin wanted the house fixed up for you women. He thought you'd like it."

Sheena choked out, "Was he intending on painting the whole complex pink?"

Brian laughed. "No, the other colors were to remain the same. Now that you're in charge, you might want to change them. But in the last six months, since Gracie took over the restaurant, the blue building has become sort of a landmark around here. I'd be careful with that one. Gracie might fight you on it."

Darcy headed for the front door of the cottage. "Might as well see what's here."

Sheena followed Regan and Darcy inside. Standing in a small vestibule, she stared in surprise at the long, open room in front of her. The walls were painted a bright white. Even the high ceiling was white. A brown ceiling fan whirled above them in the center of the room, gently stirring the air. Soft brown, wooden floors lent a warmth to the setting. At the far end of the room, an oversized picture window made obvious their nearness to the backwater bay beyond them.

Two beige couches with colorful pillows faced each other and were flanked by stuffed chairs. A long low table sat between the couches.

"Whoa! This is pretty nice," said Darcy, circling on her feet. "Let's see the rest of the house."

Brian held up his hand to stop them. "Warning. We never got to the rest of the house before Gavin died."

"We? Are you the one who did this work?" asked Sheena.

He did a little bow. "Harwood Construction at your service."

Sheena's heart sank. From the old-fashioned design of the exterior, she figured the house was pretty old. She headed into the kitchen.

A small eating area held a square wooden table and four wooden chairs. Yellow vinyl countertops sat on wooden cabinets with drawers painted green. The cupboards above were painted a matching green. Next to a white porcelain sink, a white gas stove that looked like something out of the 1950s sat against an outside wall. A refrigerator, also white and appearing to be as old, stood nearby. Surprisingly, a new coffee machine sat on the counter. "Antiques? Do they work?" said Darcy. She opened the refrigerator and looked inside. "Nothing much here."

"Yep, they still work," said Brian. "Of course, someday you may replace them. But not for a year."

"A year?" Darcy cried. "Why not?"

"Because that's the way Gavin wanted it. I tried to talk him out of it, but he insisted on doing things his way. He wanted to make sure you would see to the hotel first. He called it a true Sullivan challenge."

"What a jerk," Darcy mumbled. She opened the folding doors of a pantry closet nearby and looked at the washing machine and dryer tucked into the space. "These are newer, thank God."

"We'd better see what awaits us upstairs," said Sheena, doing her best to keep her sagging spirits from collapsing altogether.

They climbed the stairs to the second floor, which Brian explained consisted of three bedrooms and one small bathroom. He led them to the bathroom.

Sheena stared at the claw-footed tub with a shower attachment, the pedestal sink, and mirrored medicine cabinet hanging above the sink and wondered how three women would ever survive these living arrangements without killing each other.

"We can't do this," said Regan. "There's no place to put all my stuff."

"What's to prevent us from using the bathrooms in the hotel?" said Darcy. She looked to Brian.

He shrugged. "Nothing." Brian held up three envelopes. "Gavin drew up a letter for each of you. I'll leave yours on your bed, after you each choose your room."

They went from one bedroom to another. The three rooms were basically the same. Each had one good-sized window with blinds, a tall ceiling on which a fan was mounted, beige-colored, low-pile, carpeted floors, a double bed, a nightstand with a lamp, and a bureau.

"I get this front bedroom," Darcy said.

"I'd like the back bedroom. It's a little more private," Sheena said, thinking of the times when Tony would visit her.

"Okay, I'll take the middle one. It's got a nice view of what looks like a bocce ball court," said Regan agreeably.

Darcy went over to the closet in her room, opened the door and slammed it shut. Leaning against the closet door, she closed her eyes and groaned. "It's a good thing we didn't bring a lot of clothes. This makes my closet back home seem like a living room. This whole scene is awful." Tears filled her eyes. "Simply awful."

"I'll bring your suitcases up," said Brian before making a quick exit. Sheena, Regan, and Darcy collapsed on the double bed in Darcy's room and stared at each other helplessly.

"What in Gawd's name have we gotten ourselves into?" Darcy said.

Sheena searched for something upbeat to say, then realized she had no real words of encouragement. She was in the biggest mess of her life.

CHAPTER TEN
REGAN

While Brian brought their larger suitcases up the stairs, Regan eased off her leather boots and wiggled her toes with relief. As soon as she could, she'd change into the one pair of shorts she'd brought with her. She looked around her room. The beadboard walls were stained brown like those in the other two bedrooms. The Jenny Lind bedframes in brown matched the walls. The only real color in the room was the quilt on the bed. Hers was a blend of purples and greens, reminding her of a favorite quilt she'd had on her bed as a young child. She'd noted that the quilt in Darcy's room was orange and red, and in Sheena's room, the quilt was in various shades of blue.

The similar appearances of the rooms made Regan feel as if she were in some kind of dormitory. At the thought, she shook her head at the idiocy of it all. Living with strangers would be a whole lot easier than living in these close quarters with her sisters. Perfect Sheena and know-it-all Darcy were already getting on her nerves.

Carefully avoiding looking at her, Brian rolled her suitcase into her room.

"Thank you," she said and turned her back to him.

After he left, she opened her suitcase and stared dismally at the few things inside. She changed her clothes and opened the letter that Brian had placed on her bed.

Moments later, Darcy walked into the room, waving a sheet

of paper. "Here's my letter. We'd better have a meeting."

The two of them headed into Sheena's room. She was sitting on the bed reading her letter. When she saw them, she shook her head. "This is going to be a real challenge. With only a limited amount of money to get started, we're going to have to be careful how we go about getting this property running well."

"But one hundred fifty thousand dollars is a lot of money," said Regan.

Sheena shook her head. "I know you're good at bargain shopping, Regan, but in business, that isn't much money at all. Let me finish reading this."

"Wait," said Darcy. "Let's start at the beginning and go through it together." She took a seat on the rug and faced Sheena. Regan sat down beside her.

"Okay," said Sheena, "here it is."

"My dear nieces, I'd hoped to be able to work with you on this project, but as bad luck would have it, that isn't going to happen. I bought this property with you and others in mind. Certain basic things like electrical wiring, fire, and life-safety issues have been taken care of to make the hotel and the restaurant viable. But the rest is up to you. I've made it a challenge of sorts. If you succeed, it and my estate will be yours. If you fail, none of it is yours, but will be split among several other people who remain unaware of this arrangement."

Regan frowned. "What kind of man would do this?"

Sheena smiled. "Uncle Gavin. He wasn't around when you were growing up, but I remember him as a lot of fun—big, loud, funny. I used to love having him hang around before he and Dad got into a big fight over something. Then 'The Big G' as he sometimes called himself, sort of disappeared. But Mom secretly kept in touch with him by sending him letters and photos."

"I remember when I asked about him, Mom warned me to not mention his name in front of Dad," said Darcy. "What was that all about?"

"Yeah, if he was the bad guy in the family, why did he do this for us?" said Regan.

Sheena shrugged her shoulders. "Probably because we're the only real family he had and because Mom, I'm guessing, was the only one who kept in touch with him." She went back to the letter.

"I'm giving you one hundred fifty thousand dollars to get the project rolling. If you don't use it wisely, you'll fail. It's up to you to use the Sullivan smarts to come up with ways to make it happen. In other words, think outside the box. And, by the way, have a hell of a ride along the way. I always did. Uncle Gavin."

In a separate paragraph Gavin had typed: *'Sheena, you're the one who's most like me. Don't believe it? You will.'*

Sheena frowned. "Did either of you get a separate note at the bottom of your letter?"

"I did," said Darcy. "Mine says: *'Darcy, you are not who we think you are.'* Weird, huh?"

Sheena turned to Regan. "And you? What did he say to you?"

Regan couldn't help the sting of tears. "Mine says: *'Beauty is in the eye of the beholder.'* What in the hell does that mean? I'm tired of everyone thinking about how I look."

Sheena shook her head. "I don't think he means that at all."

"Then, what?" said Regan.

"I'm not sure," said Sheena. "But I believe our stay here is meant to be a whole lot more than learning about running a hotel."

CHAPTER ELEVEN
SHEENA

Sheena stood. "Okay, now that we've unpacked and changed our clothes, we'd better take a look around the property." She grabbed a pad of paper and a pen, and said, "Let's go."

Sheena led her sisters outside the pink house and stood a moment, looking around.

"Wow! There's a dock," said Darcy. She took off, pushing through sea grapes and other foliage to get to the backwater's edge. She turned and waved to Sheena and Regan to come forward.

Sheena hesitated. She had a fear of snakes. Reluctantly, careful to watch where she was stepping, she followed Regan to Darcy.

"Hey! I know! We could buy a party boat and give our guests sunset rides," said Darcy, grinning. "That should bring in a lot of business."

"Looks like the dock needs a lot of work," said Regan, frowning. "C'mon, let's go see what the rest of this place looks like. There's a bocce ball court that looks like it's in pretty good shape."

They trekked back through the undergrowth and stared at the court. "A bocce ball set shouldn't cost too much," said Sheena. She made a note of it, along with a notation about the poor condition of the dock.

Darcy dashed over to the pool. "Uh oh. Looks like this

needs a good cleaning. Ugh. There's a tiny dead frog in it."

Sheena and Regan exchanged worried glances. What they'd seen so far wasn't encouraging. Sheena made another note.

"Let's check out the hotel rooms. Uncle Gavin said he'd done some preliminary work. Maybe things are better there," said Darcy. The earlier enthusiasm in her voice was beginning to fade.

Brian strode across the lawn to them. "I forgot to give you the keys to the buildings. I'll go inside with you and show you around a bit." He handed a ring of keys to Sheena. "As time goes by, we can have extra copies made as you wish."

"Thanks. Before we go inside, let's walk around the building to see what work might have to be done."

She stood and looked up at the two-story building faced with beige stucco. It looked … uncared-for. Air conditioner units were visible below each window and appeared to be in fairly good condition. She counted the windows on each floor. Ten.

"How many rooms are inside?" she asked Brian.

"Forty. Twenty on each floor. Ten facing the pool and ten facing the back."

"What's that building?" asked Darcy.

A wide, one-story, stucco building sat at one end of the fenced-in pool, facing both the pool and the restaurant. In the same neutral color as the guest buildings, it lent some privacy to the pool.

"The back half is used for handling the pool," explained Brian. "A storage area for towels, chairs and pool chemicals sits at one end. A service counter is used to hand out towels. The front of the building is where the guest registration office is located. A hallway with two bathrooms connects the front and back. Gavin was able to upgrade the bathrooms before he died, but the registration office needs to be spruced up."

Sheena turned and pointed to the small, one-story building opposite them. "How many rooms over there?"

"Eight large rooms," said Brian. "They're set up as suites with two bedrooms, an oversized living area with pull-out couches, and a small kitchen. Good for families."

"They sound nice. We ought to get a lot of money for them," said Darcy.

"We'll see," said Sheena, doubtfully. "It depends on their condition."

Brian gave her a thoughtful look. "It's going to be difficult to beat this challenge. All the bedding, including mattresses, the over-stuffed furniture, and the carpeting will need to be replaced. And the rest? You'll see for yourself."

Sheena grimaced. "Knowing what I learned about Uncle Gavin, I figured it wouldn't be easy. Let's see what we have to deal with inside and then we can draw up the various phases for each building. The outside needs a lot of dressing up. Do you know a good landscaper?"

Brian nodded. "Me."

Sheena laughed. "Is there anything you can't do?"

He shot a glance at Regan. "Apparently, I'm not very good at greeting people."

Regan's cheeks flushed, but she said nothing and turned away.

Inside the building, the hallway was dimly lit. Blinking to help her eyes adjust to the dimness after the bright sunshine, Sheena prayed that things wouldn't be as bad as she guessed.

"Give me the keys and I'll open up some of the rooms for you," said Brian. "They're pretty much the same. Gavin took care of the emergency and security issues, but the rooms' décor hasn't been touched in some time."

"Thanks for the warning," said Darcy, her spirits definitely drooping now.

Sheena followed the others inside a poolside room. Sunlight shone through the window, exposing the worn carpet, the furniture that had dings and scrapes, and the bedding that needed to be replaced. Her heart sank. If each room was in this kind of shape, they'd never have enough money to make everything nice enough to rent out.

After seeing several rooms, Sheena's worst fears were confirmed. None of the rooms was useable as is. Trying to hide her dismay, she turned to Brian. "We might as well see what the other building is like."

The tour of the family suites gave her even more reason to think they might fail. In addition to bedroom furniture, other things, like couches, tables, and chairs, needed to be replaced. And this didn't include televisions, mirrors, lamps, and the like. They'd have to do a few rooms at a time.

Outside, Sheena glumly turned to Brian. "What about the beach across the street? Do we have access to that?"

Brian nodded. "A public right of way is directly across from the hotel."

"That's one good thing," said Darcy. "Let's go see the beach. From the limo, it looked great."

Sheena followed the others across the street, down a weathered boardwalk, and onto a beautiful, wide stretch of white sand. In the salty breeze that ruffled her hair, she felt her spirits rise. Determination filled her. Maybe they could pull off this challenge—with a lot of work and even more luck.

She laughed as Darcy and Regan took off their shoes and wiggled their toes in the sand.

"C'mon! I'll race you to the water," Darcy cried, squealing as Regan raced by her.

Their playfulness reminded Sheena of her own children and she wondered what they and Tony would think of the Salty Key Inn. A shudder rippled across her shoulder. She couldn't, wouldn't let them see the hotel as it was.

She slipped off her shoes and walked down to the water's edge. The foamy edges of the waves washed over her feet and pulled away in a steady rhythm. Cupping a hand over her eyes, she stared out at the scene. Several people were splashing about in the water—some swimming, others just standing waist deep.

Regan came up beside her. "Beautiful, huh?"

Sheena turned to her with a smile. "Makes it all seem worthwhile."

Regan frowned. "Are we going to be able to make it happen?"

Sheena shook her head. "I don't know. I don't know."

A short while later, they left the beach and headed to the restaurant.

Gracie was in the kitchen when they arrived, but she came out to greet them. "We're having a meet-and-greet at six o'clock. I'm fixing dinner for everybody."

"Thanks," said Sheena. "Who's everybody?"

"Gavin's people," Gracie said. "Help yourself to water in the cooler out here. Looks like y'all could use some."

Sheena wiped the sweat from her brow. After living in the cold weather up north, she wasn't used to the warmth and humidity of Florida.

Regan went to the cooler, retrieved four bottles of water, and wordlessly handed them out to Sheena, Darcy, and Brian before taking a seat on one of the stools at the counter.

"What else is in this building?" Darcy asked Brian.

Sheena hid her amusement at the way Darcy was fluttering her eyelashes at him. But she couldn't blame her. With his sun-streaked hair, dark brown eyes, and rugged features, Brian would make a wonderful poster boy for the state's tourism council.

"Beyond the restaurant are the office and storage rooms," said Brian. "Upstairs, there are eight small apartments—for Gavin's people. Come with me. I'll show you around."

At the far side of the restaurant, a short hallway held doors to men's and women's restrooms. At the end of the hallway was a door marked "Private". Brian took the ring of keys from Sheena and unlocked the door. Holding it open, he waved them inside.

Sheena stepped into a large space that held two desks, two chairs and a filing cabinet coated in dust. "Guess nobody has used this for a while. No computer?"

"How can anybody do anything without a computer?" said Darcy. "No wonder the place isn't even known on the internet. This is like something out of the dark ages."

Sheena shook her head with disgust and made notes on the notepad she still carried.

From the office, Brian led them down a corridor. He opened the doors to two storerooms—one on either side of the hallway. One served as a pantry for the kitchen. The other held cleaning supplies, toilet tissue, and shelves loaded with towels and sheets. Midway down the corridor, a staircase led to the second floor.

"Beyond here is a one-car garage and the large workshop you saw, accessible from the outside," Brian explained. "But let's go up."

On the second floor, four rooms sat on either side of the corridor. One of the doors was cracked open, allowing them to peek inside. The room was furnished with a double bed, a bureau, and a nightstand with a bedside lamp. An overstuffed chair with standing lamp sat outside a small bathroom. Ceiling fans circulated the air in the air-conditioned space.

"Looks cozy," said Sheena.

"These rooms are where Gavin's people live," said Brian softly. "Better be quiet. Some might still be napping after their morning and afternoon shifts."

They returned to the first floor and went outside to look at the building itself. Like the pink house, wooden clapboards covered the exterior. Studying the building, Sheena frowned. "This really needs work."

"We ought to be able to find someone to paint it," said Darcy. "I bet it doesn't cost that much money. We ought to be able to swing it."

"We might even have to do it ourselves," said Sheena, wondering at Darcy's lack of knowledge. Her eagerness to spend money was beginning to annoy her. *Didn't Darcy realize what a challenge they faced?* Sheena knew from helping with Tony's business how difficult it would be.

They entered the restaurant and sat down, grateful for the through-wall air conditioners placed high on the walls.

"Okay," said Sheena, perplexed. "Everyone keeps referring to Gavin's people. Who are they? And why are they living here?"

"Hold on," said Brian. "I'll get Gracie in here to explain."

Brian returned with Gracie. Wiping her hands on her white apron, Gracie said, "You want to know about us, do you?" The challenge in Gracie's voice caught Sheena's attention. She studied the woman who seemed to be in charge. Sheena guessed her height at five-two and her age about the same. Brown hair that was turning gray was cut short around Gracie's pleasant face. Gracie's dark eyes snapped with suspicion when she realized Sheena was staring at her.

"Brian said you could tell us what is meant by Gavin's people and why they're living here," said Sheena.

"Gavin Sullivan was the most loyal, the kindest man many of us have ever known. He bought this place with us in mind." Tears filled Gracie's eyes. "Can't get more loyal or kinder than that."

Brian put an arm around Gracie's shoulder, and she continued. "Me? I used to wait on him in one of his favorite restaurants, a little breakfast place in Tampa. Had to go to work after my husband dumped me and left me without a place to stay. Most of the other folks are older, trying to live on Social Security, without places of their own. They've met Gavin here and there, and he's given them a home at the Salty Key Inn."

"But ..." Sheena began.

Gracie held up a hand to stop her. "In exchange, most do what they can to help around the place in little ways. But they could do a whole lot more. No reason to run them off."

"No ..." Sheena began again.

"You just wait and see," said Gracie, crossing her arms in front of her in a stance of defiance. "You'll meet them all tonight. And before you make any decisions about firing them, you talk to me. Okay?"

"Okay ..." Sheena stopped talking when she realized Gracie had already turned and was heading back into the kitchen.

"She's just upset," said Brian softly. "Without Gavin's generosity, these people would be on the street. Herself included." He cleared his throat. "I think you ought to know Gavin bought the bar next door for my mother. Gave it to her free and clear."

"I see," said Sheena, realizing Uncle Gavin was full of not a few, but many surprises.

What next?

CHAPTER TWELVE
DARCY

"Wow!" Darcy murmured to Sheena, sitting beside her. "If Gracie's breakfasts are as good as this fried chicken, no wonder this restaurant is booming." She was happy they'd been invited to a "get-acquainted meeting" with Gavin's people if it meant eating a meal like this.

"It's delicious," agreed Sheena.

"The potato salad is fantastic," said Regan, putting another forkful into her mouth, not counting the calories for once.

Darcy looked around the dining room. In addition to her sisters and herself, ten others sat in the room. Brian and his mother were at one table, looking more like brother and sister than mother and son. *Some friend Holly Harwood must have been to Gavin*, Darcy thought, and then chided herself for being petty. Holly was a petite woman with dark eyes and pretty features, light brown hair sun-streaked like her son's, and a ready smile.

The other people consisted of five women and three men who appeared to be in good health. She thought the man she'd seen swabbing the patio floor might be a little mentally challenged, but the others seemed to be alert. Gracie had said they did some work around the hotel, but Darcy had seen little evidence of it except in the kitchen.

After pie and coffee were served by two of the women in the group, Gracie stood. "Time for us to get acquainted. Sheena, why don't you start by introducing yourself."

As Sheena stood, one of the men said *sotto voce*, "Gold diggers. That's what they are."

Darcy glared at the man. Swarthy, he had dark curls, dark eyes, and a hooked nose. The one gold hoop earring in his left earlobe added to the impression of his being a pirate who'd come back to life. All he needed was a red bandanna around his head.

"Why would you say something like that?" Darcy said.

Sheena turned to her with a frown and whispered, "Please, Darcy."

But Darcy was too angry to sit back in her chair. This couldn't be anyone's idea of gold-digging, not with the awful way things were. Resting her elbows on the table, she continued to stare at the man. "Who are you?"

His smile was sly, a bit frightening. "My name is Rocky Gatto, but some people call me Cat."

"Aww ... nobody calls you Cat." Ignoring the venomous look he gave her, Gracie said, "Rocky's harmless." She faced the group. "Okay, everyone. Let's meet the new owners."

"Thank you," said Sheena. "My name is Sheena Sullivan Morelli. I'm the oldest and am married with two children, fourteen and sixteen. And, no, everyone, I'm not a gold digger, and neither are my sisters. If we were, we'd sure be disappointed with this place." She waited until the laughter died down and then added, "I hope we can work together. We all have a challenge ahead of us."

At a signal from Sheena, Darcy got to her feet. "I'm Darcy Sullivan. Before I came here, I worked in IT with computers and programming. I'm not sure about being here, but I want to try to make it work." A few people clapped.

Regan rose next. "I'm Regan Sullivan and I'm here to tell you that I don't want to go back to Boston or New York. I want to stay here like Uncle Gavin wanted." More people clapped.

"Very good," said Gracie. "Now, let's introduce ourselves to you. Start at that table."

Darcy lost track of the names as they stood and introduced themselves. When it came time for the man who'd swabbed the patio floor to say his name, the man sitting next to him nudged him. "My name is Clyde," he said proudly. A bright smile lit his face, and Darcy's heart opened. She grinned along with everyone else at Clyde's enthusiasm. At the end of the introductions, she realized the people who'd seemed frightening at first were just ordinary people with bad luck— except, maybe, Rocky.

As people prepared to leave, Holly Harwood came over to Darcy. "Are you available to help me with my computer system at the bar?"

Darcy blinked in surprise. "Perhaps, but I'll be pretty busy here."

"I can pay you in dollars or in drinks and food for you and your sisters."

"Great, I'll get back to you on that." Darcy's mind spun with possibilities. Maybe bartering would be a way to get some things done for the hotel. In the meantime, working with Holly would give her the chance to know Brian. And that was an opportunity she wasn't about to miss.

CHAPTER THIRTEEN
REGAN

Brian approached Regan, smiling. "I'm glad you don't want to go back north. Listen, I'm sorry I started off on the wrong foot with you. Can we be friends?"

Regan felt heat rise to her cheeks. "Maybe." At the look of dismay on Brian's face, she laughed. "I mean, yes, we can try."

"Good." Brian's brown-eyed gaze seemed to reach inside Regan, making her stomach whirl nervously.

Regan studied him, looking for any sign of leering. His expression remained neutral—friend to friend. *Maybe he was one of the good guys*, she thought. Only time would tell. And if she was wrong, he was going to get the tongue-lashing of his life. Or worse.

Darcy came over to them. "I might be working with you and your mother," she said to Brian, smiling at him in a flirty way that might have been comical if it weren't so irritating.

Really? Darcy was flirting with him? Watching Brian turn a kilowatt smile on her sister, Regan froze. *Oh, my God! He's a player, after all.* She turned and hurried away.

"Wait!" Brian called.

Regan kept walking. As far as she was concerned, Brian could wait in hell before she would stop.

Regan lay in bed in the early morning darkness, staring at the ceiling, her mind whirling with ideas. She and her sisters were planning to sit down and brainstorm about their situation right after breakfast, but Regan didn't want to wait that long.

She rolled over, hopeful of getting more sleep. When it became obvious that sleep was not about to come, Regan finally got up and tiptoed downstairs.

As she entered the living room, she stopped in surprise. "What are you doing up?"

From a couch, Sheena smiled up at her. "Couldn't sleep, either. As soon as it's light, I'm going to take a walk on the beach. Want to join me?"

"Sure, that would be nice." Regan sat down beside Sheena and studied her. Even disheveled from her restless night, she didn't look her age. It was hard for Regan to believe Sheena had teenagers.

Sheena reached over and took hold of one of Regan's hands. "I hope we can get to know each other better while we're here. Since I was fourteen when you were born, I sometimes thought of you as my own, especially with Mom being sick all the time. But I've never really known you, woman to woman."

Regan filled with gratitude. "It wasn't always easy being the baby at home. By the time I was fourteen, Darcy was ready to leave home. She didn't go that far away to college, but since then, it's been difficult to reconnect in a meaningful way."

Sheena rose. "I'm going to fix myself a cup of coffee. Want one?"

"Sounds good." Regan padded into the kitchen behind Sheena and lowered herself into a chair at the small table.

Sheena put a mini cup container of coffee into the coffee machine and waited for it to fill a mug. When the coffee mug was full, she handed it to Regan. "Cream? Sugar?"

Regan shook her head. "No, thanks." She held the mug

between her hands and inhaled the steamy aroma of the coffee. She loved this time of day. It seemed full of possibilities.

Sheena fixed a cup of coffee for herself and sat at the table opposite Regan. Giving her a steady stare, Sheena said, "You told everyone you didn't want to go back north. What about New York? Weren't you happy there?"

Regan couldn't help the snort that left her throat. "Only a rich person could enjoy living there. It's impersonal and pseudo. At least it was for me. No, if we can make this work here, I'll be happy. There's a lot I've never been able to do. I'm hoping this will give me the opportunity to try new things."

"Okay, that sounds good," said Sheena.

"You know I wanted to go to RISD, don't you?"

Sheena's eyes widened. "The Rhode Island School of Design? No, I never knew that. Why didn't you go there?"

Regan made a face. "Because I couldn't get in. I don't test well. That's what my guidance counselor said, but I think it's just because I'm dumb. You don't know how many teachers told me to be more like my sisters. I tried. I really did." Regan fought tears. "I have a learning difficulty—something like dyslexia that makes it difficult for me. I have the ideas and I can draw, but I never could do well on exams. My SATs stunk."

'Oh, honey, I didn't realize that. I thought you just didn't like school and later, that you wanted to go and have a good time in New York. You went there to model, didn't you?"

Regan shook her head. "What a snake pit that is. I didn't want to get into the drugs, the things you have to do to make it. That's why I settled on doing what Darcy might think is a nothing job. But, Sheena, I learned a lot about people in that job. I think I can help us. I'm good with people."

"You helping us? How?" said Darcy, swinging into the room in only panties and a camisole.

"I think we'll ask Regan to come up with ideas for fixing up and decorating the rooms," Sheena said, giving Regan a sly wink.

"Fine with me. That's not my thing," said Darcy. "But, remember, I'll need money for all the computer stuff we need."

"No one is going to get money for anything until we come up with a budget. And that means, we all have to do some research," said Sheena. "We'll have to do things in stages. We'll set up a schedule after we have a better understanding of what we need. After that, I'll be able to tell you what we can and cannot do."

"You sound like the bossy big sister you used to be, Sheena," complained Darcy. "Remember it's the three of us, not only you, who will make the decisions."

Regan saw a flash of hurt cross Sheena's face. "Darcy, you know that's not fair. Where would either of us have been without Sheena taking care of us when we were younger?"

"I guess you're right," said Darcy. "Sorry, Sheena. I'm more nervous than I thought about making this work. I can't go back to Boston a failure."

"None of us can," said Sheena quietly.

As she stepped onto the cool sand, Regan thought of the wintry weather up north and smiled. No doubt that cold wind would be seeping into the coats of people on the streets of New York while she was enjoying the sun.

Regan paused and listened to the cries of the seagulls as they lifted and swooped down in the air above her, their white wings bright against the lightening, blue sky. For her, being in Florida seemed almost exotic. She'd never traveled like many of her friends.

She walked to the water's edge and stood in its frothy midst, staring at the tiny fish that swam past her in small schools. She didn't know what it would take to beat this challenge, but like she'd told Gavin's people, she wanted to be able to stay at the Salty Key Inn for as long as she could. Her life up to this moment had been one disappointment after another.

"C'mon! We're going to walk down the beach and check out the other small hotels," said Darcy, waving her forward.

Regan hurried to join her sisters.

The buildings lining the beach were a polyglot of shapes, colors; and sizes. The restaurant building, which had at first seemed very ugly with its blue clapboard siding and faded yellow trim, now seemed more appropriate.

As they continued their walk, Regan realized theirs was one of the larger properties around.

"We'd better head back and have breakfast," said Sheena. "There's a whole lot we have to discuss."

The cries of the seagulls accompanied them as they made their way past other early walkers to the public right of way.

They walked along the wooden boardwalk in single file, with Darcy leading. When she reached the end of it and stood by the street, Regan called to her, "Wait! I want to show you something."

Darcy and Sheena stopped and stood beside her.

"Yeah? What?" said Darcy.

"Look straight ahead," said Regan. "What do you see?"

Sheena smiled. "I get it. The curb appeal of the hotel is about zero."

"Yes," said Regan. "We need to repaint that building and add some plantings to make the whole entrance to the hotel more appealing. It shouldn't cost that much. Especially if we help paint it."

"Whoa!" said Darcy. "We can hire it done."

"Let's talk about it after breakfast, but, Regan, I like what you're saying." Sheena placed a hand on Regan's shoulder, like some kind of benediction.

Regan filled with gratitude. Maybe this stay in Florida would be everything she'd hoped.

CHAPTER FOURTEEN
SHEENA

Sheena noticed the look of pride that crossed Regan's face and smiled. The family had always considered Regan the "dumb blonde" of the family, even with her dark hair. She hadn't known of her sister's misery because she'd been too busy raising her own family. Maybe, she thought, with this stay in Florida, she could help Regan gain more self-confidence.

As she approached the restaurant, Sheena was pleased to see several cars in the parking lot and people eating on the patio. If they were going to use Gracie's as a focal point to renew their hotel, it seemed right to dress up the building a bit. Besides, she wanted at least one thing to be attractive before Tony and the children came for a visit.

Inside the restaurant, two women from Gavin's group— Lynn Michaels and Maggie O'Neil— were acting as waitresses. Sheena peeked into the kitchen. Bertha Baker, better known as Bebe, was in the kitchen helping Gracie. Sam Patterson— also from the group—was standing at the griddle, flipping pancakes. Sally Neal was washing dishes.

Sheena stepped away, pleased to see that like Gracie had said, members of Gavin's group really did help out on a regular basis.

After Sheena and her sisters had taken seats and ordered their meals, Sheena gazed around the interior of the restaurant. There was a lot she'd do to upgrade it, but with money being an issue, she thought they should hold off on any major expenses on the interior until they had money coming in. *If* they had money coming in, she quickly amended.

Their meals came and Sheena dug in. It felt wonderful to be waited on. And when she took a bite of her fluffy, scrambled eggs and then tasted the soft biscuit coated with honey, she couldn't hold back a sigh of satisfaction. Gracie was a miracle worker.

Sheena smiled at the looks of contentment on her sisters' faces.

"Delicious," said Darcy, digging into her pancakes.

"This French Toast is the best I've ever had," said Regan. "Not that I can allow myself to have it very often. I'd get too fat."

Sheena sighed. It was something Meaghan would say. She hated that young girls felt a need to apologize for treats whenever they dared to have one.

As they were eating their breakfast, the place became more and more crowded. They quickly finished their meal, which they were told was complimentary, and left the restaurant.

Back at the house, Sheena hurried everyone into the living room. "Let's make a list of priorities, and then we can decide what we want to do. We can't waste a minute."

They quickly agreed on the need to paint the outside of the restaurant and to do some minor landscaping there.

"We really need to get a computer and install internet service," said Darcy. "After we do, I can build a website and give this place a presence on the internet."

Sheena recalled the items in one of the storage closets. "And we need a program that will keep track of things we'll be getting."

"And the furniture in the guest rooms," said Regan.

"Whoa!" said Darcy. "I'm going to be super busy."

Sheena and Regan exchanged looks. "Right," they said together.

"I'd like permission to look into secondhand furniture for the rooms," said Regan.

"What? We don't want a lot of junk," said Darcy.

"We need to trust her judgment," warned Sheena. "Regan has had a long-time interest in interior design and decorating."

Darcy's look of surprise was telling. She turned to Regan. "You do?"

Regan's nostrils flared with irritation. "Being a receptionist was never a goal of mine, no matter how dumb you think I am."

Darcy held up a hand. "Sorry. I didn't mean to rattle your cage."

"Okay, you two," said Sheena. "Let's give each other a break. I'm realizing there's a lot we don't know about each other."

Darcy nodded. "Yeah, I don't know how I ended up working with computers when all I've ever really wanted to do was write a novel."

Regan's eyes widened. "A novel? You're kidding!"

Darcy shook her head. "No, I'm not. But I've been stuck doing computers because that's where the money is. Don't worry. I'll handle the computers here."

"And I'll do an inventory of furnishings," said Regan agreeably.

"I'll get in touch with Brian and see what he can do to help us get the landscaping and painting done," said Sheena.

"Don't forget I'll need money to buy the computer," warned Darcy.

"First, I need to talk to Brian to see what he knows about our utility expenses and other financial matters."

"I could help you talk to him," grinned Darcy. "Brian is hot, hot, hot."

Sheena noticed the flare in Regan's nostrils but said nothing. Those two would have to work out their differences over the cutest guy she'd seen in some time.

Just as Sheena was about to head out to the restaurant, Brian knocked on the front door. "You ladies decent?" he called through the door he'd merely cracked open.

Darcy sprang out of her seat and went to answer him. "Very decent," she said, grinning at him.

He opened the door and stepped inside. "Figured you'd be meeting and thought I could be of help. Gavin asked me to be at your service while you got started on the project."

Two hours later, many of Sheena's questions were answered. Yes, they had a vehicle—Gavin's old red Cadillac convertible. No, there weren't any contracts with landscapers. No, a pool service wasn't in place. Yes, the account for electricity was paid up-to-date. Yes, he would show her a record of monthly expenses, most of which were covered under normal operating expenses. No, there were no reservations for guests.

When it came time to talk about various expenses, Brian became solemn. "My business can help you with the painting and landscaping. Hell, I can even find you someone to take care of the pool. But that's just window dressing. How about the rooms themselves?"

"I'm doing an inventory of furnishings," said Regan. "Do you know of any place where we can get good used furniture? That may be a way for us to refurnish those rooms with something better. At least a few at a time."

Brian's face lit up. "Great idea. Let me poke around. I heard rumors about one of the bigger, older hotels doing a refurbishment."

"We don't want to go from one crappy set of furniture to another," said Darcy.

Brian held up his hand. "No, no. I'm talking about a place similar to the Don CeSar Hotel. And that's very nice." He turned back to Regan. "We'll go together if you like."

"And I can go too," Darcy said hopefully.

"You're probably going to be busy with all the new online computer programs," Sheena gently reminded her.

Darcy grimaced. "Right."

"Yeah, my mother's hoping you'll help her at the bar," said Brian, bringing a smile to Darcy's face.

Watching their interplay, Sheena wondered when she'd become such an old lady. She and Darcy were only ten years apart but it felt like fifty. Playfully, she said, "Maybe I'll go too."

Brian grinned at her. "You're on."

This time, Sheena noticed to her amusement that both Darcy and Regan wore frowns.

After Brian left, Sheena said, "I have to pick up some things at the drug store, and we need to have some food in the house. I'll pay for it for now. We should be reimbursed by Archibald Wilson for them. But we can't wait until then. Among other things, we need sunscreen. The Sullivan pasty-white skin is already turning pink on us."

"I need some clothes too. But there's no use buying a lot of fancy stuff. Not if we're going to be working around here," said Regan.

"I'm sure there's a Walmart around," said Darcy. "I'll check on my phone."

"I wonder what shape Gavin's car is in," said Sheena.

"Yeah, they're the only wheels we have," said Darcy.

"I bet it's a mess. Like the hotel," Regan said, sighing.

"We'll soon find out. Follow me." Sheena held up the ring

of keys and led her sisters to a single-car garage at the end of the front building.

There, she unlocked the overhead garage door and lifted it up.

"Wow!" said Regan.

Sheena flipped on the light switch. A single light bulb dangling on an electric cord hooked on the ceiling of the garage shone on a car Sheena had only seen in antique car shows.

A red Cadillac with a white top and white-walled tires sat in the middle of the garage. The red body of the car glistened in the light, exhibiting the care it had been given.

"Brian says it runs. Right?' Darcy's voice was a whisper as her fingers trailed over the surface of the car. She opened the car door, peered inside and turned back with a grin. "It's in good condition for what I'm pretty sure is a car from the 1950s."

Sheena unhooked the car keys from the ring and handed them to Darcy. "Here. You drive. I'm not comfortable doing it."

Darcy gave Regan a questioning look.

Regan shook her head. "Not me. I didn't have to drive in the city."

Darcy grinned. "Okay, get in. We're going for a spin."

CHAPTER FIFTEEN
DARCY

As she turned the key in the ignition, Darcy held her breath. Sean, her ex-boyfriend, had loved old cars, and she'd willingly gone to various car shows with him. And this car of Uncle Gavin's was a real classic in superior condition. *He must have loved it a lot*, she thought as the engine purred to life.

Regan, sitting in the front passenger seat, grinned at her. "Nice!"

"Be careful backing out," said Sheena. At Darcy's glare, she laughed. "Sorry. I'm in Mommy mode. There's nothing like teaching a teenager how to drive to shake your confidence in all drivers."

Darcy eased the car out of the garage, and drove it through the parking lot, and onto the road.

"Let's see the neighborhood from this angle," she said.

She drove slowly enough to give them all a good look at the properties around them. They passed through one small beach town after another and approached St. Pete Beach.

"What is that huge pink building?" asked Regan.

"I think that's the Don CeSar. Let's go see," said Darcy.

As they approached the imposing, glamorous façade of the hotel, the inside of the car was quiet. Regan's sigh broke the silence. "This is what I thought our hotel would look like."

"Me too," admitted Sheena. "I had no idea things would be like they are. Guess we'd better enjoy this view because that's as close to staying here as we're going to get."

Darcy drove onto the main road and headed back to their hotel. "You know we might be able to make it work. Sheena, you've been helping Tony with his business. You're going to have to organize the Salty Key Inn. And, Regan, you're going to have to make it look nice. Think we can do it?"

There was an ominous pause, and then at the same time, Sheena and Regan said: "*Yes!*"

The ring of laughter that filled the car was satisfying.

CHAPTER SIXTEEN
SHEENA

Sheena sat in the backseat of the car, staring out the window, smiling and waving back when people tooted their car horns at them. She felt so young, so carefree. Getting pregnant at such a young age, she'd missed out on a lot of simple things like cruising the neighborhood with girlfriends.

She thought back to last night's phone conversation with Tony. He'd said the one thing he missed was her cooking. Talk about being married too long! Somewhere along the line, they'd lost even the idea of romance.

"Sheena, are you going to draw up a budget or whatever you do for Tony?" said Darcy from behind the wheel.

"Absolutely," she answered. "We'll need a strict budget if we want to succeed. And while we won't ever be as big or as fancy as some of these other places, we can make something of the Salty Key Inn that we can be proud of."

Regan turned around in the front seat and gave Sheena a fist bump. "Yeah, girl. Let's do it."

"Okay, now to more practical matters," said Darcy. "The Walmart is across the bridge. Hang on, I'm turning right."

As Sheena left the store with her sisters, she was struck by how simple their lives were becoming. Both Darcy and Regan had chosen two pairs of shorts and three T-shirts to supplement the wardrobe they thought would be filled with glamorous clothes. All three of them had purchased baseball hats, suntan lotion, beach towels and enough food to keep them going for a week at home.

When they returned to the hotel's entrance, Brian waved them to a stop.

Sheena rolled her window down. "What's up?"

"Good news. I've found a couple of painters to power-wash and then scrape and sand down the building as prep for painting it. We'll see what your budget allows. If necessary, we can all pitch in and do the actual painting ourselves."

Sheena smiled. "Thanks. If they can do the tough work, we can help with the rest. We want as little disruption to our dining guests as possible."

"Gotcha," said Brian. "You let me know what your budget is for landscaping and I'll come up with a plan. Glad to see our Gertie has gone for a drive."

"Gertie?"

Brian grinned. "That's what Gavin used to call her." He patted the side of the car. "She's a good one." He gave them a wave and walked away.

Darcy fanned herself with her hands. "Whew!" she said, still staring at Brian's retreating body.

Regan remained silent, but Sheena noticed her watching him walk away. Who wouldn't? Sheena thought, enjoying the movement of his hips as he crossed the lawn to his mother's property next door.

"Maybe I should go visit The Key Hole," Darcy said. "I need to talk to Holly about helping her with her computers."

Regan heaved a sigh and got out of the car. "I'll take our purchases back to the house."

Darcy frowned. "What's wrong with you?"

"Nothing," said Regan. "Absolutely nothing."

Darcy gave Sheena a questioning look.

Sheena shrugged. After getting out of the car, Sheena helped Regan load the groceries on a golf cart, and then they traveled along the driveway to the pink house. Regan stopped the cart outside the front entrance and looked up at the house. "With a little work this house could be adorable."

"I know, but that's the last thing to get done. Agreed?"

"Agreed."

Later, as Sheena sat with her sisters in the living room, sipping a glass of pinot noir—a welcome-to-Florida present from Holly next door—Sheena thought of her mother. Had her mother known that Gavin was rich? Would she ever have guessed what he'd do for her and her sisters? If the gold coin was worth a lot of money, she could sell it and solve their problems. But Sheena vowed not to do it. A life lesson is what Gavin had wanted for them, and she had the feeling classes were just beginning.

"What kind of novel would you write?" Regan asked Darcy, curling her feet under her in one of the overstuffed chairs that sat beside the couches.

"Oh, I don't know," Darcy mused. "Not a serious romance. Not after the way Sean crushed me. Maybe a comedy of some kind." She gave Regan a steady look. "Why didn't you let everyone know you wanted to be a designer?"

Regan shrugged. "What was the point? My grades were lousy. And besides, by then, Mom and Dad had spent a wad of money on your education. I heard Dad complain about it and I didn't want to make things worse for Mom. You know how he could be, going on and on about something."

"I saved them a lot of money by screwing up and getting pregnant," Sheena said. "You could've used some of that money."

Regan shook her head. "Mom's medicine cost a bundle, and there were other problems too. I don't know the whole story, but Dad lost a lot of money on some kind of investment with Uncle Gavin." Her brow wrinkled. "Or maybe it was a deal Gavin told him not to invest in. Anyway, I heard that's one of the reasons Dad and Gavin never got along. Money at home was tough sometimes."

"Gavin has done some nice things for people. I wonder about the real size of his estate," said Sheena. "This whole arrangement is so unusual."

"Maybe it's another trick of his and this is all there is," said Darcy. "From what you tell me, I wouldn't put it past him."

"Either way, tomorrow, we begin the projects in earnest. Right?" said Sheena. "Darcy, you're going to price a wireless system for the internet and the cost of equipment. Thank goodness, we all brought our computers."

"Yes," said Darcy. "I already asked Brian to help me. He has a friend who's in the business."

"I wonder how he and Gavin began to work together," Regan commented.

"It's a good thing. He seems to know everyone in the area," Sheena said. "Regan, you're going to begin an inventory of all the rooms furniture. Right?"

"Yes. And you're going to start on a budget."

Sheena smiled. It was beginning to sound like a team.

When a call came from Tony, Sheena stepped outside of the house and sat in one of the chairs on the so-called porch.

"Hi, honey. How are you?" Sheena said, hoping Tony wouldn't ask her the same question. She wasn't good at lying.

"Not very good. It's chaotic with you gone. Meaghan is freaking out over the dance, and Michael thinks he can drive anywhere he wants without considering what the rest of us are up to. Mom is trying to help by feeding us, but we're already out of most of the groceries you bought for us."

"You all know where the grocery store is. Right?" Sheena kept her voice light, but vindication for her decision flooded her. What her family was missing was obviously all the things she usually did for them, not herself.

"How did you keep things running smoothly? Tony said. "I don't know where to begin."

"Begin by having the kids follow the schedule I drew up. Then keep a running list of things needed at the grocery store. Michael can drive there with or without his sister and get the groceries. It's not all that complicated. It just takes teamwork."

"I'm busy working. I can't do this. You need to come home."

"Tony, I've been gone only a couple of days. You all are going to have to "do this" because I'm not leaving. I have an enormous project here."

"What do you mean...enormous? What in the hell is going on? Is that why you haven't sent us any pictures?"

"Partly," said Sheena honestly, "and partly because we're still trying to understand what we're dealing with. Let's just say it's not what we envisioned."

"I knew it! You've told me all about Gavin. It's just a joke, isn't it?"

"I'm not sure, but I intend to find out. Are the kids around? I've tried to reach Meaghan, but she won't answer my calls."

"Meaghan is next door at Mom's, and Michael isn't home from practice yet. Sheena, I want you to come home."

"Tony, I love you, but I'm staying here. It's as much about me and us as it is about a hotel I inherited. I need to find me."

Tony's voice lowered to a growl. "You need to be home with your family,"

"Look, I've got to go," Sheena said. "I'll call you tomorrow. And give the kids hugs for me."

Sheena disconnected the call before Tony could make more demands of her—demands she had no intention of meeting.

She sat in the chair for a moment staring through the dark at the shapes of the buildings she'd once imagined would be different. As frogs chirped in the background and stars twinkled in the ebony sky above, sadness and frustration enfolded her. For years, her role had been to keep her family happy by filling their demands, keeping things running smoothly. But they now took her for granted. They demanded, not asked her to do something for them, as if she were a genie in a bottle. And if things didn't happen with a magical poof, they got upset with her. She couldn't allow herself to continue in that pattern. She was more than their slave. She would not, could not, go back to that situation now or ever. She had to begin to change things by meeting this challenge. She owed it to her sisters; she owed it to herself.

The next morning, determination filled Sheena as she set to work preparing a budget. But as she delved into listing real and imagined expenses, she realized she needed a lot more input than Brian could give her. She needed to talk to the man who'd handled the finances for Gavin.

She headed to The Key Hole, Holly Harwood's bar next door, to see if she could find Brian.

The pale green building with turquoise trim that held the bar was similar in style to the hotel's restaurant but in much better condition. Its bright colors and the painted, carved wooden parrot by the entrance fit nicely into the funky neighborhood. At eleven o'clock in the morning, the bar was open, but not busy. Sheena stood inside the entrance to get a good look at the interior.

Inside, stained walls toned down the colorful exterior. A

central, u-shaped bar held a number of stools. Several booths lined the far wall. The place was clean and smoke-free, which Sheena appreciated.

Holly appeared from the back kitchen. "Well, hello, neighbor! What can I do for you? It's a little early for wine, but we've got it."

Smiling, Sheena held up a hand. "Thanks, anyway. I'm wondering if Brian is around or if you might be able to help me. I understand you knew Gavin quite well. I need to know the name of the person who handled his finances. I could call the lawyer handling his estate, but I thought it might be quicker for me to ask you or Brian."

"Got some time? I can help you out. In fact, it's probably a good idea for us to have a little chat." Holly led waved her over to a booth and slid onto the red-plastic-covered seat.

Curious, Sheena sat opposite her. Holly's sun-streaked hair, classic features, and trim body made her attractive, but it was the kindness that Sheena saw in Holly's dark eyes that caught her attention.

"I guess Brian told you that Gavin bought this place for me," Holly said. "He knew I needed a source of income. Since I wouldn't marry him, he made sure I'd be okay."

"He asked you to marry him?" Sheena said.

Holly nodded. "I know there's quite an age difference, but, of course, in Gavin's mind, he was only half his age. And, I must say, for the most part, he acted it. But after Brian's father left me high and dry when he was a toddler, I had no interest in settling down with anyone else. But Gavin and I had a nice, long-term relationship. More platonic than not. And, most of all, we were best friends."

A sadness crossed Holly's face. "I was very upset to learn his heart was so damaged the doctors weren't sure surgery could fix it. And then the heart attack ended it. He only had a short time to live after learning of his problem, but it was enough time to take care of me and to set things up for you Sullivan sisters. He talked a lot about you, Sheena. You and your mother. He loved her, you know. And she loved him."

Sheena felt her eyes widen. "He did? She did?"

Sheena felt the blood drain from her face. She recalled the gold coin Gavin had given her. Did it mean more than a nice gift for a little girl? Her stomach filled with acid. Was she Gavin's daughter? Was that why her father had hated Gavin? There was a ten-year difference between her and Darcy. Was that part of the equation of love between her mother and Gavin? Her mind spun with possibilities.

"Apparently, there was some kind of family misunderstanding. Gavin knew he wasn't welcome back in Boston. Before he died, he had me help him destroy letters to him from your mother. He said he didn't want to mar her memory. I was to tell only you."

Sheena thought back once more to the gold coin. Questions bombarded the inside of her head. *Was the coin some sort of symbol of Gavin's love for her mother? Had Gavin used the monkey to deliver the gold to her? Was it to be used to give her mother the opportunity to get away if she wanted?*

Holly reached over and patted Sheena's hand. "Are you all right? Let me get you some water.

Sheena took a sip from the glass of water Holly handed her and then said, "Gavin seems to have done many nice things for a lot of people. Tell me what he was like."

A dreamy expression filled Holly's face as she sat back down across from Sheena. "Gavin was a bigger-than-life kind of guy—a tall, handsome man with big dreams, big plans, big successes. He was always dabbling in something. He even went diving for gold on shipwrecks. He succeeded in whatever he did. Some called it the luck of the Irish. But Gavin was a very bright, energetic man who seemed to smell possibility. The hotel he's given you is in a prime location. I know about the will. He talked to me about it. Should you fail at it, the people taking over could sell the land alone for a small fortune. But Gavin always saw it as a place for people to come to and enjoy. He wanted it to be special."

"What about Gavin's people as they call themselves?"

Holly grinned. "He hand-picked them himself. Right now, they're helping Gracie in the kitchen. But each one has a special story, a special talent. You should take the time to get to know them."

"Rocky looks like a pirate," said Sheena.

Holly laughed. "Indeed he was, sort of. He was one of Gavin's buddies searching for gold. I'm not sure they ever found any, but they became trusted friends."

"Who handled Gavin's finances? I'm trying to draw up a budget for the property, but I'm missing a lot of information."

Holly slid out of the booth and onto her feet. "Let me give you his business card. Gavin left it here for you. He hoped you'd be smart enough to ask for it."

"Wait! What's his name?"

Holly turned back to Sheena with a smile. "Blackie Gatto."

As Sheena made the connection to Rocky, a shiver, like a dancing spider, crossed her shoulders.

CHAPTER SEVENTEEN
DARCY

How could a hotel run without high-speed internet access, a good wireless system, and excellent computer programs? Darcy was ready to dive into the IT issues at both the hotel and the house. Though she wasn't as anxious to keep in touch with her old roomies as she thought she'd be—not with the way things had turned out in Florida—without access to the internet, she felt lost.

With Sheena's and Regan's encouragement, she called a friend of Brian's to help her set up a wireless system in both the house and in the hotel's office. Chip Carson sounded like a typical, non-communicative geek on the phone, but he agreed to come to the hotel within a day or two.

Until she could meet with Chip, Darcy spent the time cleaning up the office and going through files. Whoever ran the place before had left behind a lot of worthless papers relating to a restaurant that existed before Gracie took it over. Any papers she thought might be of interest to Sheena, she set aside.

When Sheena saw what Darcy was doing, she joined her. "Good idea to get things in shape here. That will allow all of us to work in here from time to time."

Together, they wiped down the two wooden desks, cleaned out the drawers, and did their best to make sense of the files.

"Now we need office supplies," said Sheena.

"Make a list and I'll go get them," Darcy said.

"Between the Dollar Store and a few other stores nearby, we should be able to pick up most for a good price. We'll use your money, this time," said Sheena, giving Darcy a challenging smile. "At least until we can talk to the lawyer about reimbursement."

"Okay, I'll buy them, but don't complain if it's not exactly what you want. And Regan can put money toward more groceries."

"Deal," said Sheena. "Remember to save your receipts. After meeting with Mr. Gatto, I'll know what money we've been given, if any, has to be used for living expenses."

If the hundred-fifty grand Gavin left us for the hotel includes the cost of our living here, it'll just make the hotel project that much more difficult to get going." Darcy's sigh came from deep inside her. "This is such a frickin' mess."

"We'll take it one step at a time," Sheena said. "Once we can get some rooms ready, clean up the front area, and have financial control over what's happening, we should be able to pull in some revenue. It's going to be touch and go for a while, though."

Darcy and Sheena exchanged worried looks. This was a game they might not win.

Darcy was pulling Gertie into the garage when she noticed a soft-top, blue Jeep Wrangler pull into the nearby parking lot. She retrieved her packages from the back seat of the Cadillac and watched a tall, young, robust guy with dark brown hair get out of the car and head down the walk toward the office. In his shorts and T-shirt, he looked ... well ... yummy. "Hey! Can I help you?" Darcy said, intrigued.

He stopped and turned around. "I'm here to meet someone."

Darcy noticed the computer case he was carrying. "Are you Chip?"

A grin spread across his face. He lifted his sunglasses atop his head and studied her with bright blue eyes. "Yeah. Are you Darcy?"

She smiled. "Yes. I was expecting you a little later."

"I finished up another job earlier than I thought I would." He seemed to suddenly notice the packages she was trying to juggle in her arms. "Need some help?"

"Thanks, that would be great." Darcy handed him two of the four packages she was holding. "Let's go inside."

Chip followed her into the office, and, still holding the packages, looked around the room. "I haven't seen old wooden desks like this before. Very cool."

"Well, it's what was left behind when my uncle bought this place," said Darcy. "I hope we can replace them someday."

"Gavin Sullivan was your uncle? I wondered about that relationship when I heard your name. He and I talked about setting up a wireless system here. This shouldn't take a lot of time. I still have the schematics for it. We can talk about routers and all and then I can get you hooked up with a computer dealer."

Darcy set her bags on the floor near the desk she was taking over. "Do you have experience with inventory systems, restaurant sales, and the like?"

He nodded. "I set up the temporary point-of-sale or POS system for Gracie's. Gavin and I were going to work on it, and then he died. I was told not to do anything else to it until his estate was settled. I guess you are part of that picture."

"Yes, I am. How much time can you give us?"

Before he could answer, Regan appeared at the doorway. "Am I interrupting anything? I wanted to show you an inventory sheet I've created for the furnishings, Darcy. I'm just beginning the project, but I wanted to see if you thought this made sense."

"Want me to take a look at it?" said Chip. "I'm working with Darcy on things like this," he quickly explained.

"Okay." Regan handed Chip the paper and gave Darcy a questioning look.

"Regan, this is Chip Carson, the IT guy who's going to set up a wireless system and various programs for us." Darcy turned to Chip. "And this is my sister, Regan Sullivan."

Chip smiled and quickly returned to studying the sheet.

Darcy couldn't hide her amusement at Regan's surprised reaction to Chip's indifference. Regan was used to guys falling at her feet. And with those cut-off jeans and the halter top she was now wearing, most guys would drop to their knees.

Chip looked up from the sheet of paper. "Good job of capturing what you need to know. I can help you set up a spreadsheet that will automatically tally numbers for you. You'll be able to break down pieces of furniture by condition, style, whatever you want."

"Really?" A smile spread across Regan's face.

"Before you do that, Chip, we need to set a time to get those wireless systems up. And we need a cost estimate for doing so," said Darcy.

"If it's too expensive, we may have to wait on the house," said Regan. "But we hope we can do both."

"I'll definitely give you a good price," said Chip before turning to Darcy. "How about we meet first thing tomorrow morning? I'll bring the specs and we'll come up with a definite plan." He pulled out his phone. "I'll mark it on my calendar. Now I'd better go see to my girl."

After Chip left, Regan collapsed into a desk chair. "Wow! Too bad he already has a girlfriend. He hardly noticed me."

"And that bothered you, did it?" Darcy said, unable to keep

a teasing edge out of her voice.

"Bothered me? No, I loved it! And he even thought I did a good job with the inventory." Regan sighed. "That's the kind of guy I'm looking for."

"I'm looking for someone like Brian," Darcy said, fanning the air in front of her face.

Regan made a face. "See you back at the house."

Darcy watched her sister go, and realized the girl she thought she knew didn't exist. Why hadn't she known how unhappy Regan was with her reputation—beauty but no brains? The truth was Regan was plenty smart, but everyone had judged her by her beauty alone. Or had she, like the rest of her family, simply fitted Regan into that slot without thinking how much it would hurt her?

CHAPTER EIGHTEEN
SHEENA

A few days later, as she drove across the bridge and into St. Petersburg, Sheena wondered about the man she was about to meet. With a name like Blackie Gatto, he had to be tough. In fact, she wondered if he was legit. His brother Rocky looked like a pirate from old, seafaring days.

She parked the Caddy in the garage near the office building. The building's exterior of cream-colored stucco with dark green trim was exactly how she'd once envisioned The Salty Key Inn—classy, simple, clean.

After entering the office of Gatto and Ryan and checking in with the receptionist, Sheena sat down in one of the chairs in the reception area. Gazing around, she took in the soft green Oriental carpet, the nice furniture, the beautiful artwork on the walls. The firm of Gatto and Ryan was obviously doing well.

The receptionist answered a call, said, *"Thank you,"* and then rose. "Mr. Gatto can see you now," she said to Sheena.

Sheena got to her feet, brushed off her skirt, and at a signal from the receptionist, followed her down a long hallway. The corner office she entered overlooked a small inlet where several boats were tied to docks.

The man behind the large, modern metal and glass desk smiled, strode over to her, and took her hand in both of his. "You're even more beautiful than your pictures."

Taken aback, Sheena blinked. "Where have you seen

pictures of me?"

His dark-eyed gaze stayed on her. "Gavin was eager to show me pictures of his nieces. Your mother, I believe, kept him supplied with them. Especially after she learned to use an iPhone."

Sheena laughed. "That was quite a project. But once she learned how to take pictures on her phone, she went crazy."

He smiled and said, "Have a seat and let's talk. Gavin was pretty sure we'd meet. He gave me a list of things to discuss with you."

"He did? How did he know I'd come to you?"

Blackie grinned. "He guessed you would. You're smart, like him."

Sheena lowered herself into one of the soft-cushioned, brown-leather chairs in front of his desk. As he got settled behind his desk, Sheena studied him. His face was a softer, kinder version of his brother's—a younger, darker George Clooney. "I've met your brother, Rocky. I was surprised to learn your name is ..."

"... Blackie to my friends." His smile was charming. "I got the name when I was in high school acting as a pirate during the Gasparilla Pirate Festival in Tampa. Believe me, with a given name like Byron, I welcomed the new one."

Taken in by his easy manner, Sheena chuckled with him.

He leaned back in his chair and steepled his fingers as he studied her. "So you and your sisters accepted Gavin's challenge. How are you finding things?"

Sheena noticed the twinkle in his eyes and wondered what games he and Gavin had in store for them.

"I'm sure the two of you knew how surprised we'd be at what we found," she said. "However, we're going to do our best to make it work. It matters to each of us for different reasons."

At the steady stare of interest Blackie was giving her, Sheena shifted in her chair. She hadn't had a man look at her with such attraction in a long, long time.

Blackie stood, went over to the window, and stared out at the scenery. When he turned back to her, he exuded a long sigh. "Gavin was one of the most interesting men I've ever met. He was a gambler and a giver, a loudmouth and a tender soul, and a cautious businessman who dared to try new things. Sometimes he failed, but most times he succeeded.

"The hotel meant many things to him. As he grew older, he wanted to give back to those who weren't as fortunate. Each of the people he chose to live cost-free at the hotel meant a lot to him. But he was smart too. Each person there is very special. Gracie, as you know by now, is a fabulous cook. My brother Rocky has his own tricks, but he can be useful to you. The others can be put to work at the hotel until you're successful enough to hire others."

Sheena heard the earnestness in Blackie's voice and felt some of the tension leave her shoulders. Blackie might have assisted Gavin in developing the challenge, but he would help them.

"Before I set a budget, I need your input," she told him. "For instance, I know nothing about the arrangements he made with his people. Are we responsible for their expenses? And what about the restaurant? Does the revenue come to us?"

Blackie shook his head. "The costs of running Gracie's are borne by Gracie's as part of the hotel and have nothing to do with the capital budget you've been given or your challenge. It is a separate entity with revenues and profits going to the hotel. Gracie and the others are paid nicely out of revenues for their work, along with room and board."

"Good," said Sheena. "How are we to get around? We have

only the Cadillac, and we don't want to use that for hauling stuff. And can you give me a complete list of regular expenses for the hotel? Those shouldn't have to come from the money he gave us."

By the time Sheena rattled off her questions, Blackie was laughing. "God! You sound just like him, you know."

"Gavin?" She recalled the note at the end of her letter and sat back in her chair. Maybe she was more like Gavin than she thought. Maybe she was more than his niece. The idea pleased her.

Blackie handed her a sheet of paper. "Gavin and I already set up a budget of pre-opening expenses. These are expenses one could consider normal in preparation for opening the hotel such as personal food for you, office supplies, your phone bills, and the lease of a vehicle. Your challenge budget covers capital expenses—the costs of bringing the hotel up to operating condition. Capital expenses cover those things that will have a useful life longer than a year."

Sheena left the office full of ideas. What had sounded straightforward and rigid in the will and in Gavin's letter wasn't as difficult as it had once seemed. The phrase '*Think outside the box*' had been used a lot in conversation with Blackie. Sheena realized she hadn't done that kind of thinking for years. Change might not be easy for everyone, but it was good for her.

When Sheena returned to the hotel, she parked the car in the garage and headed into the office. Darcy was there, typing away on her computer.

"What are you doing?" Sheena asked, pleased to find her busy.

Darcy smiled. "Coming up with a shopping list. Chip thinks

he can get most of the computer stuff we need at a discount for us. He has 'connections.'"

"Great. Where's Regan?"

"Working her way through the guest rooms." Darcy gave Sheena a troubled look. "Did you know that Regan didn't even apply to college because she thought she was dumb? She says it wasn't really about the money. While you were gone, we talked a bit, and she finally admitted that her insecurity was the real reason she didn't even go for it. Kinda sad, don't you think?"

"Yes," said Sheena. "Let's give her all the leeway she needs to spruce up the rooms."

"Okay. But she can't hog all the money."

"I agree," Sheena said. "I can't wait to tell you about my meeting with Blackie Gatto. Call Regan on her cell and ask her to come to the office."

While they waited for Regan to arrive, Sheena left the office and went into the kitchen for a cup of coffee.

Gracie looked up at her from the small desk in the corner of the room. "Yes?"

"Okay if I grab some coffee?"

Gracie nodded. "Help yourself."

Sheena poured a cup from the coffeemaker still warm from lunch and took a long sip. Even in the humid heat of Florida, it felt good to have the hot coffee slide down her throat in a satisfying swallow.

"What are you doing?" Sheena asked Gracie, going over to her.

"Making sure I have all the supplies I need for the next couple of days," said Gracie. "Why?" The challenge in her expression told Sheena she'd better go slowly. This was Gracie's territory. Gavin had made sure of it.

"It will be nice when we get things better organized around

here. We're counting on you to help us, Gracie. Blackie told me Gavin wanted it that way."

Gracie nodded but said nothing.

"What restaurant did you work at in Tampa and how long have you known Gavin?"

"The restaurant is gone and I've known Gavin forever," Gracie replied, making it clear she didn't want to discuss it.

Sheena hid her disappointment but understood some stories might be private. "Well, I'd better get back to the office. Thanks for the coffee."

As she walked away, Sheena realized that, though she'd been told all of Gavin's people had a story, and they all would cooperate with her, it would take time to gain their confidence.

By the time Sheena got back to the office, Regan had joined Darcy.

Sheena glanced at her and smiled. Usually, Regan presented herself perfectly. Now, her nose was smudged with dirt, her hair was tangled, and she was covered with dust.

"Working hard?" Sheena asked her.

Regan grinned. "You won't believe the messes in those rooms. I need to order a dumpster, maybe two, to be brought here. I'll also need a couple of the men to help me dispose of things. I'll mark those things that need to be thrown away in each room and they can haul them to the dumpster."

Sheena was impressed. This wasn't the quiet sister she thought she knew. "Good thinking, Regan. Let's add that to the list. It can't be too expensive, and I believe that cost will not come from our budget. I have good news." She pulled out a chair and sat down at the free desk.

"My visit with Blackie Gatto was very productive. He and Gavin were very close. In fact, they worked together to set things up for us. The list of questions we had for Blackie was part of a test of sorts, and we passed it with flying colors."

"Yeah? What does a 'test of sorts' mean?" asked Darcy skeptically.

"It means that Gavin wanted us to be creative and willing to ask others for help. By doing so, I've come up with a new way to look at our budget. Normal hotel costs and our living expenses won't have to come out of the one hundred fifty thousand dollars we've been given to make this hotel operable. Running Gracie's is not part of our plan, nor are its costs. And he's agreed our personal food costs should come out of a different fund, a petty cash fund, as long as they are reasonable." Sheena held up a hand to stop Darcy's clapping. "We're still going to have trouble making this work, but things like leasing a more practical car can come under ongoing hotel expenses."

"A car? How about a jeep?" said Darcy.

Sheena shook her head. "Blackie suggested a van, and I agree with him. We need something we can use to haul stuff around. Now, let's go over our list of renovation expenses. They come under capital expenditures, which means from the one hundred fifty thousand dollars. "

After only a few minutes, it became obvious that preparing the guest rooms for use was going to be a huge financial problem.

Regan slumped in her chair. "It's going to take some kind of miracle to get the rooms ready. We can't use anything in them. Not like they are."

"And until they're ready, we can't bring in guests. And that means we can't bring in money," said Darcy. "What a mess."

Sheena, Darcy, and Regan exchanged worried glances.

"Let's take it easy," Sheena suggested. " I don't see a problem with ordering dumpsters. And there's nothing to stop us from leasing a van and buying groceries and other supplies.

Let's go do that now. Blackie didn't like the idea of our using Gertie on a daily basis."

As they were preparing to leave, Brian knocked on the office door and entered the room.

"Just the man we want to see," said Darcy, smiling at him.

"Yes," said Sheena. "We need to lease a van for the hotel. Do you have any suggestions? We want to get one right away."

"Depends on what you're looking for. There's a whole bunch of dealers around. My mom likes her Honda. And I know a guy at the Toyota dealership. I've got some free time this afternoon."

"Why don't you two go ahead with Brian. I'll take 'Gertie' to the grocery store," said Regan. "I pretty much know what we all like."

A smile crossed Darcy's face.

"Sounds like a plan," said Sheena. "Are you sure you have the time to help us out, Brian?"

He nodded gamely. "I'm here to help."

Sheena shook hands with the salesman at the Toyota dealership and accepted the keys for the silver van they'd chosen. She and Brian had struck a good deal with the promise of, among other things, keeping the sticker advertising the dealership visible at all times. Sheena was proud of her participation. At home, Tony liked to handle buying a car for her through the company, and except for color choice, she played no part in it.

Sliding behind the wheel, Sheena smiled at Brian. "Thanks very much for your help! This is going to make a big difference. Later, we'll get the hotel logo put on the side."

"Hotel logo? We don't have one," said Darcy from her place in the passenger seat.

Sheena turned to her with a grin. "Not yet, we don't. But, we will." After her talk with Blackie, her mind had been spinning with all kinds of ideas.

At the hotel, Sheena bypassed the front parking lot and drove the van along the driveway to the house. The driveway was wide enough to accommodate the van, but they'd need to cut back some of the foliage to make it easier, safer. Maybe Brian's landscaping group could do that, she thought happily.

Regan raced across the lawn to greet them. "Wow! This is ours?"

Sheena corrected her. "It's the hotel's van for our use."

"I get to drive it next," said Darcy.

"Uh...I'm going to need it," said Regan, giving them a sheepish look. "I got lost going to the grocery store and went by a garage sale. A man was selling his kayaks. I stopped and got two for one hundred dollars."

"Great!" said Darcy. "We can fix up the dock and get a sailboat and everything."

"Whoa!" said Sheena. "The three of us have to approve an expense like this before you go ahead and buy something."

Regan's face fell. "But I got a real bargain."

"Why do you always have to be in charge?" said Darcy. She put an arm around Regan and glared at Sheena. "Can't you ever do anything spontaneously?"

"I thought I was in charge of keeping track of our money," said Sheena. She stared down Darcy. "Do you want to take on that job?"

"No, but we've got to have some fun doing this."

Feeling as if she'd been slapped, Sheena lifted a hand to her cheek. *Am I really that much of a downer?* Memories of the many times she'd had to insert common sense into her children's plans itched her mind. *But that was sometimes the role of a responsible mother, wasn't it?* She drew a deep breath. Her sisters were not her children even though her memories of them were exactly that.

"It's okay," said Regan, acting in her usual role of peacemaker. "Maybe I can go back and tell the man to forget it."

"No," said Sheena with fresh determination. "We're going to buy them."

"Great," said Darcy. "I'll drive."

CHAPTER NINETEEN
REGAN

Regan tugged on the kayak to remove the lightweight boat from the back of the van. The man at the garage sale had helped Darcy and her load it into the van. She'd go back for the second one—alone if she could manage to get away from her sisters. She had an idea in mind and she didn't want them with her while she saw to it.

As Darcy and Sheena carried the kayak away to store it in the workshop, Regan called to them. "I'll be right back with the other one."

"Wait for me," said Darcy.

"No need to come. I've got it," said Regan, ignoring the frown on Darcy's face. She climbed into the van and sat behind the wheel. It felt good to be in charge for once. And if her sisters got angry with her, so what? She was going to prove to them and everyone else she could contribute her share and more in making this hotel nice.

Regan pulled up to the house and got out of the van. The old man running the garage sale strode toward her with a smile. "Back already, huh? Well, now, I'll help you load the kayak and you can be on your way."

She shook her head. "There's something else I'm interested in. She walked inside to the back of the garage and held up a wooden plaque. The outline and shape of an egret were carved into the brown wood. "Got any more of these?"

"No, my grandson makes these, though. Like it? A pretty

girl like you can have it."

"Do you have your grandson's business card?" she said, taking the plaque from him.

"Let me get one from the kitchen. My wife keeps a bunch of them. Don't know why. It's just a hobby of his, not a real business. He's studying to be a dentist."

Hiding her excitement, Regan smiled politely.

When the man returned, he handed Regan a small, white card. "Here. His name is Austin Blakely, but everyone calls him Blake."

"Thanks," said Regan. "I really appreciate it."

They loaded the plaque and kayak into the van, and then Regan said goodbye.

On the return trip to the hotel, she thought of the best way to approach her sisters. They would either hate or love her idea.

CHAPTER TWENTY
SHEENA

Sheena called a meeting before dinner to discuss the day's happenings with her sisters. They took seats on the couches and munched on apples Regan had bought at the store. Sheena reiterated what she and Blackie had discussed. "It's going to take a lot of creative thinking, but I'm more optimistic about our chances to turn this place around."

"Me, too," said Regan. She stood and held up the wooden plaque. "I found this carving of an egret at the garage sale. And, no, Sheena, I didn't spend any money. The man gave it to me for free. His grandson, Austin Blakely, does this work. I want to order another one—a heron this time. I think we should name the two guest buildings for these birds. That way, we can tell our guests 'you're in the Egret Building-Room E101 or the Heron Building-Room H101,' or whatever. What do you think?"

A smile spread across Darcy's face. "I like it. It's logical and will make it easier to track room sales on the computer."

"Great idea, Regan," said Sheena. "We can mount the plaques by each building's main entrance. And I like the idea of the simple, stained wood."

"I'll paint the birds," said Regan with a new authority in her voice, "but I'll do it very tastefully with just enough color for interest."

"You really are good at this decorating thing, aren't you?" Darcy said to Regan with a new note of respect.

At the smile that crossed Regan's face, Sheena filled with satisfaction. Her little sister was stepping up to the task she'd chosen for herself.

After going through the list of items they needed to work on, Sheena said, "I think we need to call a meeting with Gavin's people. Blackie indicated Gavin had already made arrangements with them to give us help with projects when we need it."

"They weren't exactly friendly, especially that Rocky guy," said Darcy. "I can't imagine he'll want to lend a hand."

"I need him to help with the dumpster," said Regan. "Leave it to me."

Sheena and Darcy looked at each other and laughed.

"Okay, boss, we'll let you tangle with him," said Darcy. "I'm not sure what's gotten into you, but I like the new Regan."

Regan's lips curved, and then she frowned. "In the past, no one in the family gave me credit for anything. I vowed to make things different here in Florida."

"And you're doing a good job of it," said Sheena, seeing her sister in a new light.

"Yeah, I figure we should all take advantage of this time to learn about a lot of things. Us, included," said Darcy. "We're sisters and we hardly know each other. Not really. And we know none of the little things about each of us. Let's start. Sheena, what's your favorite color?"

Sheena laughed. "Powder blue. How about yours?"

"Green in any shade," said Darcy, turning to Regan.

"Mine's pink," Regan said.

"See?" said Darcy. "That wasn't so difficult.Okay, let's do another little quiz. What's the one thing you're most afraid of?

"That's easy. Snakes," said Sheena. She'd been afraid of them since she'd been a child and had come across one in the woods.

"Oh yes. Snakes for me too and spiders," said Regan.

"I haven't seen an alligator up close," Darcy said, "but I really, really don't want to."

"Florida's full of them," warned Sheena. "So, you'd better be careful."

Darcy shuddered. "I know."

Sheena checked her watch. "Okay, enough of this getting-acquainted stuff. Time to think about dinner. Who's going to cook tonight?"

"Not me," said Darcy. "I'm going to The Key Hole for dinner and to work on the computer system there."

"I'm not hungry," said Regan. "I'll just snack later."

"Well, I'm going to make a chef salad. Sure you don't want one, Regan?"

She shook her head. "No, I'm going to go with Darcy.

After the two of them left, Sheena was alone in the kitchen. She punched in the cell phone numbers for Meaghan. Until now, Meaghan had refused to take her calls, and they hadn't discussed the Valentine's Dance.

The phone rang and rang. Sheena gritted her teeth and texted her: *Meaghan, please pick up the call. I'm tired of trying to talk to you and getting no response.*

Moments later, she received an answer to her text: *Mom, I'm still mad at you for leaving. The dance was a disaster. My two best friends are teasing me about being an orphan. Why did you have to leave us?*

Sheena paused before attempting to answer. She couldn't harm Tony's relationship with his daughter. Meaghan thought he was a wonderful businessman, able to give her anything she wanted. But, like it or not, Sheena's being in Florida might, among other things, save the family from financial problems.

She began typing: *Meaghan, I love you and I miss you. I*

wish you understood that. Can't wait to see you in a few weeks. We'll talk more then. Hugs and hugs. Mom.

Sheena cleaned the lettuce and mixed up a simple garlic and mustard salad dressing. She was eating her salad when her cell rang. *Meaghan.* Eager to hear from her daughter, she clicked on the call. "Hi, darling!"

"Mom! You've got to come home. Things are a mess here. Dad's cooking is terrible, the laundry isn't done, and there's no one to take me shopping!"

Sheena's happiness with the call disappeared with a sharp pain in her heart. Meaghan was missing all the things Sheena normally did for the family, that's all.

"I'm sorry, but I have a commitment here—a commitment I can't break. And, Meaghan, it's only a few weeks until you come to Florida." Sheena swallowed hard, determined to keep her voice light and full of understanding. "This might be a good time for you to learn some cooking. I'm sure Grandma Rosa would be delighted to help you. And I've already shown you how to do your own laundry. That shouldn't be a big issue. As for shopping, I thought you liked to go shopping with your friends."

"Dad won't give me money. He says I have enough clothes," said Meaghan with a distinctive whine.

Sheena could hear the tears in her daughter's voice but hardened herself against being too sympathetic. Before she'd left for Florida, she'd made sure that Meaghan's clothing was set for spring. She loved her daughter, but it was clear how spoiled Meaghan had become.

"Why can't you be like other mothers? They take care of their families," said Meaghan.

Sheena sighed. No doubt she'd heard Tony say the same thing. "We've gone over this before. If I didn't think the three of you could handle being on your own, I wouldn't be here.

But you are perfectly capable of helping each other take care of things while I'm gone. And Grandma and Grandpa are right there to help you too."

The buzzing sound of a disconnected call rang in Sheena's ear. Her eyes widened with dismay. Meaghan had hung up on her.

Drawing deep breaths, Sheena calmed herself. She debated about calling Meaghan back and decided to let it go. Angry words were building inside her, and she didn't want to make things worse.

Sheena pushed her salad away, no longer hungry. She left the kitchen and went out to the front porch and sat in one of the lightweight metal chairs. In the darkness, she inhaled the salty air and felt her muscles loosen as warm air wrapped around her like a comforting blanket. She was growing to love the tropical feel to the place. Even the house, which at one point had seemed primitive, now seemed very...adequate.

Her cell phone rang again. At the sight of Tony's face on the screen, Sheena grimaced but took the call.

"Hi, darling! How are you?"

He sighed. "Trying to cope with everything here. But, Sheena, your family needs you to come home. This idea of Gavin's is ridiculous! We don't need the money that bad. My business will pick up. I'm sure of it."

Guilt washed through Sheena. *A mother should stay home with her family. Right?* Then another thought assailed her. *Time to think differently.* "This is a good time for the children to learn some responsibility. They've been much too pampered. When they come to Florida, I intend to put them to work."

"Aren't you going overboard with this whole idea of yours?" Tony cleared his throat. "Are you sure you're not preparing to leave us ... forever?"

"Oh, Tony, no! Of course not. I'm just following through on this challenge—a challenge, by the way, that I'm sure will lead to something wonderful for all of us."

"You're being very selfish," said Tony. "You made the decision, and now we're all stuck with it."

"No, Tony. *We* made the decision after going over the books for the plumbing business. There are many reasons for sticking with the plan. I was thinking that if things got too tough, the kids might want to transfer to a school here."

"And where does that leave me?" said Tony. His voice held a bitterness Sheena couldn't ignore.

"I haven't figured that part out yet. But I will because I want all of us to be together. I'm trying to think creatively."

"What about the 'finding me' bullshit?" Tony asked.

Anger bubbled inside Sheena, but she held her tongue. Tony didn't get it and never would.

"Well?"

She drew a calming breath. "It isn't bullshit, Tony. It's time for me to do something with my life, make a contribution to other causes than my family's happiness. I'm only thirty-six. There's time for me to make a difference for us and for others."

"You promised to take care of us. We should be your first priority," Tony retorted.

"But not my only one," said Sheena. "I owe something to my sisters too."

"Look, I've got to go," said Tony. "There's a call coming in on the service line."

"Tony? I love you," said Sheena.

"Yeah, right," he said and hung up.

Sheena's eyes stung with tears. Was she such an awful a person for wanting to find herself, do something for her sisters, meet a challenge of a different kind for what she felt would be a big benefit to her family? The whole challenge thing was weird, but it was opening her mind to the possibilities of things she hadn't thought of before.

Later, as Sheena sat on the porch grappling with her emotions, Darcy returned to the house.

Darcy jumped when she noticed Sheena in the dark. "Hey! What are you doing out here this late?"

"Trying to decide if I'm an awful wife and mother," Sheena said. "My family is very angry with me for being here."

Darcy lowered herself into a chair next to Sheena. "Your family has had you at their beck and call forever. It's time for you to discover who you are and how you want to spend the rest of your life. Michael will be off to college in another year, and Meaghan will follow. Then what?"

"I know but..." Sheena began.

"No buts. You got married and had children too young and have paid the price of losing yourself in their demands. We have one year for each of us to make some changes—not only with the hotel but for ourselves. Do it, Sheena."

"Thanks. I needed to hear that." Sheena reached out and gave Darcy's hand a squeeze. "How'd you get so smart?"

Regan came out of the house and joined them. "What are you two up to?"

"Growing up a bit," said Darcy. She winked at them. "Our oldest sister has a lot to learn."

Regan laughed. "We all do." She gave Sheena an encouraging hug and sat down in a chair beside her.

CHAPTER TWENTY-ONE
DARCY

Darcy lay in her bed thinking about Sheena. She was nine years old when Sheena suddenly got married, leaving Regan and her to cope with a mother whose frequent migraines sent her to bed. Looking back at that time, Darcy realized how devastated she'd been by Sheena's disappearance. She'd felt abandoned to be suddenly left with the care of her younger sister. Unable to talk to anyone about it, she'd been terrible to Sheena, acting out whenever she came around to visit their mother. It was the only way she could express her feelings.

Her ex-boyfriend, Sean, had once accused Darcy of needing a lot of reassurance about his love for her. Darcy snorted with disgust into the silence of the room. Had she been that needy? If so, was it because she didn't want to feel abandoned again? When he'd dumped her, Darcy had tried to make it appear as if she didn't care, but Sean's actions had hurt her deeply. After that, she'd dated often, but no guy seemed worth the effort of doing more than casual dating.

She hugged her pillow, wishing it was Brian Harwood. He was someone she'd be glad to give a lot of attention to—not that he cared. He had his eyes on Regan, who couldn't care less about it. Sighing heavily, Darcy rolled over. Life was sometimes just frickin' messed up.

###

Darcy awoke to the sounds of laughter downstairs. She sat up and listened, surprised when she heard a male voice. She got out of bed and went into the bathroom to freshen up. Looking at herself, she groaned at the way her red, curly hair stuck out in all directions. She worked hard to tame those curls but the humidity in the Florida air made the battle even tougher. Wishing she could scrub away her freckles, she quickly washed her face and then swiped a brush through her hair. If something fun was going on, she didn't want to miss out.

She finished with her morning rituals, quickly slipped on a pair of shorts and a T-shirt, and headed down the stairs.

Her heart thumped in her chest when she saw Brian. Dressed in cut-off jeans and a shirt that stretched over the muscles in his chest, he looked better than a cup of high-test coffee.

"Hi, Brian! What are you doing here?"

He bobbed his head at her. "Telling Sheena and Regan that they can begin painting the front building tomorrow. The guys should be finished prepping it soon. I've got a full team working on it."

"And we want him to go ahead with the landscaping in the front and trimming the foliage along the driveway," said Sheena. "You okay with that?"

"Sure," said Darcy. The longer Brian was around the easier it might be to have him think of her as a possible date.

"You'll be excused from painting whenever you're working on computer stuff," said Sheena. "And so will Regan when she's working on the rooms. Later this week, though, we're all meeting with Gavin's people. I set it up with Gracie earlier this morning."

Darcy felt some of her old resentment build inside her. Sheena was the big sister, but did she have to be so bossy?

Regan gave Darcy a knowing look and silently handed her a cup of coffee.

"Thanks," said Darcy, and took a satisfying sip.

Brian smiled at her. "My mother says you're going to be a big help to her. Guess she's paying you in free booze and meals. Nice."

Darcy's whole body tingled with pleasure. "I'll be spending quite a bit of time at her place."

"Good," he said and turned to Regan. "I understand you want to hire some of my men to help you and Gavin's men move stuff? I can spare them for an hour or two whenever you need them and they are free. Just let me know."

"Thanks for stopping by," said Sheena. "What time should I meet you tomorrow morning to begin painting?"

"By eight o'clock. And wear plenty of sunscreen. The temperature is starting to rise. You won't want to work in the heat of the day."

Brian left the house, and Darcy took a seat at the kitchen table. "Wow! Things are moving awfully fast. At this rate, we'll be ready to open within a month or two."

Sheena shook her head. "Not exactly. There's a lot to be done, and we won't know if we've succeeded unless we make a profit. I'm doing more work on the figures. But, Darcy, you told us you wanted to write a novel. How good are you at writing advertising material? I've helped Tony a little, but this is very different from writing about plumbing stuff."

Regan gave her a teasing grin. "Hah! Maybe the hotel will even be in one of your novels someday."

"You never know," said Darcy, warming to the idea.

CHAPTER TWENTY-TWO
SHEENA

After spending a restless night thinking of her family circumstances. Sheena awoke determined to see the challenge through. Darcy's reassurance had helped her realize that she could use this opportunity to change her life in a way that hurt no one. There were times when she'd thought of her sisters as her children rather than her siblings. But after getting to know them a little better, she felt more an equal with them.

She got out of bed and hurried into the bathroom for a quick shower before her sisters claimed the room. As she soaped her body, she thought of Tony. They'd always had sexual chemistry between them, but deep affection—the quiet, everyday kind—had disappeared with their hectic lives. She wanted more from her life with him— more fun, more time alone. They were still young, still able to do many things together now that the children were older and could be left on their own. But times like that hadn't happened.

As she finished dressing, she decided that part of finding herself was finding the young woman she used to be.

Downstairs, she was sitting in the kitchen sipping coffee when Regan and Darcy walked into the room.

"I'm going to see if Gracie has room for me for breakfast," said Regan, "and then I'm going to continue marking things to be thrown away. We all agree the bedding has to go. Right?"

Sheena and Darcy nodded their heads together. It was in

terrible condition.

Regan took off, and Sheena turned to Darcy. "Thanks for your encouragement the other night. I needed to hear what you had to say."

"That's a first," said Darcy, giving Sheena a fake punch in the arm. "After breakfast, I'm going to work in the office. I've got to come up with a marketing plan for both our business and The Key Hole. Cute name for the bar, huh? Salty Key...Key Hole?"

Sheena grinned. "It's perfect. I've been thinking that maybe we can work out a deal with Holly Harwood to give our guests a discount or something like that."

Darcy's eyes lit up. "Great idea. And because Gracie's doesn't serve dinner, maybe we can work something out on that too."

Sheena grabbed a cup of yogurt out of the refrigerator and headed into the living room. She needed to work on her computer to put together some budget ideas.

She was setting up a spreadsheet when her cell rang. She checked the number and frowned. *Blackie Gatto.*

"Hello," Sheena said. "More ideas for us?"

"Actually, I thought it might be easier if we met, maybe share a meal. I think it's a good idea for you to get out and see what's happening in the area."

"Okay, sounds good. Want to meet for coffee?"

"How about dinner tomorrow night?"

Sheena felt her eyes widen. *Was he hitting on her?* "I can't. We're meeting with Gavin's people for dinner. We're hoping to get their support behind us."

"Okay, then, how about the next evening? There's a restaurant I want you to see. It's next door to a property like yours. Gavin wanted you to see it."

At the idea of a dinner with him, Sheena's stomach

fluttered. *There was nothing wrong with meeting a business associate for dinner, was there?* Even as a thread of unease wove through her mind, she found herself saying, "Yes, that will work."

Several times that day Sheena thought of calling Blackie back and telling him to cancel the dinner, but each time she stopped. She was in business now and needed to stop acting like a frightened housewife who'd never done anything like this. *God! Was she so sheltered she couldn't even meet a man, a very handsome one, socially?*

Her thoughts flew to Tony. He would definitely not approve. But then, he didn't approve of anything she was doing, so what did it matter?

That evening, as Sheena and her sisters stepped inside Gracie's restaurant for their meeting with Gavin's people, delicious smells met their noses. Sheena's lips curved. Gracie was a gem.

Gracie greeted them with a smile. "Rocky brought us fresh lobsters that a friend of his caught. We're grilling them out back, along with some shrimp. I'm making a potato casserole that goes nicely with the seafood."

"Wonderful," said Sheena. She wondered how the Caribbean lobster would compare to the cold-water lobster she was used to back home in New England.

"My kind of meal," said Darcy, patting her stomach comically. "Lobstah!"

"Can't wait. After all the lugging around of furniture I did today, I'm ready to dig in," said Regan.

"We'll eat first, and then talk," said Gracie. "Okay with you, gals?"

Sheena nodded. "Of course."

While Darcy and Regan headed into the office to check on things, Sheena found a seat at the table where Maggie O'Neil and Lynn Michaels were sitting. Other than their names, Sheena knew nothing about them except they acted as waitresses for the breakfast and lunch crowds.

"How are you today?" she asked them.

They gave her perfunctory smiles.

"I'm curious. How did either of you know my Uncle Gavin? I remember him from my childhood, but lost touch with him."

"I guess you could say my husband, Benny, and Gavin were best friends," said Lynn, giving Sheena a thoughtful look. "They used to hunt for gold together many years ago. Whenever they were ashore, Gavin pretty much lived at my house. After my husband got very sick and died, Gavin came to me with an offer to have me stay here at the hotel. It was a godsend. I had no place else to go." Tears came to her eyes. "He also paid off all our medical expenses."

"I met him through Lynn and Benny," said Maggie. "He knew I was a nurse, and though I'd gotten into trouble for stealing drugs from the hospital, he still hired me to take care of Benny. And then he offered to give me free room and board if I stayed with his people."

Lynn smiled at Maggie and turned to Sheena. "Gavin knew we might need her. She's the youngster of the group and a very good nurse."

Sheena took a moment to study them. Thin, with weathered, tanned skin, Lynn looked frail beneath the top knot of gray-streaked, dark hair. But Sheena knew how strong she was. She'd seen Lynn pile dirty dishes on a big tray and carry it off as if it weighed nothing.

Sheena guessed Maggie's age to be in her forties. Heavy-set and of medium height, there was a vulnerability to her that was striking—something in her blue eyes that said: *"Don't hurt me."* Sheena wondered about her past.

Regan and Darcy returned from the office and joined them.

"Chip is here, working on the computer stuff," said Regan. "He's very good at it."

Darcy rolled her eyes. "He knows his stuff, but I'm the one who's designing the program for us."

"And doing a good job," Sheena assured her.

Rocky and Sam Patterson walked into the restaurant, each carrying a platter of food that he set down on the breakfast bar. Clyde tagged along behind them.

Gracie and Bebe emerged from the kitchen. Gracie placed a casserole next to the seafood platters and indicated a spot for Bebe to set the large bowl of salad she was holding.

"Okay, everyone," said Gracie. "Buffet dinner. Help yourselves."

Sheena and her sisters politely waited for the others to serve themselves, and then Sheena eagerly selected a grilled lobster tail, a few shrimp, and some salad for herself.

Her plate loaded, she found a seat next to Rocky. He was a puzzle to her—a puzzle she intended to unravel. After meeting his brother, very different in appearance, she wanted to know more about him.

"Lobster is such a treat. Thank you," she said to him.

He bobbed his head. "Yeah. A friend of mine owes me, so he gives me a bunch of them every now and then."

Sheena took a bite of the lobster drizzled with butter and lemon juice and murmured, "Delicious." The lobster meat was softer, sweeter, than the cold-water lobsters back home. "How do you keep the lobster this tender?"

"Sam, here, showed me how to cook them, back when we were cruising together," Rocky explained.

Sheena turned to Sam. Tall and lanky, the man who looked to be in his fifties had large ears and a long nose. The name

Ichabod Crane came to mind—recently, Meaghan had been reading *The Legend of Sleepy Hollow*.

"Were you both part of Uncle Gavin's gold-hunting adventures?" she asked.

"Yes," said Sam. "I started probably about the time you were just a kid. Rocky, here, got on board toward the end."

"Were you successful?" Sheena asked, thinking of the gold coin she'd been given.

"Not that we could declare ourselves rich," Sam said. "Most of the gold coins we found were taken away from us."

"But, for a couple of days, we thought we'd made it big-time," said Rocky. "Damn government wouldn't let us keep them."

"Most of them," chortled Sam.

Rocky flashed him a look of warning.

"I guess Gavin kept a few for himself," said Sheena matter-of-factly. "Is that how he bought this hotel and made some other money?"

"No," said Sam, ignoring Rocky's furious expression. "He was a genius when it came to the stock market. Ain't that right, Rocky?"

"Guess so," growled Rocky. "Now, shut up."

Sam grinned. "Rocky ain't very good at stocks and bonds."

"Well, whoever cooked this lobster and the shrimp is very good at it," said Sheena in an attempt to keep things light.

"Good food is good for the soul," said Rocky.

"I've met your brother," Sheena said. "He's being very helpful to us. Gavin apparently trusted him with everything."

"Yeah, Blackie's a good guy. Smart too. A lot smarter than me."

Sheena was pleasantly surprised by the pride she heard in Rocky's voice. "Guess you and he had a lot of fun at the Gasparilla Pirate's celebrations."

Rocky grinned but said nothing.

Sheena had just taken the last bite of her salad when Gracie stood. "Okay, folks, we're meeting at Sheena's request. Sheena, I'm going to turn this meeting over to you."

Sheena patted a paper napkin to her lips, took a hasty drink of water, and got to her feet. "I've met with Blackie Gatto, whom you all obviously know, as he's the one who made the arrangements for you to be able to live and work here. He told me that as part of the deal he made with each of you that you are available to help my sisters and me. But much more than that, I hope, like Gavin wanted, we'll all become part of this special family."

"Gavin told us all about this before he died," said Rocky.

"Yeah, we told him we'd be glad to help," said Lynn.

"What do you need from us?" asked Sally, a quiet, little woman who helped in the kitchen.

Regan stood. "I need help removing some of the furniture and all the bedding and carpeting from all the guest rooms. We're bringing in dumpsters to haul it away. It's going to take several days to clear the rooms of the things we can't use. I was hoping you three men could help me."

"We should be able to do that," said Sam, giving Rocky a wary look.

Rocky nodded. "Yep. If one of the women can take over for Sam in the kitchen, he, Clyde, and I will help whenever we can."

"Yes, me too," said Clyde with such excitement that everyone laughed.

"What about maintenance on the buildings?" said Sheena. "Who can I talk to about that? And the swimming pool?"

"Better talk to Rocky," said Gracie. "He's the guy we trust to do things like that around here. He used to be an engineer of some kind. Right, Rocky?"

Rocky shrugged. "Sorta."

"I'll help in any way," said Sally, the smallest and shyest of the group. "I usually take care of our rooms, clean them and all, when I'm not helping in the kitchen."

"And I do best in the kitchen," said Bebe. "Right along with Gracie."

"Thank you, everyone! My sisters and I will be in touch with you." Sudden tears stung her eyes. "Gavin was right about you. You are his people and now, hopefully, ours."

As Sheena sat down, Maggie began to clap. Soon everyone joined in. Even Rocky. The magical sound filled Sheena's ears and her heart. Maybe this would work.

CHAPTER TWENTY-THREE
REGAN

Regan's nerves jangled as she walked across the grounds of the hotel to the guest building she'd labeled Egret in her mind. The sun was still low in the morning sky, but she didn't mind getting up early. Moving things around in the guest rooms was a hot, sticky business, and the cooler air felt good to her. But she was nervous about bossing the men around—especially Rocky. With his tough looks, he scared her.

She walked past the pool and wondered when they'd be able to swim in it. Brian was supposed to find someone to clean it up. She thought about him. He was handsome, no doubt about it. But the way he acted around her—his interest obvious—was a total turnoff. She'd been stung by guys who treated her like a china doll for a date or two and then tried to get into her pants. And when she'd tried to speak to them about something serious, they'd lost interest.

From an early age, her mother had drilled it into her head to play it safe. That and going to Catholic school had formed images in her mind of awful things happening if she ended up with the wrong guy. Her parents' marriage hadn't been that happy. And Sheena was an example of someone getting married too young. Regan had no intention of doing the same thing no matter how her friends laughed at her when she made it plain she was not going to be like some of her friends who had casual sex.

Still mulling over these thoughts, Regan studied the

ground as she moved along. She came to an abrupt stop when she bumped into someone.

Jolted by the impact, she stared up at Brian and stepped away. "Sorry. I didn't see you there."

"Yeah, you were miles away. Anything I can help you with?" His smile was bright, pleasant.

"No thanks." She turned to go and was stopped by a hand on her shoulder.

"Wait! Look, Regan, I already apologized for getting off on the wrong foot with you. What can I do to make things better between us? For the next year, we're going to be working together at various times. What do you say we call a truce, though God knows I don't understand why we seem to be at some kind of idiotic war."

Regan's body stiffened. "War? I don't think so. I just have a lot on my mind." She was not about to get into a battle of wits with Brian. She didn't like him. That was all.

He shrugged. "Okay. Let's leave it at that."

As Regan went on her way, she could feel Brian's gaze on her. Shaking off the uncomfortable feeling, she entered the Egret Building and found Rocky and two of Brian's men waiting for her.

Smiling broadly, she said, "Wow! You guys are up early. Thanks for being here."

"Ready to help," said Rocky. "What do you want us to do?" he asked impatiently. "I have to go to Ybor City today."

"We need to go through all the rooms on both floors and pull out the mattresses and bedding. We'll keep the box springs as long as they look good. In addition, I will be marking furnishings too ruined to do anything with, and these will also have to go to the dumpsters, which should be here at any moment. Some of the wooden furniture I'm going to keep and have refinished. Or maybe we can paint it. We'll place all those pieces of furniture in connecting rooms and paint them there."

"What about draperies?" one of the men asked.

"They're going, along with any over-stuffed chairs. Anything with fabric. But leave the drapery rods in place; we'll re-use them if possible," Regan said. She hadn't cleared everything with Sheena and Darcy, but they'd agreed in principle to her plan and now that she was in charge, for once, she intended to do things right.

Rocky gave her a little salute. "Okay, we'll get to work on it. Gracie said to tell you that we could get coffee and water anytime we want."

Regan handed him a master key to all the rooms. "You guys get started. I'll check on the dumpsters."

Rocky accepted the key from her and headed down the hallway.

Watching them walk away, Regan filled with pride. It felt good to be listened to as if she knew what she was talking about. The truth was, this renovation project was the biggest challenge of her life.

Mid-morning, while the guys took a break, Regan went to the office. She'd seen the blue jeep in the side parking lot, and she hoped Chip was around. His lack of interest in her was confusing.

When she entered the room, Darcy and Chip were bent over her computer, deep in conversation. Darcy looked up at her. "Yeah? What do you want? We're busy."

"Uh, I just thought I'd see how things are going," Regan said, searching for a smooth reply.

Darcy waved her away. "Thanks, but like I said, we're busy."

At Darcy's dismissive tone, old resentments boiled inside Regan. She turned and fled the room before Darcy or Chip saw how upset she was.

Standing alone outside, she felt as if she were ten years old all over again, with Darcy as her babysitter. Even as a child, she knew how much Darcy resented how often she had to watch over her because their mother was sick.

Regan drew a deep breath. She would not, could not, let Darcy ruin her attempt to break free from the past where she felt like a stupid nobody.

CHAPTER TWENTY-FOUR
SHEENA

R eady?" called Brian to Sheena, who was taking a short break. "Let's get back to work on this building. We need to get a lot of the trim painted before the heat rises."

Sheena tried to shake off her exhaustion. Brian had put a couple of his men on the project, but it was her job to do the detail painting around the window trim. She was determined to complete the job to prove to Darcy and Regan the value of saving money in any way they could.

Hours later, Sheena wished she'd just allowed Brian and his crew to do the job as she and her sisters had agreed. Every muscle in her body ached. She realized how long it had been since she'd gone to the gym—the very same gym that had promised to help her get rid of a few extra pounds. Not that Tony minded her weight. He loved the idea he had something to hold onto when they made love.

Longing filled her. She missed Tony, the way he held her, stroked her, and satisfied her during their lovemaking, which had become rarer and rarer as their children demanded more of their attention.

"What do you think?" Brian asked her, jarring her from her memories.

They stood together and looked at the front of the building. With a fresh coat of paint, it looked like a new structure—funky, but nice. Some of the yellow trim needed a touch-up, but Sheena reveled in the improvement. The painting of the entire building would be completed within a few days, well ahead of the scheduled spring break visit from Tony and the kids.

Darcy and Chip emerged from the building, chatting easily with one another.

"What's up?" Sheena asked.

Darcy grinned. "We've got a wireless system set up in the downstairs areas of the building. We'll even be able to offer our guests WiFi in the restaurant. We're looking into costs of putting WiFi in the guest buildings."

Sheena smiled. "Pretty exciting stuff. Love it."

"Yes. Soon, I'll be able to work with Chip to set up inventory systems and other programs."

"Hey, this building is looking a whole lot better," said Darcy, beaming at Brian.

He grinned. "Big difference. Should be done in a day or two." He gave Sheena a little bow. "See you tomorrow."

Sheena hurried down to the house. She was a mess and didn't have much time to get cleaned up before Blackie picked her up for dinner.

She crossed the threshold of the house and paused a moment in the living room to let the ceiling fan wash the cool air over her sweaty skin. Then, checking her watch, she hurried up the stairs.

After stripping off her damp clothes, she grabbed a towel from the hook behind her bedroom door and went into the bathroom, grateful neither Regan nor Darcy was at home.

She drew cool water into the tub and crawled into the old-fashioned fixture. She'd discovered it was easiest if she took a bath first and then knelt in the tub and used the extended water wand to shampoo her hair. Not convenient, but she was getting used to it.

After washing the blue paint from her hair, she towel-dried

it. In just a matter of weeks, it seemed much longer. She stood before the small mirror over the sink and combed the long auburn strands, then pulled it up in a ponytail. The new light-tan coloring of her skin deepened the color of her green eyes. She smiled at her image—she'd worn her hair like this when she'd first met Tony. What would he think of it or her now? A troubled sigh escaped her. He probably wouldn't even notice.

Sheena finished in the bathroom and went to her bedroom to get dressed. She'd just pulled on the one good summer dress she'd brought with her when she heard someone climbing the stairs.

"Hey, Sheena? You up there?"

Regan stepped into the room and, frowning, stared at her. "What's going on? Where are you going?"

"Blackie Gatto is taking me out to dinner to discuss some things for the hotel and to show me a restaurant he thought I should see in case we expand meals at Gracie's."

Regan's eyebrows shot up. "You're going on a date?"

"Nooo," said Sheena with a firmness she felt to her toes. "I'm doing business over dinner. That's all. Nothing else."

"Okay, if you say so," Regan said, "but I don't think Tony would like something like this."

"Blackie is a huge source of information and guidance to the three of us, and I want to take advantage of every bit of advice he can give us."

"Who can give us what?" said Darcy, joining them.

"Sheena is going out with Blackie." Regan paused. "For a business dinner."

"Business dinner? Why not lunch? That way it won't seem like a date," said Darcy. "Besides, if any dates are happening, it should be Regan and me. You're married."

Sheena sighed. "It's not a date. Just a nice dinner."

"I don't like it. If anything goes on between the two of you,

I'm telling Tony," said Darcy.

"You're such a bitch," Regan said to Darcy. "And by the way, you didn't have to be nasty to me when I stopped in your office. And you did it in front of Chip. Gawd! I felt like I was ten years old again being told to go away. Growing up, you were mean to me."

"Yeah? When Sheena took off to get married, that left me in charge of you. It wasn't fair. I couldn't do anything without you tagging along. Mom made me take you everywhere because she was never feeling good with those headaches of hers."

"Talk about being unfair! Think of all the times I had to take care of you, Darcy," said Sheena tensely. "I wasn't even ten when you were born. And then when Regan came along I often had to take care of both of you."

"It may seem irrational, but I hated you for leaving, you know," said Darcy. "And I couldn't talk to anyone about it. Dad wouldn't listen and I didn't want to hurt Mom's feelings."

"I blamed you, too," said Regan. "It was never the same after you were gone."

Sheena placed her hands on her hips and stared at her sisters. "You're going to try and blame every bad thing that happened in your childhood on me for leaving?" She shook her head with disgust. "You two sound like my fourteen-year-old daughter. Maybe it's time you grew up and realized how lucky we were to have a mother like ours. Even though she wasn't healthy, she was kind and loving. Think about that while I get ready for my *business* dinner."

"There's no use talking to you," said Darcy, shaking her head as she left the room.

Regan silently followed Darcy.

Sheena sat down on the bed to gather her thoughts. Her sisters' anger was surprising but understandable. Their family was unusual. Growing up, both she and Darcy had been made to feel more like mothers to their siblings than sisters. In reality, she'd been glad to leave home at an early age. But she hadn't wanted a family before having the chance for a college degree and a fulfilling career.

Sheena was slipping pearl earrings through her earlobes when Regan called up the stairs. "Sheena, your...your ride is here."

Sheena straightened, brushed the skirt of her black linen dress, and grabbed her purse. Even though it wasn't a real date, she wanted to look her best.

As she descended the stairs, Blackie stepped inside the front entrance.

"You look fabulous, Sheena," he said, giving her a wide smile.

"You too," she said politely. Tan slacks and a light blue sports jacket fit him perfectly, showing off his toned body. The gray in his dark, glossy hair gave him a distinguished look.

Darcy and Regan were all but gawking at him.

"Blackie, I want you to meet my sisters." She introduced them and watched as they exchanged handshakes.

"Gavin was very proud of the three of you," Blackie said. "I can certainly see why. And I understand that each of you is contributing to the success of the challenge very nicely. Regan, it will be interesting to see how you handle the rooms. I understand you love interior design. And you, Darcy, love books."

Sheena was as shocked as they by what he'd said. It was as if Gavin had shared their dreams with Blackie. But how had Gavin known? Their mother must have told him.

Blackie crooked his arm in an old-fashioned gesture.

"Ready, Sheena?"

Sheena took his arm and allowed him to lead her out the front door. Outside, she stopped and stared at the bottle-green Jaguar that sat in the driveway like a certain pumpkin chariot in a fairy tale. When she and Tony went out on a rare date, they usually rode in Tony's truck, or if they were feeling fancy, in her old Ford Explorer. Blackie led her to the car and then held the car door for her while she tried to gracefully slide into the passenger's seat. As she waited for Blackie to go around behind the car to get to his seat, she noticed Darcy and Regan staring out the window at them. It reminded her of the days when Tony would pick her up for a date.

Blackie got in the car, started the engine, and smoothly drove the car away from the house. As they exited the hotel property, he turned to her with a grin. "Ready to see some competition?"

She returned his smile. "I told my sisters that we'd listen to any advice you have to give us. I'm sure that's what Uncle Gavin would want us to do."

"Yes, indeed," said Blackie. "He asked me to show you around a bit. Big, fancy hotels like the Don CeSar and the Vinoy are not competitive properties, but you should know about them and visit them when you get the chance. Tonight, I want you to see and experience The Key Pelican Restaurant. It started out as a breakfast and lunch place like Gracie's but expanded to dinner service about three years ago. It's one of the top five places to eat on the west coast of Florida. You'll be surprised when you see it."

A comfortable silence filled the car as Blackie drove along the road following the coastline. When he pulled up to a turquoise building with pink trim, Sheena's eyes widened.

Blackie grinned at her. "Doesn't look like much from this angle, does it?"

Sheena shook her head, studying the exterior of the restaurant. With its painted clapboards, colorful trim, and old-time metal roof, it wasn't too unlike the front building of the Salty Key Inn.

Blackie pulled around to the side of the building and stopped the car. A teenage boy acting as valet hurried over to Sheena's door and opened it for her. "Welcome to The Key Pelican," he announced before hurrying over to speak to Blackie.

Sheena studied the colorful, carved wooden statue of a pelican perched on a piece of wood beside the front entrance and smiled. Statues like this seemed to be a decorative theme special to the area. Gracie's even had one called Davy.

Blackie joined her, and they entered the restaurant together.

A stunning woman greeted them with a smile. "Well, hello, Blackie! Long time no see. Where have you been hiding? With this lovely girl, no doubt." Her less-than-friendly gaze settled on Sheena's face and then traveled up and down her body.

"We're just business associates," Sheena felt compelled to say.

"Some business, Blackie," said the woman with a definite edge.

"Do you have my regular table for me?" Blackie said with no acknowledgment of their previous conversation.

She drew in a breath and gave him a smile that could only be called fake. "For you, anything, Blackie. Remember that?"

Sheena shifted uncomfortably on her feet, not knowing where to look. The hostess and Blackie obviously had been together at one time.

The hostess led them to a small round table in the corner of the room, near a window that looked out to a tiny, enclosed garden.

Blackie helped Sheena get seated and sat down opposite her. "Sorry about that conversation with Rosie. She has a problem with being overly possessive."

"That's all right," said Sheena. "I just don't want anyone to get the wrong impression."

"I understand," said Blackie agreeably. "But you do look lovely tonight, Sheena."

Sheena's cheeks heated. She couldn't remember the last time Tony had said something like this to her.

"How about a nice glass of wine?" Blackie said. "Any preference?"

"A nice red wine sounds wonderful," Sheena said. In anticipation of a nice meal, she hadn't eaten much that day and intended to enjoy this evening out.

While Blackie perused the leather-bound wine list, Sheena took a good look around. The wooden walls of the small restaurant gleamed a warm brown. The tile entrance gave way to a richly carpeted room. Tables were covered in crisp pink linen and held sparkling crystal glasses and heavy silverware. In the center of the table, colorful hibiscus blossoms nestled inside a glass container shaped like the blossom itself.

Like Blackie had indicated, the interior was the total opposite of what one would suspect looking at it from the outside. Sheena liked that element of surprise.

Blackie smiled at her. "Nice, huh?"

She nodded. "Very interesting. Is this why you wanted me to see it?"

"Yes. Gavin had the idea of building a place something like this along the water. An upscale, private place for people who enjoy exceptional dining. Those in the know would come by boat or by driving around the hotel complex to get to it. That would, he hoped, keep the typical tourist away."

Sheena couldn't help laughing. "Why would Gavin want me

to see this? We don't even know if we're going to beat this challenge of his."

Blackie's shoulders lifted and dropped. "If, by chance, you do make it, you and your sisters will come into a lot of money. And if you decide to live out Gavin's dream, he wanted you to know about the possibilities involved in making it very special. He was a dreamer, you know."

Sheena's lips thinned. "And a bit of a tease. This is such a crazy idea."

"Maybe not so crazy. He always thought you and he were alike."

Unable to think of a single response, Sheena remained quiet. But the thought probed her like a sharp-edged knife, twisting uncomfortably inside her mind. After all those years of caring for her sisters, then her family, was there still a remnant of the whimsical girl she sometimes had been?

Blackie reached over and patted her hand. "Nothing to worry about now. First things first. Right?"

"Sure."

Sheena sat back and watched as Blackie selected a red wine for them. After the waiter left, an older gentleman came to their table.

"Blackie. Good to see you again. How are things? And who is this delightful, young woman?"

Blackie stood and shook hands with the man and then turned to Sheena. "This is a client of mine. Sheena Morelli, Gavin Sullivan's niece."

The man's eyes widened and then a smile spread across his face. "Well, I'll be darned. Nice to meet you, Sheena. Gavin talked about you a lot."

"Sheena," said Blackie, "this is Arthur Weatherman."

Sheena smiled and held out her hand. "Nice to meet you, Mr. Weatherman."

They shook hands, and then Arthur said to Blackie, "I've got a new deal to talk to you about."

Blackie nodded. "Give me a call."

After Arthur walked away, Blackie said, "Arthur Weatherman has his fingers in a lot of pies in the state. For one thing, he owns a number of fast-food franchises."

"And you handle his legal work?"

Blackie grinned. "Of course."

Sheena couldn't help laughing. Blackie Gatto had a lot of business dealings too.

Throughout dinner, Blackie kept up a pleasant, well-informed stream of conversation. That, and the delicious food, along with the wine, made it one of the most pleasant evenings Sheena had ever enjoyed.

After coffee and slices of key lime pie for dessert, Blackie sat back and patted his stomach. "Excellent. Thank you for sharing the meal with me, Sheena. It's been a pleasure."

She smiled. "For me, too. I'm curious. You're not married?"

He shook his head. "Once was enough for me. After my divorce, I haven't found anyone I'm willing to share my life with permanently. Jaded, perhaps, but I like it this way. I don't lack for company anytime I want it."

"I see."

Blackie checked his watch, ending further conversation. "We'd better get you home."

"I have to admit I'm ready for a good night's sleep. I'd forgotten what it's like to paint something. I used to paint the kids' rooms, but haven't had to do that in some time."

Blackie ushered her out of the restaurant.

As they waited for the valet to bring Blackie's car, Sheena inhaled the warm air with pleasure. A snowstorm had hit Boston a few days ago, and the last time she checked, the temperature was hovering in the thirties.

###

Blackie pulled into the Salty Key Inn. As they drove toward the house in the back of the property, Sheena tried to imagine all the improvements to the grounds and the addition of a waterfront restaurant along the bay.

"It could work," Sheena said. "The restaurant, everything."

Blackie nodded. "Lots to think about."

He parked the car beside the house, got out, and went around it to assist her.

After holding the door for her and offering his hand, he pulled her toward him. Gazing up at him, Sheena knew he wanted to kiss her. She froze, uncertain how to handle it when a voice called to her.

Sheena swiveled and faced a familiar figure.

"Tony?"

CHAPTER TWENTY-FIVE
SHEENA

Sheena watched in shock as Tony's sturdy, broad-shouldered body all but sprinted toward them.

"What are you doing with my wife?" he growled at Blackie.

At the ferociousness in his voice, Sheena automatically moved in front of Blackie. "Hold on, Tony. This is a business associate of Gavin's. He's been helping us."

Tony came to a stop in front of her. "Yeah? It looks like he's been helping himself to a lot of stuff."

Blackie moved away from Sheena and held out his hand. "Hey, look, bud. Sorry if you got the wrong idea. I just wanted Sheena to see a competitive property—something she and her sisters might want to consider in the future."

"Well, the future is over." Tony glared at her. "It's time to end this foolishness."

Sheena's dismay turned to anger. "*I* will be the one to decide that. Not *you*." She gave Blackie a weak smile. "Blackie, I'd like you to meet my husband, Tony Morelli. Tony, this is Blackie Gatto, Gavin's financial advisor, and now, mine."

To his credit and Sheena's relief, Tony shook the hand Blackie offered him.

"Thank you for a lovely evening, Blackie. I'll talk to you tomorrow." Sheena didn't look at Tony as she walked away from them, her back stiff.

Her sisters stood on the little patio in front of the house gaping at her. She brushed past them and entered the house.

Darcy rushed inside, and over to her. "I told you not to go out with him."

Sheena whirled around to her. "What did you say to Tony?"

Darcy looked away from her and then faced her. "He asked if you were out on a date and I didn't know what to say, so I turned away. That's all."

Sheena formed her hands into fists. She wanted to slap Darcy so hard it hurt to keep her fingers clenched. She couldn't remember when she'd been this angry. "Thanks, Darcy. You might have just broken up my marriage."

"Don't blame me for your foolish mistake," Darcy retorted.

Their conversation ended abruptly when Regan appeared, followed by Tony.

"We need to talk," Tony snarled, marching over to Sheena.

"We'll leave," said Regan. "C'mon, Darcy, let's go over to the Key Hole and give Sheena and Tony some privacy."

"Good idea. I need to get out of here."

Alone, standing in the living room like two fighters in a boxing ring waiting for the starting bell to ring, Sheena and Tony faced each other.

Sheena raised a hand to stop Tony from saying anything. "Before you start, there's nothing going on between Blackie and me. I would never do that to you or the children."

"Yeah? What you're doing is already hurting me and the children. Don't you get that?"

The frustration that had kept Sheena from shrieking overcame her. "What I don't get is any idea that you miss *me*. You miss all I've done and do for you—cooking, cleaning, laundry and all—but neither you nor the children have mentioned missing me, the person. Think about it, Tony. You know I'm right. And it hurts."

"Hey, wait a minute..."

"No, you wait. Look at this place. You must know it's not

an easy challenge, but we have people who are willing to help us—people of all ages and from all walks of life. We can't let them down. We're all going to benefit if Darcy, Regan and I can pull this challenge off. It's time for my children to grow up and think of others, and it's time for us to become partners in a different way."

"What do you mean? An open marriage?"

The look of dismay on Tony's face almost made Sheena laugh. "No, you dummy! Time for me to become more independent so I can be a happier, better person."

"You haven't been happy with me?"

The hurt in Tony's eyes caused Sheena to reach out for him. "Of course, I have. But it's been a while since we've sat and really talked to each other, had romance in our lives, worked together on projects, even dated."

"Dated?"

Sheena nodded. "Yeah. Sounds silly, doesn't it? But you and I haven't gone on a date since I can remember. You work every weekend and are too tired to go out."

Tony narrowed his eyes. "I do that for you and the kids."

"Yes, but you could have one of your workers take over emergency calls now and then. You've become stuck on the idea that you have to be present at every job. The guys you've hired and trained are capable of doing most jobs on their own. We've talked about this before, Tony."

"I came down here to see you because I care about you and me, about us as a family. But I see that you don't give a damn!"

Sheena shook her head. "That's not true, and you know it. Let's sit and calm down. Would you like a cup of coffee? A sandwich? Anything?"

"No. I had something to eat at the airport. I'm going to head back there. This is a wasted trip."

"Aw, Tony. Let's not make it a wasted trip. I want to show

you the hotel, have you meet some of Gavin's people ..."

"Gavin! He's the one who's to blame for all your nonsense," sputtered Tony.

"Tony, please ..." She gave him a steady look. "I want you to stay."

His long, loud sigh spoke volumes. Sheena's hopes rose.

"Okay, I'll stay," Tony said, "but I'm sleeping on the couch."

"Fine," Sheena said. "I'll get you a pillow and some blankets. In the meantime, we can sit on the porch and talk."

Upstairs in her room, Sheena quickly changed into jeans and a T-shirt. Slipping the pearl earrings out of her earlobes, she stared at herself in the mirror, wondering if she could keep her marriage together. She loved Tony; she loved her children. But after experiencing a new sense of herself, she knew there was no turning back. Other women had careers, a family, outside interests. Why couldn't she?

CHAPTER TWENTY-SIX
DARCY

Inside the bar next door, Darcy slumped in her seat opposite Regan feeling miserable.

"Why'd you have to go and imply to Tony that Sheena was out on a date? Couldn't you have said something like she was at a business meeting?" Regan spoke quietly, but the words hurt because Darcy was asking herself the very same question.

"I was trying to be fair by not saying anything, but I messed it up." Darcy's stomach roiled. "Do you think Sheena's marriage is really in trouble?"

Regan sighed. "No. I'd love to have some man fight for me the way Tony was fighting for Sheena. Tony loves Sheena and she loves him. He's just a bit old-fashioned."

"Good." Darcy looked across the room and straightened in her seat. She felt a wide smile spread across her face. "Hi, Brian! How are you?"

"Mind if I sit down?" Brian smiled at Darcy and turned his gaze to Regan.

"Not at all." Darcy was pleased to have him join them.

"We're just escaping the house," Regan explained.

"What's going on?" Brian asked.

Regan told him about Tony's surprise visit and then said, "We're giving them some privacy to work things out."

"Sheena told me Tony is a plumber. That right?" said Brian.

"Yes," said Darcy. "Why?"

"Just wondering."

Darcy was sure there was more to it than that.

Darcy almost tripped as she and Regan made their way into the house. "Whoa!" she uttered in a loud whisper, clinging to her sister's arm.

Regan giggled. "We never should have tried all those drinks Brian fixed for us. I can hardly stand up."

"Yeah, but they tasted so good," said Darcy. "Uh, oh ... I think I'm going to be sick." She stumbled into the living room and jerked to a stop. "Someone's here."

Regan shoved her playfully. "It's just Tony sleeping on the couch. Guess things aren't that great between Sheena and him."

Darcy paused and then raced into the kitchen, where she upchucked into the sink. "Gawd," Darcy said before doing it again.

"What's going on?" Tony turned on the lights in the living room.

Darcy turned as Tony entered the kitchen, wearing jeans but nothing else. She washed her face with cold water and tried to calm her stomach. "Sorry for disturbing you," she mumbled, and turned back to the sink, feeling sick once more.

"Good God! You're throwing up in the sink?" Tony said. "Too much partying? Is that it?"

"Don't blame her." Regan joined them. "We were just staying away from the house to give you and Sheena some time alone."

Tony shook his head. "This place is a goddamn zoo."

He left them in the kitchen and went back to the couch.

"You okay?" said Regan, sounding sober now.

Darcy nodded, but she knew she wouldn't be okay until things were better between Sheena and Tony.

CHAPTER TWENTY-SEVEN
SHEENA

Sheena lay in bed watching rosy fingers of dawn streak between the slats of the window blinds. The enticing color beckoned to her. Exhausted from lack of sleep, she got out of bed and pulled on some clothes. After brushing her hair and teeth, she slipped her feet into sandals and crept downstairs.

Tony was lying on the couch, curled up like a younger version of himself.

She tiptoed over to the couch and peered down at him. A wave of tenderness washed over her.

He opened his eyes and stared up at her. "What are you doing?" he asked, his voice raspy.

"Get dressed," she whispered. "I want you to come with me. There's something I want you to see."

Grumbling, Tony got up and slipped on the shirt and sweater he'd thrown onto a chair. After grabbing his sneakers, he silently followed her.

Outside, Tony turned to her. "Where are we going?"

"To one of my favorite places. The beach. We can talk there."

As they walked through the hotel grounds, Sheena pointed out the guest buildings and described the rooms to him. "We have forty standard rooms and eight family suites. It's a small number of rooms, but this property can be upgraded nicely, making it special. It's a great location, and I'm told the land alone is worth a lot." Sheena took his arm. "The walkway to the beach is right across the street."

Tony remained quiet, but Sheena noticed he took a careful look around.

Passing Gracie's, Sheena heard activity in the kitchen and smiled. Gracie's breakfast would do wonders for Tony.

They crossed the road and walked down the boardwalk. The sun behind them sent shafts of golden light on the water ahead of them, burnishing the crests of the waves that rolled toward the shore.

Sheena drew in a breath of salty air with satisfaction. In a light sweater, she lifted her arms and sighed. "I love it here." She turned to Tony and took hold of his hand. "C'mon, let's take a walk. It's very peaceful at this time of day."

Tony allowed her to hold his hand as they headed down the beach. Seagulls flew up in the air around them, rising and falling like puffs of popcorn. Little sandpipers skittered along the hard-packed sand at the water's edge, keeping just ahead of them, amusing them both.

"How far are we going to go?" Tony asked, pulling her to a stop

"We can turn around if you want," Sheena said agreeably. "But before we do, I need to clear the air with you. You embarrassed me last night when you charged Blackie and me. I am and will be faithful to you, Tony. That's the vow we made to each other, and I intend to keep it."

"Going out to dinner with other men isn't being faithful, Sheena, and you know it," Tony retorted.

"It was a business dinner," Sheena said as evenly as possible, though she wanted to scream with frustration. "It was a nice evening. I admit it. But the purpose was to show me a restaurant that Gavin thought he'd like to duplicate on the hotel's property one day. Blackie and Gavin were close, and Gavin trusted him to help us for as long as we ask him."

"Well, don't go out with him again," said Tony.

Sheena merely nodded, deciding it was better to win the war than this one battle. Later, when Tony had a better idea of what she and her sisters were doing, he might be more open to her or them having meetings with Blackie and other people who could help them.

"Let's have breakfast. Gracie's really is the best, like the sign says." Sheena smiled at Tony. "Wait until you meet her and the other people Gavin's rescued. They've promised to help us to get this place ready for our first guests."

"There's no way you can turn this property around in less than a year," said Tony.

"We only have to be able to bring in enough guests to start making money. Then if we've met the challenge, we will have enough funds to renovate the property the way Gavin wanted. And if we don't, someone else gets the property."

"What if you want to sell it?"

"That's a choice my sisters and I will have to make at the time. In only a short while, though, I've fallen in love with the place. And each day we're here, it gets better and better."

"Where are the kids going to stay when they come down here? Your house is small. They won't have bedrooms of their own."

Sheena shrugged. "We'll have to figure it out. They aren't going to be allowed to merely sit on the beach—they're going to work for room and board. Our children have become selfish and entitled. A visit here will do them good."

Tony studied her thoughtfully, and then nodded his agreement.

A few customers were already in Gracie's when Sheena and Tony walked into the restaurant. The aroma of bacon, coffee, and cinnamon wafted in the air, wrapping around them in a welcome no one could resist.

Sheena led Tony over to the kitchen. "Hi, Gracie! This is my husband, Tony. And, Tony, that's Gracie, and Sam and Sally and Bebe," she said, pointing out each one.

After they'd all acknowledged each other with smiles and bobs of their heads, Sheena led Tony to a table in the corner.

Lynn Michaels and Maggie O'Neil came over to them.

"And who is this handsome man?" Maggie said, giving Tony a big smile.

"This is my husband, Tony," said Sheena.

"Oh, yes!" said Lynn. "Gavin talked about you. He thought you'd approve his ideas for transforming this place. Said you were a good worker."

Tony's look of surprise eased into pride. "Thank you."

Lynn pushed a strand of gray hair behind her ear. "Gavin was a good soul. A little different, but a good man all the same. And if he liked you, he'd take good care of you."

New customers walked into the restaurant, and Lynn hurried away from their table.

Maggie handed them menus and said, "I'll be back to take your order. Coffee for either one of you?"

Tony placed his order for black coffee and orange juice and turned to Sheena.

"The same," she said.

"What's all that B.S. about Gavin liking me?" Tony said in a low voice after Maggie walked away. "I never met him."

Sheena held up a finger. "Gavin knew more about all of us than I ever suspected. My mother kept in touch with him. They exchanged letters. And, after she got her iPhone, she went crazy sending everyone pictures of all of us. Remember?"

Tony nodded. "Tell me about the people here. You told me they were rescued by Gavin. How did they all end up here?"

"They needed places to live, jobs, security," said Sheena. "They were people he met and liked."

Maggie returned with their coffee and juice. "Ready to order?"

Tony said to Sheena, "Go ahead. I'm still looking."

Sheena ordered a cheese and tomato omelet and listened as Tony ordered the heavy-duty surfer's breakfast of eggs, sausage, potatoes and toast and pancakes.

As she sipped her coffee, Sheena studied Tony. He'd just turned forty and was sensitive about his age. He'd developed a little belly but was still a trim, striking man with his dark hair, brown eyes and strong features.

"Great menu," said Tony, patting his stomach. "And the smells in this place have made me hungry."

Sheena smiled. Tony liked his meals on a regular schedule.

A short time later, Maggie brought their food to the table. "Anything else? Warm-ups on the coffee?"

After she refilled their coffee cups, she left to wait on other customers. They were quickly filling the tables.

Tony took a few bites of eggs and let out a satisfied sigh. "Mmm. Good."

Some of the tension that had knotted Sheena's shoulders eased. Tony would be easier to talk to on a full stomach. She had to convince him to see the value in what she was doing without hurting his pride.

They'd just finished their meal when Brian entered the restaurant. He waved to her and walked over to their table.

"Hey, how's my painting buddy?"

Sheena sensed Tony tenseness. "Hi, Brian! What's up?"

"May I join you?"

Sheena glanced at Tony and turned back to Brian. "Sure. This is my husband, Tony."

Brian smiled and held out his hand. "Brian Harwood. Your

wife is one smart lady, but actually, it's you I wanted to talk to."

The men shook hands, and Brian sat down.

Lynn came over to the table with a pot of coffee and a mug. "Black, right, Brian?"

He nodded. "Thanks."

Brian took a sip of the steaming coffee and then turned to Sheena. "I ran into Darcy and Regan last night. They told me Tony was here." He faced Tony. "I understand you're a plumbing contractor. I thought you could do me a huge favor. I'm in construction and am wondering if you'd help me on a project today? It shouldn't take too long."

Tony's eyebrows lifted. A smile crossed his face and evaporated. "That may be a problem. I'm not licensed in Florida."

Brian shrugged. "Not a problem. My usual guy, who is licensed here, was called out of town. He'll inspect your work and approve it when he gets back. I don't want to put up with any more delays on this project. It's important to me."

Tony glanced at Sheena. "Do you mind?"

"No, I guess not," said Sheena, secretly pleased by the idea. "But before you leave the hotel, I want to walk you through the property so you'll better understand what we're dealing with."

Tony nodded. "Deal."

He rose and, giving her a little wave, left the restaurant with Brian.

Watching them go, Sheena had the oddest feeling that helping Brian would either convince Tony the hotel project was worthwhile or kill any enthusiasm she might be able to build in him.

CHAPTER TWENTY-EIGHT
REGAN

Regan awoke with a start. She tried to move, but her arms were pinned against her. She managed to roll onto her side and realized the lightweight blanket she used at night was wrapped tightly around her. After wiggling and rolling enough to unwind and free herself, she sat up and held her pounding head in her hands. Why had she tried to keep up with Darcy and Brian as they tried a number of different exotic drinks? Gawd! She was stupid sometimes.

She got to her feet and made her way into the bathroom, ran her washcloth under cold water and pressed it to her forehead. She was supposed to meet Rocky and two men on Brian's team, and she didn't want to be late. Regan peeked into Sheena's room. Empty. She ducked her head into Darcy's room and found her still in bed.

"Hey, Darce! You'd better get up! It's late!"

"Go away!" Darcy snapped. "No way am I getting out of this bed. It's still spinning on me."

"Don't you have a meeting with Chip this morning?"

"You'd better go talk to him," said Darcy. "Tell him I'll see him sometime this afternoon. He knows what to do anyway."

The thought of having an excuse to talk to Chip sent new energy through Regan. There was something so intriguing about him. She left Darcy and went back to the bathroom for a shower. Afterward, she dressed carefully in a clean pair of shorts and a fresh T-shirt, brushed her hair, and took a moment to apply eye makeup. The unusual color of her eyes was fascinating to others, and she wanted to break through Chip's indifference—a whole different role for her.

She left the house and hurried across the hotel grounds to the Egret guest building. Rocky and the other men were already at work unloading mattresses into one of the two dumpsters on site.

"Thanks, guys!" said Regan. "I'll be back soon. I have to do an errand for Darcy."

As Regan left the building, she met up with Sheena. "Hi! Where's Tony? Did he leave?"

"He's helping Brian with a project," Sheena said. "If you need me, I'll be at the house working on numbers."

"Darcy's there. She's feeling really hungover because of all the drinks she had last night. I stopped before she did, but I don't ever want to see or smell tequila again."

Sheena shook her head. "Darcy's looking for trouble."

"Aw, don't go big sister on her," said Regan, quickly coming to Darcy's defense. "We were just trying to help you out by leaving the house."

"Sorry," said Sheena. "See you later."

Regan went into Gracie's, grabbed a cup of coffee, and carried it into the office. Chip was at work at Darcy's desk, tapping away on a computer.

"Good morning! How are you?" Regan asked, pulling as much enthusiasm out of her as she could in her hungover state.

"Okay. Where's Darcy?" he said, barely looking at her.

"She's not feeling well. She said to tell you that she'd meet up with you this afternoon, that you knew what to do."

He nodded. "Yeah, I'm working on some system stuff."

"You're going to set up a program for me to track furniture for the guest rooms, aren't you?" She smiled. "I thought maybe you'd do it for me."

"Yeah, okay, later," he said, turning back to his work, obviously not charmed by her.

Disappointed, she paused a moment and then turned to go.

"Wait!" said Chip. "I was going to ask you and Darcy if you wanted to come to a party at my house tomorrow night. My roommate is celebrating landing a job at Disney World in Orlando."

"Thanks," said Regan. "It sounds like fun. You can give all the details to Darcy and we'll make arrangements to be there."

Excited about the prospect of seeing Chip again and meeting friends of his, Regan left the office, dropped her coffee mug off at the restaurant, and headed to the Egret Building for another day in the guest rooms. Maybe, out of the office, she'd have a better chance to talk to Chip.

CHAPTER TWENTY-NINE
DARCY

Darcy opened her eyes and groaned at the sight of Sheena standing by her bed. "What do you want?"

"I'm just checking to make sure you're all right. Tony said you were sick last night."

"Ugh. Was I ever! But, Sheena, the worst part of my getting drunk was asking Brian if he wanted to be friends with benefits."

"You did whaat?"

"You heard me." Tears stung Darcy's eyes.

"My God! What did he say?" said Sheena.

"He turned me down, of course. He's fallen for Regan and she doesn't even care."

Darcy rolled over, unable to look at the horror on Sheena's face any longer. "Don't you dare scold me, Sheena. I know I made a jerk of myself. You don't have to go there."

Sheena's sigh said a lot. "I'll be working downstairs at the kitchen table. Call me if you need me."

After Sheena left the room, Darcy closed her eyes with relief. Knowing how stupid she'd been, she couldn't face Sheena's perfection. The whole thing with Brian was crazy, but she'd been attracted to him from the beginning.

Her sisters thought she was impulsive. Well, maybe they were right. Because right now, Darcy would give anything to take her words back and start all over again.

CHAPTER THIRTY
SHEENA

Sheena stared at the computer without seeing the numbers on the screen. Instead, in her mind, she saw the satisfied expression on Tony's face when Brian had asked him for his help. She'd known then how vulnerable Tony was about his plumbing business beginning to falter. Oh, he still brought in money—everyone needed a plumber at one time or another. But required health insurance for his workers was just one thing among several others that were eating away at their profit. The simple fact was that it was difficult for a small business to succeed when other larger, companies were able to be more competitive.

Though she recognized Tony's worries were contributing to his frustration at her being gone, Sheena realized that, in many ways, the failing business of his greatly limited their choices. And once she'd tasted independence, she couldn't go back to the way things were. She needed both her family and her freedom. Was that one of the reasons why Gavin had set up his challenge? To help her discover herself? Sheena was still lost in thought when Darcy came downstairs.

"Guess I'd better try to eat something. I was supposed to meet with Chip," Darcy said, stumbling into the kitchen.

Moments later, she sat opposite Sheena with a cup of tea and a piece of toast. "What happened with Tony? Did he go back home?"

Sheena explained about Tony helping Brian.

Darcy's eyes widened. "You talked to Brian this morning? Did he say anything about me?"

Sheena shook her head. "I can't imagine he would. That benefits thing is really between the two of you."

Darcy covered her face with her hands. "I don't know if I'll ever be able to look at him again. He laughed when I asked him."

"I'm sure he knew you were drunk. Just forget about it," said Sheena. "He's a nice guy. He'll probably pretend it never happened."

Sheena hated the whole idea of friends with benefits. It put a girl in such a cheap situation. She knew from other mothers that two girls in Meaghan's class actually had such an arrangement. The thought made her stomach turn.

Thinking of her daughter, Sheena couldn't wait to have Meaghan come to Florida. She hoped it would be a time of healing, of self-discovery. She planned on putting her to work with Regan. Meaghan had always liked her.

"Sheena?"

Jolted out of her thoughts, Sheena focused on Darcy. The paleness of Darcy's cheeks and the woebegone expression on her face worried her. "You okay?"

Darcy shook her head. "Sean told me once I try too hard to make relationships work. What's wrong with me? Why would I do something like ask Brian to be a fuck buddy?"

"If that's what you call it, that says it all." Sheena couldn't hide her distaste. "You're a wonderful woman, Darcy. You just don't believe it. Maybe because Regan and I always got more attention than you."

"Yeah, typical middle-child I guess." Darcy gave her a glum look. "I'm going to the restaurant to see if they have ginger ale or something like that to help settle my stomach. See you later."

After Darcy left, Sheena thought of her sisters. It had hurt when they'd told her how angry they'd been that she left the family to start her own. Didn't they understand how disappointed she'd been to have her life change so abruptly? She'd never known their freedom to try different things.

Pushing aside those thoughts, Sheena focused on the financials and then tried her hand at coming up with some advertising scripts. She wondered about a logo for their hotel and decided to talk to Regan about it later.

The morning flew by as Sheena did some research on other hotels' room rates on her phone. They'd have to be competitive, but reasonable enough to lure customers in. Once they were able to generate income from room sales, they could continue to make improvements. And then, if they won the challenge, they'd have even more money to make the hotel the wonderful place they wanted it to be. After getting started on the project, Sheena hoped she'd be able to see it through on a more permanent basis. But with her family opposing her, she didn't see how that could happen.

Sheena ate a simple salad for lunch and was back at her computer when Tony walked into the house.

"Hi! How did the plumbing project for Brian go?" she asked, noticing a new confidence in Tony's stride.

"Great. Brian and his partner have a good little business going here in Florida. And he's a nice guy. Apparently, Darcy got a little out of hand when she got drunk, but he helped her and Regan get to the house."

"Good," Sheena said. She wouldn't say anything more about Darcy's indiscretion. Her sister was already mortified by her behavior. "Have you had lunch?"

Tony smiled. "A grouper sandwich with the guys. It was great."

Sheena stood and came over to him. "I'm glad you had a

chance to get to know Brian a little. He and his mother were close to Gavin, and he promised my uncle he would help us. Do you want to take a look around the property?"

"Later. Right now, I want to make good use of our afternoon. Alone."

The sexy look he gave her surprised Sheena. She couldn't remember when they'd last made love in the afternoon. At the thought, her body reacted to his silent invitation.

"Hold on! I'll post a note to the door." She grinned at him. "And then I'll lock it."

They looked at each other and laughed. The sound of it brought back memories of their early years together.

Upstairs, lying beside Tony, Sheena sighed. Their lovemaking had been more exciting, more urgent than anything in the last few years. Like she'd told Tony, they were too young to act old and boring. Apparently, Tony thought so too.

She rolled over and faced him. Lifting her hands to his cheeks, she stared into his eyes. "I love you, Tony."

"Me, too. You, I mean. I hate having you gone."

"Missing my cooking, are you?" she asked and held her breath.

"Missing you," he replied. An impish grin spread across his face. "And your cooking." He drew her to him, surprising her with a fresh manly response to her closeness.

"Whoa! I guess you did, big boy!"

He laughed. "Like you said, we're too young to act old. Come here, woman!"

As Tony's hands trailed down her, Sheena's body turned liquid. His old touch was back in a whole new way.

When they finally got out of bed, they went into the

bathroom together. Tony stared at the antiquated toilet, sink, and bathtub and shook his head with amazement.

"This is ridiculous. Why don't you let me install some new stuff for you? I'm sure I can get a discount either through my business up north or with Brian's company."

"You and I can't afford that, Tony, and the budget we have for the hotel can't afford it either. If things go well, after the year is complete, we can upgrade the bathroom and the kitchen. Heck, we probably can do a lot of things."

Tony shook his head. "This whole thing is crazy. You know that, right?"

Sheena placed a hand on his shoulder. "Let's not go there now. I'm still enjoying being with you. You were... well ... wonderful."

His happy grin was good to see. "Sorry, I'm not up to anything else right now. But maybe later?"

Sheena laughed. "What a greedy guy." She wrapped her arms around him and rested her head against his muscular chest, listening with satisfaction to the strong beat of his heart.

As soon as she'd bathed and dressed, Sheena hurried downstairs to unlock the door and remove the note from it.

After opening the door, she pulled off the taped note and stared at the words someone had scrawled across it: *Hope you and Tony are having fun!*

She laughed, not caring if anyone else knew what they'd been up to. Like she'd told Tony, it had been a wonderful, long-overdue romp.

Sheena and Tony rode to the airport in silence. There were a lot of things Sheena wanted to say, but she decided to let the afterglow of their afternoon speak for them. In a couple of weeks, the kids and Tony would return for their break. By then, she, Tony, and the kids should have more opportunities to resolve any issues among them.

She pulled up to the curb at the Tampa International Airport, regretting that she and Tony wouldn't have more time together. She turned to him. "Say hi to Meaghan and Michael for me and let them know how much I miss them. I'll keep trying to get in touch with them, but I wish you would encourage them to answer my calls. They could at least text me."

Tony nodded. "Okay. They owe that to you." He leaned over and kissed her, then quickly pulled away. But she'd already seen the sadness in his eyes.

"See you." He got out of the car, flipped his backpack over his shoulder, and walked away without looking back at her.

At the sound of a car horn behind her, Sheena stepped on the gas and pulled away, wondering how many more times they'd be torn apart by the challenge she couldn't refuse.

CHAPTER THIRTY-ONE
REGAN

Regan checked herself in the mirror. Her new, short denim skirt was sexy but not outrageous. With her conservative background, outrageous was never going to happen. The blue and yellow print blouse she'd bought had a scooped neckline and cute, little puffed sleeves. After working hard with the men cleaning out guest rooms, it had felt good to come home, have a nice hot bath, and wash her hair.

Chip had given Darcy directions to his house. It was in an area just north of Treasure Island in a neighborhood that backed up to Boca Ciega Bay. Regan was pleased to be asked to the party. She'd come to Florida with the intention of having a good time, but so far, she'd been stuck working her butt off with a bunch of older people.

"You ready?" asked Darcy, coming into Regan's bedroom.

"As ready as I ever will be," said Regan, setting down her hairbrush. She'd decided to wear only a little makeup. It didn't work well in the humidity anyway.

They went downstairs and said goodbye to Sheena, who was watching a movie on her iPad. They'd talked about pitching in to buy a television together, but they hadn't done it. Sheena, she knew, was in no hurry to buy one anyway because she didn't want television available when her kids came for a visit. Until tonight, Regan had been too tired at the end of the day to care about TV programs. Now, she was ready to party.

She and Darcy went outside and climbed into the van. Darcy, of course, insisted on driving.

Darcy pulled up in front of a small, white-clapboard house. The wide front porch was filled with people, standing around, drinking, and talking. Rock music rang out above the noise of the crowd.

"Wow! Chip said his roomie had a lot of friends, but this is something else," said Darcy. She grinned at Regan. "Let's have some fun!"

"Just remember to watch how many drinks you have," warned Regan. "I don't want to have to literally drag you out of here."

Darcy frowned at her. "Stop! You're sounding like Sheena."

Regan hung back as Darcy led the way to the front porch. A keg of beer had been set up at one end of it. People were going in and coming out of the house in a constant circulating stream.

"Let's go find Chip," Darcy shouted into Regan's ear. "I want to see if they have something other than beer."

Regan followed Darcy through the crowd and into the house. Chip was standing in the kitchen at the back of the house talking to two guys. When he saw them, he grinned and waved them over.

"Hi, I want you to meet my roommate, Bill, and a friend of his..." he paused.

"Kevin," the guy said, giving each of them a wide smile. His gaze rested on Regan. "Well, hello! Where have you been hiding?"

Unable to hide her distaste, Regan stepped back.

Chip frowned. "This is Regan Sullivan and her sister, Darcy. They're the new owners of the Salty Key Inn."

Bill elbowed Kevin aside. "Glad you could come. Chip told me he asked you to the party."

"Congratulations on your new job," said Regan. "Working at Disney sounds wonderful."

"You girls want something to drink?" Chip asked them. "Beer's on the porch, and we got some harder stuff back here. I've just mixed up some margaritas."

"I'll have one of those," said Darcy.

Regan hesitated. After getting drunk with Darcy and Brian, tequila was definitely not her thing. The queasiness that had followed wasn't anything she wanted to experience again.

"I've got the fixings for a rum and coke," Kevin said to her. "Would you rather have that?"

Regan smiled. "That sounds great. Thanks."

Darcy accepted a drink from Chip and turned to Regan. "I'll catch up with you later. I'm going to see who's on the porch."

Regan nodded and waited in the kitchen for Kevin to fix her drink.

"You own a hotel? For real?" Kevin said. "How did that happen?"

"We inherited it," said Regan. "Or what there is of it. It needs a lot of work. Chip is helping us with the computer system."

"Not bad," Kevin said. "Here. Enjoy the drink. It's a specialty of mine. I add a little lime juice to it."

Regan accepted the paper cup he handed her and took a sip. "Delicious. Thanks."

She turned to go.

"Wait. Let's just stay here and get acquainted. When you're done with that, I'll fix you another."

"Thanks, maybe later. Now, I need to find my sister," Regan said and walked away from him. He was trying too hard, and she didn't like it.

On the porch, people were milling about, talking loudly or laughing together. Regan figured there must be at least thirty people there.

She made her way to Darcy's side. Darcy glanced at her and kept on talking to the guy standing with her. Not wanting to interrupt, Regan kept moving. She tried smiling at a couple of the girls, but after looking her over, they made no effort to talk to her. Disappointed, Regan made her way back to the kitchen. Another drink was what she needed.

Kevin looked up at her and smiled. "How was that drink?"

"Good," said Regan, and suddenly realized how potent that one drink had been. Or maybe it was just her being nervous about meeting other people that made her want to hide in the kitchen. Feeling weak, she sank down into a kitchen chair. As the room began to spin, she clung to the edge of the table.

"Hey! Are you all right?" Kevin asked her.

"I...I don't know," she answered.

"How about some fresh air?" Kevin helped her out of the chair and led her outside. "We can sit over there," he said, leading her to a grassy area under a tree. "No one will bother us here."

Regan tried to pull away from him, but he had a firm grip on her arm and she was too weak to keep trying. He helped to lower her to the ground.

All Regan's instincts told her this scenario was dangerous. She fought to keep her eyes open.

"Hey! What's going on?"

Another guy's voice brought Regan back to the moment.

"Help me!" she cried, struggling to get to her knees.

"It's okay, man. She's just sick from having too much to drink," said Kevin. "I've got the situation under control."

With all the strength she could muster, Regan looked up at the stranger and said, "Help me."

The guy knelt beside her. "You're Regan Sullivan, aren't you?"

She nodded weakly.

"Your sister sent me to find you. There's something she wanted me to talk to you about."

"I think I'm drugged," Regan managed to say, fighting with a strength she didn't know she had.

The stranger stood and glared at Kevin. "You'd better not have hurt her or I'll see that you're arrested. Now get out of here before I call the cops."

Regan's vision blurred as the stranger bent and picked her up. "Don't worry," he whispered. "I won't hurt you."

Regan awoke in her bedroom and gazed around in confusion. She started to get up and fell back against her pillow, her mind spinning with unanswered questions. *Why was she in her room? Hadn't she and Darcy been at a party? How had she ended up here? Was she sick again?* She felt very funny.

With effort, Regan managed to get to her feet. She headed for the bathroom and used the walls to guide her.

Darcy came out of her bedroom. "You're awake?"

"I think so, though I feel as if I'm in some weird dream. I thought we were going to Chip's party. What happened?"

"We went to that party all right. Don't you remember?"

"Hold on." Regan closed the bathroom door, completed her task and faced Darcy once more. "I remember going to Chip's house, all the people on the porch and meeting that guy who fixed me the drink. From then on, I don't remember much of anything."

Sheena came running up the stairs to join them. "Oh my God! You're awake." She wrapped her arms around Regan and gave her a hug. After Sheena pulled away, Regan was surprised to see tears in her sister's eyes. "Thank God Austin found you in time."

Regan frowned. "What are you talking about?"

"She doesn't remember anything about it," Darcy said to Sheena.

"Who's Austin?" Regan said, straining to make sense of it all.

"Austin Blakely, the wood carver. He's the one who found you lying in the backyard with that creep Kevin. You told him you'd been drugged."

Regan felt her eyebrows lift in surprise. "I did?"

"Let me explain," said Darcy. "I was talking to Austin on the front porch when you walked by. I told him about the other sign we wanted him to make and sent him into the kitchen to talk to you. That's when he saw you outside on the lawn."

Regan clasped her head in her hands. "I don't remember any of it. I did dream about a man with brown hair and bright-blue eyes. He was wearing a cowboy costume."

Darcy shook her head. "I don't know about any cowboy costume, but Austin has dark-brown hair and bright-blue eyes."

"Weird, huh?" said Regan.

"It could mean your mind thought of him as a hero, coming to save you," said Sheena. "You've always liked cowboys, and drugs can do strange things to your brain. What do you remember, Regan?"

"Darcy and I met Chip and some other guys in the kitchen. One of them offered me a drink. I took it and went to find Darcy. By the time I was able to reach her through the crowd, I was feeling out of it. I went back to the kitchen to get another drink and suddenly realized I'd had too much. Things began to spin. After that, I don't remember a thing. Nothing weird happened, did it? I wasn't...assaulted, was I?" The thought made Regan clutch her stomach.

"No, hon, you weren't," said Sheena, taking hold of her hand. "Austin found you before anything like that happened."

"How did I get home?" Regan asked.

"I drove you," said Darcy. "Austin followed me to make sure you were all right. He's studying to be a dentist and knows the effects of some drugs."

"He's a very sweet guy," said Sheena. "Look, I'm going to make you a nice, hot breakfast, and then I want you to take it easy for the rest of the day. Okay?"

Regan nodded her head, still trying to wrap her mind around the idea that she'd been drugged. She was usually careful about such a thing happening whenever she was in a new group. In New York City, where people came and went easily, she'd been especially wary. To have it happen in sunny Florida seemed way too bizarre.

CHAPTER THIRTY-TWO
SHEENA

When Darcy and a stranger had all but dragged Regan into the house that night, Sheena's heart had stopped and then started again with jerky beats. And then, when she understood what had almost happened, all the maternal feelings she'd always had for her sisters rose to the surface in a rush of horror.

Even now, as she made breakfast for Regan, she thought of how close Regan had come to a sexual assault. She intended to speak to Chip about it. He hadn't been the one to drug Regan, but one of his friends had.

Later, when Regan and Darcy calmed down, she'd talk to them about any actions they might take against the guy known to them only as Kevin. He'd apparently claimed he'd done nothing wrong, that it must have been someone else who had dropped a roofie in Regan's glass as she'd walked through the crowd. He had stood by his assertion that he was only trying to help her.

Sheena couldn't help thinking of her own children. Their teen years were and would continue to be very different from her own. More and more exposure to the internet and various phone apps made it difficult to keep track of the information filling their minds. And drugs were always present.

Regan came downstairs to the kitchen, looking as if she still wasn't sure where she was.

Sheena helped her to a chair and handed her a plate with

scrambled eggs and buttered wheat toast. "Here. Try to eat what you can. We'll keep your diet simple today."

Regan gave her a weak smile. "Thanks, Mom!"

Sheena grinned at the attempted joke, certain Regan didn't understand how frightened she'd been.

After Regan ate what she wanted, she climbed the stairs to go back to bed. Sheena watched her go and then turned back to an advertising program she was working on. She'd also been thinking about the pool. Brian had told her it needed to be drained, scrubbed and painted. And, as usual, he knew someone who could do that for them.

She was researching logo designs when her cell rang. She checked Caller ID. *Rosa.* A thread of worry wove through her, tying her stomach into knots. She snatched up her phone.

"Hi! Is everything all right?" Sheena asked.

"Well, actually no. It's Meaghan. She's been sent home from school for the next few days," said Rosa. "It seems she and two of her friends were intercepted bullying another girl in their class."

"Whaaat? Bullying? Meaghan? Oh my God! She knows better." Sheena felt sick to her stomach. She'd discussed bullying with both her children on many occasions. What had happened to her once-sweet daughter?

Sheena's shock turned to anger. "Is Meaghan there?"

"Yes," said Rosa. "She's terribly upset."

"Put her on the phone, please." Sheena's voice was deceptively calm. She waited impatiently to hear her daughter's voice.

"H...hello."

"What happened Meaghan?"

"It's all Lauren's fault. She told me I couldn't be her friend unless I posted something about Marina Palo. Marina said something mean about Lauren."

"Okay, you went ahead and did it. Now, who's fault is that? We've talked about bullying before, Meaghan. I thought you were a better person than that." Sheena couldn't hide her disappointment. "How could you do something like that?"

"I won't do it again. It isn't fair that the principal kicked me out of school."

"What isn't fair is that you hurt someone else," said Sheena. "I'm going to call the principal and explain that you will not return to school until after the break, that you will miss five extra days. Five extra days that you will have to work extra hard to overcome."

"What? You're going to make me stay here with Grandma?"

"Nooo," said Sheena. "You're coming to Florida to spend some time with me. You'd better start packing. And don't bring any fancy clothes. You will be working hard here."

"This would never have happened if you'd hadn't left home," taunted Meaghan.

"It should never have happened. Period," said Sheena, furious that her daughter was trying to pin her bad behavior on her. "Now, let me talk to Grandma Rosa."

"Hi, Sheena. What's going on? Meaghan is crying."

"I've come up with a plan." Sheena explained what she intended to do and then, after making sure there were no other problems, she hung up.

As she punched in the number for the school, Sheena wondered if Meaghan was right. If she'd stayed home, would things have gotten this far out of control?

Shaking her head, Sheena told herself not to fall into that trap.

A short while later, Sheena hung up from the call with the principal, filled with anguish. Meaghan had been acting out in class and had become belligerent when called to task for it. A note had been emailed home regarding a detention. Why,

Sheena wondered, hadn't Tony brought it up? Hadn't he been keeping on top of things?

When she was finally able to talk to Tony, he immediately went on the defensive. "I told Meaghan she'd better behave, but when she began to cry, I stopped talking. I thought she got my message. I haven't heard anything more from the school."

Sheena held back a sigh. Tony was trying his best, but where his daughter was concerned, Meaghan could do no wrong. "Are things okay with Michael? No problems?"

"Other than curfews? No."

"Good. I'm making arrangements for Meaghan to come to Florida a few days early for the break. It'll mean she'll have to make up five days of school, but the principal and I feel it would do her good to get away from the group of girls she's been hanging out with."

"Okay. Good idea," said Tony. "It'll be good for everyone. Mom's been having a bit of a bad time with Meaghan too. And that Valentine's Dance? What a mess." He gave her the details.

"Good thing Meaghan's coming here. I'll give you the flight information. Will you see that she gets to the airport?"

"Yes," said Tony. "Believe me, it will be my pleasure. Thanks for handling this, Sheena."

"Of course. I'm her mother." Sheena did her best not to be defensive, but the silence that followed pricked her heart.

Tony broke into the quiet. "Michael and I will see you in two weeks. Good luck.!"

"Love you," Sheena said, but Tony had already hung up.

Staring out the window at the palm trees, Sheena knew it would take more than a change of scenery to bring about changes in her daughter. But no matter what it took, she wouldn't allow Meaghan to be less of a person than she could be.

###

Sheena stood in the baggage claim area inside the airport waiting for Meaghan to arrive. She told herself to enjoy her daughter's presence, to not harp on the reasons why she was in Florida, to simply enjoy the time with her. She looked up and saw Meaghan walking toward her, looking uncertain.

Sheena's heart went out to her. She ran toward her daughter, arms held out. "Hi! Glad you made it!"

As she drew Meaghan to her, Sheena heard a sigh escape her daughter's lips.

"It feels good to hold you in my arms," said Sheena, giving Meaghan another squeeze. "C'mon! I've parked the car in the lot. We'll head down to the hotel and you'll have a chance to get comfortable. Have you had lunch?"

Meaghan shook her head. "No, just a snack. I was too nervous to eat breakfast."

"Okay, then, we'll hurry to the hotel and you can sample some of Gracie's wonderful cooking. I've got water and a few snacks in the car."

Meaghan followed her out to the van and sat silently in the passenger's seat as they drove south.

"Things are in a rough state at the hotel," Sheena said. "You'll either be sharing a bed with me or sleeping on the couch until we can get a space cleared for you. I'm hoping to get one of the suites set up for our family when Dad and Michael join us."

Meaghan nodded but remained silent.

Sheena turned to her. "Darcy and Regan know why you've come to Florida, but the staff and others know it's simply for personal reasons. How, and if, you explain anything to them will be up to you."

Meaghan stared out the window.

When she turned back, tears glistened in her eyes. "Lauren and her friends won't speak to me anymore. They say it's my fault that they're in trouble."

"Maybe it's time you thought long and hard about them. These are girls who think it's perfectly normal to spend four hundred dollars for a dress for a school dance. Their parents don't set curfews I agree with. They've even allowed parties at their houses to go on without them."

"Where did you hear that? From the principal?"

Sheena shook her head. "Dad told me. The party after the Valentine's Dance was not properly supervised. You were late getting home from it, and you had alcohol on your breath. You're fourteen years old, Meaghan, not an adult. Even then, you have to be careful who you choose for company, what you do."

A defiant expression crossed Meaghan's face. "Why should I care? You don't even love me enough to stay home!"

"Oh, girl," Sheena said, "you have no idea what love is all about. I love you dearly. I love Dad and Michael, Grandma Rosa, the whole family. By coming to Florida, I hope to do something wonderful for everyone. And you're going to help me."

"I am?"

"Oh, yes," said Sheena. "You're going to be busy."

Meaghan crossed her arms. "What if I don't want to help."

Sheena gave her a mocking smile. "Sweetie, being here is called one of life's lessons. And I really hope and believe you will be a better person because of it. Now, here we are."

As Sheena pulled into the entrance of the Salty Key Inn, she watched Meaghan's eyes become round with surprise. Sheena hid a smile. Even with a fresh coat of paint on the main building, more work needed to be done to make it look upscale. The landscaping Brian had done was attractive but still needed to fill in to give the appearance of lushness they desired.

Sheena drove the van along the side driveway and up to the house.

"Pink?" said Meaghan. "You live in a pink house?"

"*We* live in a pink house—Darcy, Regan and me, and, now, you. Watch out! Here come your aunts!"

Darcy and Regan sprinted across the hotel grounds toward them.

"Hi, Meggie!" shouted Darcy, reaching Meaghan first. She wrapped her arms around Meaghan in a sweeping hug.

"Hi, Meaghan," said Regan, joining them and putting an arm around Meaghan. "Glad you made it!"

Sheena watched with affection as Meaghan's eyes lit with pleasure at the welcome. It would, she knew, be good for Meaghan to have her aunts around to keep things on a harmonious footing. She had no intention of constantly criticizing Meaghan. If it was going to be a real learning experience, Meaghan had to be free to make some decisions on her own.

"We're going to Gracie's for lunch," said Sheena. "Want to join us?"

"Sure," said Darcy. "I was about to take a break."

Regan shook her head. "Not me. I'll join you later. The guys are helping me clear the rooms and move some furniture around. We want to get a lot of it done before we go to the big sale tomorrow."

"Good idea," said Sheena. The renovation of one of the bigger, more luxurious hotels in Orlando was, they hoped, going to be a chance to buy some nice, used furniture. Though Regan was in charge, they all were going to the sale. They'd already put their bid in on some of the nicer stuff.

"Let's put your suitcase inside," Sheena said to Meaghan. "Then we'll head over to the restaurant."

She led Meaghan into the living room. "You can choose to

sleep here on a couch or, as I said earlier, with me. Go ahead and carry your suitcase upstairs to my room. For the time being, we'll have to cope with these arrangements."

Meaghan's steps behind her on the stairs slapped the wood defiantly, but Sheena decided to ignore her behavior. Her daughter had a lot to learn, but it wasn't going to happen all at once.

Sheena showed Meaghan her bedroom, the other two and then opened the door to the bathroom. "Here it is ... the only one for now."

"You're kidding!" wailed Meaghan. "How am I going to wash my hair in that ... that thing."

"You'll manage, just like the rest of us."

Meaghan stamped her foot. "Mom! This is serious."

"Yes, it is," said Sheena. "That's why we're working hard to bring the hotel, not the house, up to standards for guests." She placed a hand on Meaghan's shoulder. "C'mon! Let's get something to eat and I'll show you where you're going to work."

Tears filled Meaghan's eyes. "I really have to go to work?"

Sheena nodded. "You'll have some time to yourself, of course, but you'll also have a job or two to do. It's all part of being a member of the family. A valued one."

Meaghan sniffed.

Darcy shouted up to them. "Are you guys ready for lunch? I'm starving!"

Sheena followed Meaghan down the stairs, and the three of them left the house for the restaurant and an uncertain future.

CHAPTER THIRTY-THREE
DARCY

As they headed for Gracie's, Darcy slung an arm around Meaghan's shoulder. She hoped her niece knew enough to keep her mouth shut and to follow the rules her mother had set up for her. Darcy had never seen Sheena angrier than when she'd informed Regan and her of what Meaghan had done and why she was coming to Florida.

Truth is, Darcy had been disappointed the two times she'd texted Meaghan—just checking up on her—and hadn't received a response. She remembered how she and Meaghan used to communicate on a somewhat regular basis and how much it had meant to her.

"Meggie, I hope you'll find it nice here. The pool is being repainted, but it should be ready to use by the time your brother gets here."

Meaghan grimaced. "Figures."

"I know how you feel. We haven't been able to use the pool either. But we're fixing things up around here as fast as we can. I'm pushing to get the dock fixed. Then maybe we can use the kayaks Regan bought."

"Kayaks?" Meaghan's face lit up. "Cool."

"We'll see how fast the waterfront area can be cleared. A lot of other things come before that," said Darcy. "In the meantime, you know you can talk to me about anything. Right?"

Meaghan grinned. "Yeah."

As they approached Gracie's, they saw Clyde helping Lynn clear dishes off a couple of the tables on the patio.

Darcy waved and led Meaghan to the front door.

"Wow! Look at the pirate," said Meaghan, fingering the tall, wooden statue. "Cool."

"Let's sit outside. What was the temperature in Boston when you left?" said Sheena, holding the door for them as she spoke to Meaghan.

"It was in the fifties and raining. Typical."

"Sheena smiled. "Ah, I think you're going to enjoy the weather here. I'm glad you wore a light shirt with your jeans. But as nice as it is here, we Sullivans need to be careful of the sun."

"I'm a Morelli," said Meaghan defiantly.

"Indeed," murmured Sheena, exasperated with her. Inside, she spoke to Maggie. "Okay if we sit outside?"

Maggie smiled and nodded. "Sure. There's plenty of room for you. Most of the crowd has gone." She turned to Meaghan. "And who is this?"

Sheena placed a hand on Meaghan's shoulder. "This is my daughter, Meaghan."

"Oh, our new busboy. Or should I say busgirl."

Meaghan frowned.

"What was that about?" Meaghan whispered as they followed Maggie out to the patio.

"One of your jobs will be to help Clyde in the restaurant. We'll talk about it later."

Meaghan narrowed her eyes at Sheena, about to speak.

Darcy elbowed Meaghan. "Your mother said later. Don't make a scene here."

Maggie led them to a table outside and set menus in front of them. "I'll be right back to take your orders."

"Mom ..." Meaghan began.

Sheena held up a hand to stop her. "What are you going to have? We need to order because it's late and I don't want to keep the staff any longer than they need to be here."

Meaghan slumped in her seat but picked up a menu.

Soon, Maggie returned, took their orders, and hurried away.

Darcy noticed Meaghan darting glances at Clyde as he cleared a table nearby. "Clyde is one of the staff and a really nice guy. Proud of the work he does."

Meaghan's forehead creased with worry.

Before Darcy could reassure her, Gracie appeared at their table. "Ah, here's my new worker. Stand up and let me get a good look at ya."

Meaghan did as she was asked, surprising Darcy and everyone else with a smile.

"Yep, you'll do. Glad to have you on board. Your mother told me you were a good worker. I hope so because we're getting busier every day."

Gracie left them and a short while later, their food came. Darcy dug into her hamburger with gusto. She'd started running along the beach in the morning and by lunch time was ravenous.

"You're eating a hamburger?" said Meaghan, her voice incredulous. "Aren't you afraid of getting fat?"

"Nooo, are you?" Darcy answered, studying the green salad Meaghan had ordered with the dressing on the side.

"Of course. Lauren says ..." Meaghan stopped talking when Sheena cleared her throat and gave her a steady look.

"I mean, *I* say we won't have any boyfriends if we're fat."

Darcy shook her head. "Hey, kiddo, don't go overboard in either direction. Eat good food wisely. That's all. You need protein and natural sugars and some good fat, along with veggies like that."

"Thank you," said Sheena. "I've been trying to tell her that for some time. Everything in moderation."

Darcy took another bite of her burger and watched as Meaghan pushed bits of her salad around on her plate, hardly eating at all.

As they were leaving the restaurant, Rocky drove into the parking lot, stopped his truck, and pushed a large bird out of it onto the ground near the entrance.

"What are you doing?" Darcy asked, wary as usual with him.

"This guy needs a new home. He was being picked on by others in his party. I've named him Petey."

"A peacock? My word, what are we going to do with him?" said Sheena.

"We're going to let him roam around and make himself comfortable. He'll keep the place clear of some of the little critters that are a nuisance around here. That and insects."

In typical fashion, Rocky ignored their concerns, put the truck in reverse, and drove around the side of the building, leaving Petey to strut over to the shade of the trees lining the property as if he already ruled the place.

Darcy and Sheena looked at each other and sighed. A peacock named Petey wouldn't be a problem, would he?

CHAPTER THIRTY-FOUR
SHEENA

Sheena showed Meaghan some of the rooms in the Egret Building, where Regan was working.

When they entered one of the rooms, Regan looked up at them and smiled. "I'm counting on you to help me, Meaghan."

Meaghan made a face. "I already have a job."

"Only in the morning," said Regan. "You can be my helper in the afternoon."

At the firmness in Regan's voice, Sheena smiled. She'd told her sisters how important it was for them to support her not only by keeping Meaghan busy but by giving her a good idea how important it was for everyone in the family to work together.

"I'm going to give Meaghan a quick tour, including a walk on the beach, and then we'll be back to help you."

"I feel like I'm in prison," grumbled Meaghan as they left the room.

Sheena ignored her remark. As harsh as the punishment might seem to Meaghan, Sheena was determined to stick with it. She'd do anything to get her sweet daughter back.

After they changed into bathing suits, Sheena showed Meaghan the way to the beach. She watched carefully as Meaghan took in the expanse of white beach for the first time.

"Beautiful, huh?"

Meaghan's eyes shone. "Yeah."

"Let's take a walk. I want you to see some of the houses and small hotels in the area."

Meaghan frowned. "Why?"

"Because, my dear daughter, you may end up with a share of our hotel in the future. Part of having you help out is to see if this kind of business is something you'd be interested in. It's not a game, Meaghan. Once we decided to meet the challenge, we three women want to make this hotel work. Someday, it could be a great opportunity for you and Michael."

Meaghan looked down and kicked at the sand with a bare foot.

Sheena walked down to the water's edge and put a toe in the frothy mixture. Meaghan joined her.

"Look! I see some tiny fish!" Meaghan cried in a voice full of wonder.

Sheena smiled. "Look up there!"

A trio of pelicans, like planes in an air show, formed a triangle as they skimmed the surface of the water together.

Meaghan cupped a hand over her eyes and studied them. "Wow," she said softly.

With raucous cries, seagulls lifted up in the air above them, their wings spread wide.

Meaghan turned to her with a smile.

Sheena returned the smile and started walking, letting the magic of the place seep in and around them. She'd always found solace in the soothing sound of the waves breaking against the sand, the cries of the birds, the warmth of the sun.

Meaghan hurried to catch up to her. "Did you mean it, Mom? Someday Michael and I could own part of the hotel?"

"A lot of things have to take place for that to happen, but I believe it could. But, Meaghan, up until now, it's just been a ton of work. Nothing more."

Meaghan remained silent, but Sheena could almost see her daughter's mind whirling. She stopped and pointed down the beach. In the distance, a tall, pink structure rose like a stucco flamingo.

"That's one of the bigger hotels in the area. Someday, I'll take you to lunch there."

Meaghan's lips formed a familiar pout. "Do I really have to work in the kitchen? It's messy and I'll have to work with that guy who doesn't seem normal."

"That guy is Clyde and he's one of the sweetest men I know. He's a little slow, but he does a good job, and he does it willingly. I expect the same of you."

"It's not fair," grumbled Meaghan.

Sheena told herself to control her frustration. "Life isn't fair, Meaghan, and poor Marina knows it."

Meaghan looked away from her. "I told her I'm sorry. What more can I do?"

"Let's take it one day at a time and answers will come," Sheena said. "We'd better get back to the hotel to help Regan."

At the house, Sheena handed Meaghan a pair of shorts and a T-shirt. "Better put these on. They're your painting clothes. I've bought you a skirt and blouse to wear for work in the restaurant. Gracie's ordered some T-shirts with her logo on it, but they won't be here for a few days."

Meaghan studied the label. "Where did you get these?"

"Walmart," said Sheena. "We don't need expensive clothing here. Not when we're working to keep the hotel."

"If Lauren ..." At Sheena's scowl, Meaghan stopped. "Lauren is the most popular girl in my class and my best friend, Mom!"

"Has she called you or said she was sorry for getting you in trouble?"

Meaghan shook her head. "She's telling everyone it's all my

fault." Tears shone in her eyes.

"Some friend," said Sheena. "I'll meet you downstairs."

The look of hurt on Meaghan's face had touched Sheena's heart, but she had to be resolute in her determination to make Meaghan see that she had made some bad choices. This whole episode with Marina was a crucial turning point in Meaghan's young life.

When Meaghan joined her downstairs, Sheena put an arm around her. "Let's see what Regan is doing. If things go well, we can get the furniture painted in a week or two. And you can help set up one of the suites temporarily. That's where we'll be when Dad and Michael join us."

She, Regan and Darcy had decided to open up the eight suites as soon as possible so they could charge more for the rooms. Sheena and her family would test the facilities, listing any problems and possible solutions for them.

They found Regan in what they now called the paint room. "Good. Glad you're here. I want to show you a new technique I heard about at an art class I took. It's painting furniture with chalk paint, giving it a distressed look. It's easy to do. And it will sort of fit the decorating style I'm looking for."

Sheena studied the dresser Regan indicated. It was a lovely shade of blue, with a distressed surface and white accents. It looked old and valuable, unlike the tired piece it had once been.

"How did you do this?" Sheena asked, grinning happily.

"Like I said, it's easy and it doesn't take that much time."

Sheena turned to Meaghan. "What do you think?"

"Nice, but it looks hard to do."

Regan smiled. "That's the secret. It isn't that hard. You paint fast and in all directions. The paint dries in about twenty minutes, then you wax it to show the texture. After that, you can add the second color. I did a chest of drawers for my apartment a few months ago. It was fun!"

"Is it expensive?" Sheena asked.

Regan grinned. "Cheaper than buying new furniture. In each of the rooms, we can paint the headboards that are screwed to the walls in this shade of blue with white accents. And here, in the paint room, we can do the dressers and bedside tables. That would save us money and give us more to spend on nice lamps and accents, and even TVs."

Sheena clapped Regan on the back. "How'd we get lucky enough to have you head up the decorating?"

A flush of pleasure colored Regan's cheeks. "I've already found a source here in the Tampa Bay area for the paint and the round brushes that are recommended."

"Let's get Darcy over here for her approval. And, Regan, we need to figure out the cost for doing the twenty rooms on this floor. And then we'll figure the cost for the suites. Maybe we can get a good deal if we buy in bulk."

Regan called Darcy and then said, "Should we do the suites in different colors? We could do a nice soft gray."

Sheena nodded. "I like that idea. It would lend itself to fun colors for the bedspreads we need to get."

Regan gave Sheena a pleading look. "Can you help me draw up what we need. I can tell you what each dresser and table requires in paint and wax and all. And then I can give you a pretty good guess as to how much paint the headboards will take."

"Brian has given us a good price to help you paint the furniture, but he might not like the idea of having to work around those headboards." Sheena grinned as a thought came to her. "*You* will have to convince him, Regan. He'll do it for you."

Regan put her hands on her hips. "Why does everyone say things like that. You know I don't like him."

"But he likes you," said Sheena.

"Who's Brian?" asked Meaghan, just as Brian came through the doorway with Darcy.

The look of awe on Meaghan's face was adorable as she focused in on the man's handsome features and his trim, taut body.

"Meaghan, I'd like you to meet Brian," Sheena said. "Brian, this is my daughter, Meaghan. She's here to help out for a couple of weeks."

As his gaze turned to her, Brian's smile brought a pink flush of color to Meaghan's cheeks.

"Hi, there. Welcome," Brian said. "We can use all the help you can give. I understand you're going to be working in Gracie's. Good girl."

Meaghan's cheeks grew even redder.

He turned to Regan. "I figured I'd better take a look at what you're doing. Darcy said it involves painting furniture in a different way."

Darcy and Brian listened as Regan told them about the painting projects and then demonstrated how she'd used chalk paint on the dresser.

"I've never seen anything like it, but I love this," said Darcy, rubbing her hand over the piece Regan had completed. "Is it difficult to do?"

Regan once more went through the routine of how to work with the paint and the wax. With satisfaction, Sheena watched a look of pride cross Regan's face. She had every right to be proud of herself.

"I'm all for this," said Darcy. "It will give the rooms a unique look without pretending to be anything but artistic. Great job, Regan." She turned to Meaghan. "While they figure all this stuff out, want to see my office?"

"Sure," said Meaghan. "Is Brian coming too?"

Brian and Sheena exchanged glances and hid their amusement. He'd made another conquest.

Regan followed Sheena over to the house to go over the figures. Sheena set up an excel spreadsheet listing the number of pieces of furniture and then, together, she and Regan figured out how much paint in each color they'd need, along with the wax, paint brushes, and all.

Excitement filled Sheena. "If we can get this done for less than $3,000 like you think, Regan, it's an enormous benefit to us. You clever, clever, girl."

Regan grinned. "When we pick up nice mirrors, paintings, and lamps, along with any chairs at the sale, things will be even better. And don't forget, there are a number of hotel suppliers in Florida who'd be glad to do business with us."

"Okay, let's go ahead and order the paint and supplies, and then after tomorrow we'll tackle the rest of the furniture and fixtures. The soft goods will come last—sheets, towels, pillows and bedspreads. We may not be able to do much about the rest until we see how we stand financially. But for the first time, I think we may be able to go forward with this project and do it right. I'm not worried about not having any business during the summer months, but by fall we want to be up and running and pulling in money."

Later, when Darcy and Meaghan joined them for dinner, Sheena popped open a bottle of chilled white wine to share with her sisters and offered Meaghan a lemonade.

"Here's to Regan and the Salty Key Inn!"

Sheena smiled when Meaghan clicked her glass against the others.

CHAPTER THIRTY-FIVE
REGAN

After dinner, Regan couldn't resist going back to the Egret Building to do a little more work. She was anxious to see how one of the headboards would look painted. She had a picture in her mind and needed to see if it would really work.

When she entered the paint room, she was surprised to find a strip of blue tape masking the wall edging the headboard. She smiled. Brian must have instructed one of his men to do it. Having the walls protected this way would make things much easier for her and the rest of her team.

Regan brought an old, tarnished, standing lamp over to the area and went to work. She'd just finished putting on the first coat of paint when she heard a noise behind her. She whirled around.

"What are you doing here?" she asked.

Brian grinned. "I saw the light on in the room and figured you'd be here. I just wanted to let you know that I'll meet you and your sisters tomorrow morning at six o'clock sharp. With rush hour traffic in Tampa, it could take up to three hours to get to the hotel sale. We don't want to be late. I've talked to the guy running the sale and he warned me it's going to be very busy."

"Okay, thank you. And thanks for taping around the headboards. That will be a big help," Regan said, eager to return to work. She started to turn back to her painting and stopped.

Smiling, Brian moved toward her.

She froze. "What?"

"You have a streak of blue paint on your nose." In one careful movement, he swiped at it with a finger.

Their gazes met.

Regan's heart pounded as he drew her to him. And when his lips pressed down on hers, she couldn't help kissing him back. His lips were soft; they tasted good. Lost in a whirlwind of sensation, it took her a few moments to realize this was the man she's vowed not to fall for.

She jerked away from him. "No!"

"Hey! What's going on?" Brian gave her a puzzled look.

She put her hands on her hips and drew a deep, steadying breath. "What's going on? Nothing. Absolutely nothing with you. I can't do this. You're just a player."

He narrowed his eyes at her. "Is that what you think?"

Sure of herself now, she nodded. "Everyone falls in love with you, and you encourage it." She stepped back. "Now, either you go or I will."

Brian shook his head at her. "I can't believe ... aw, forget it." He turned and stalked out of the room, leaving her feeling ... empty.

The next morning, Regan stood in the parking lot with her sisters, waiting for Brian to show up. She heard a loud squawk and looked up to see Petey sitting on a branch of one of the trees. His peacock blue body looked out of place up there, but it's where he spent most nights.

Brian pulled his truck into the parking lot and got out to talk to them.

Regan did her best to ignore the angry looks Brian cast her way. No matter how he felt about their kiss, she knew she was better off to ignore the lusty feelings that she'd worked hard to shake off during a restless night. Time after time, she'd seen him in action as he effortlessly drew women to him. Even Meaghan was almost breathless each time she spoke to him.

"Anyone want to ride with me in my truck?" Brian asked, looking at her.

"I will," said Darcy, giving him a broad smile.

"Regan and I will follow you," said Sheena. "I just need to check in at Gracie's to make sure Meaghan is doing okay."

After running into the restaurant and returning, Sheena got behind the wheel of the van. Regan slid into the passenger seat.

Brian's truck headed out of the parking lot.

Sheena followed him.

Catching a glimpse of Darcy riding in Brian's truck, Regan thinned her lips. *Darcy was such a fool,* Regan thought, irritated that her sister didn't see what a player he was.

They'd driven for some time before Sheena spoke into the silence. "Anything you want to talk about?"

Regan shook her head. She was not going to discuss her feelings about Brian with Sheena or anyone else. "Not really. We've already gone over the list of things we're looking for. Anything with egrets and herons would be great for decorations. Other than that, it's pretty standard stuff."

Sheena shrugged. "Okay. Sounds good."

The hotel outside of Orlando was a large, sprawling building that reeked of class. They were checked in through the gates and directed to park along the edge of a road leading behind the building. Several other vehicles were parked there.

"Oh no!" said Regan. "It's already crowded. I hope we can get what we want. We'd better separate in the crowd so we can get a good look at the stuff that will be auctioned off."

The four of them walked to the back of the hotel, where two huge white tents had been erected. In one, smaller items were displayed—paintings, mirrors, lamps, even old ashtrays and bathroom items. In the other tent, pieces of furniture were displayed.

"I'll take this tent," said Regan, indicating the one holding the smaller items.

"I'll help you," said Sheena. "Brian and Darcy can check out the furniture."

Brian nodded and took Darcy's arm as they headed off.

Regan watched them walk away, her emotions in turmoil.

Sheena elbowed her. "Come on. We'd better hurry. We don't have much time before the auction begins."

Feeling as if she were on a treasure hunt, Regan entered the tent eager to find decorative items. She quickly passed by some items that were, in her mind, plain junk. But she came to a complete stop before a stack of pictures. Four different designs were on display. Her breath caught at the sight of a print of egrets wading in water. Two other designs were of flowers. The last one was of sandpipers sprinting across the sand.

Regan waved Sheena over. "Look! These are perfect."

"But there are no pictures of herons," said Sheena.

"No problem." Regan grinned. "We'll ask Austin to make us a sign for a sandpiper and move the heron sign to our house."

Sheena's eyes lit up. "All right. You've got it figured out. Let's see if we can outbid people on these, though I can't imagine anyone is going to be eager to buy them. Look at the frames. They're all marred in some way."

"A distressed look that will match the furniture," Regan said with satisfaction. "These prints are nice. I recognize the artist's name."

"Nice," said Sheena. "Now come look at the lamps I like."

A man walked through the tent ringing a bell. "Auction starts in ten minutes. Take your seats."

Regan and Sheena took a quick look at the lamps and then hurried toward the hotel.

The hotel ballroom was abuzz with activity when Regan and Sheena walked in. Darcy stood among the seats and waved to them.

Regan followed Sheena to where Darcy and Brian were sitting.

Sheena motioned for Regan to go ahead of her. Regan sighed and moved across the row of people to the seats Darcy had saved for them. Brian looked straight ahead as Regan lowered herself into the chair next to him.

"Any luck?" Sheena asked him.

"Darcy found a few tables for the suites, but nothing else. A lot of it looks really expensive and formal."

Darcy held up the paddle she'd been given. "Let me know when to use this."

Sheena grinned. "We found some good stuff."

The auctioneer opened the auction, and Regan was soon drawn into the fast action as paddles waved in the air and lowered in a game of numbers hard to follow. When the tables Darcy wanted for the suites were offered, Darcy raised her paddle and was quickly outbid for them. She raised the paddle again. When the price was raised yet again, she gave Sheena an uncertain look.

"Sold to the gentleman on the left," announced the auctioneer, and Darcy sat back in her chair with a sigh of disappointment.

After all the big pieces of furniture were sold, the auctioneer went through the smaller pieces. Enthusiasm dimmed. Some people even left the room.

The lamps Sheena wanted were offered along with a few standing lamps. Sheena took the paddle from Darcy and in a fierce bidding war of tiny increments, she finally won all one hundred of them.

Regan waited anxiously for the framed prints to come up for bids. When at last they were shown, most of the crowd had dispersed. Looking at them now, Regan could understand why. As Sheena had pointed out, the white frames were nicked or scratched in places.

The auctioneer opened with a low bid that Regan quickly met. A few other people responded, but Regan kept waving her paddle.

"Sold to the pretty lady with dark hair," the auctioneer finally announced.

Regan raised her fist triumphantly. The wood of those frames, highlighted with different colors would be perfect for the guest rooms. And because the artist was someone she'd once heard about, they were valuable in her mind.

Brian and Sheena made arrangements to pick up the lamps at a later time and waved Regan and Darcy forward.

"We'll go get the truck and the van to load up what we can. Sheena and I will come back for the rest," said Brian.

Darcy faced Sheena. "I can go in your place. I don't need to be in the office today."

Sheena shrugged. "Okay, I want to keep an eye on Meaghan on her first day of work."

Darcy gave Regan a triumphant look and said, "I'll drive the van."

She and Brian left to get their vehicles, leaving Sheena and Regan to stay with their items.

"I hope Darcy knows what she's doing," said Regan, shaking her head. "Brian is a player."

Sheena placed a hand on Regan's shoulder. "That's something she will have to work out. Not us."

Regan shook her head with dismay. She was just trying to protect her sister, wasn't she?

CHAPTER THIRTY-SIX
SHEENA

The next day, Sheena decided to eat lunch at Gracie's. Meaghan might accuse her of spying, but Sheena didn't care. She wanted to see that Meaghan got off to a good start.

Regan joined her, declaring that she needed a break from painting,

Even though it was late, there were a number of customers inside the restaurant when they walked in. Meaghan didn't see them. She was busy clearing dirty dishes from a table on the patio.

Sheena paused and noticed Meaghan's flushed cheeks. A pang of regret flashed through Sheena and then quickly disappeared. Hard work was good for her daughter. Sheena watched as Clyde went over to Meaghan and appeared to be asking her a question.

Meaghan answered him, but after he went on his way, she shook her head with obvious disgust. That's when she noticed Sheena staring at her. Her face fell.

Sheena did her best to hide her irritation at Meaghan's behavior and followed Regan to a table in the corner of the restaurant.

Lynn hurried over to their table. "Glad to see you two! What'll you have?"

"I guess I'd better take a look at the menu," said Regan, accepting one from Lynn.

"I know I want the Spring greens salad with crispy

chicken," said Sheena. She'd had it once before and couldn't wait to taste it again.

While Regan looked over the menu, Lynn smiled at Sheena. "Meaghan's been doing real well. Clyde's been helping her."

"Thanks for telling me. It's important to me that she does a good job."

"I'm ready," said Regan, interrupting them.

Regan placed her order, and Lynn hurried away.

Sheena was careful not to stare as her daughter went about her tasks. She looked very different from the girl who lived in Boston. That girl wore makeup and went around with wealthy friends as if the world owed her what she wanted. This girl had not taken the time to put on any makeup, wore cheap clothes, and was too busy to notice the strand of hair that had escaped her ponytail. In other words, she was adorable.

"Meaghan seems to be doing a good job," said Regan.

Sheena nodded. "She'll be off soon and then, after a break, she can help you paint. Tomorrow, she'll only work the lunch shift at Gracie's. But Gracie and I thought she should get acquainted with double shifts first."

Regan reached over and clasped Sheena's hand. "Meaghan made a mistake many girls do."

"Yes, I know. But, as her mother, I want it to be the only bullying she does. It's disgusting how mean teenage girls can be to each other. Were you ever bullied?"

"Not really bullied, just treated meanly by some of the girls." Regan shook her head. "It's awful when that happens. And then with the learning issues I had, even the teachers made it plain that there was something wrong with me."

"I'm sorry, Regan. To my knowledge, Meaghan has escaped all those things. That's why I want her to understand how deep those wounds can be to others."

Regan sighed. "I know Darcy and I tease you sometimes about being the big sister, but I'm glad you're mine."

Tears stung Sheena's eyes. It wasn't easy being a disciplinarian, but what choice did she have? That was her role as a parent. And like many mothers, the task fell to her, not to Tony.

Sheena had just taken the last bite of her salad when Meaghan came over to their table and sat down.

"Gracie said I could go." She let out a long sigh. "I'm exhausted. It's hard work."

"Yes, I know," said Sheena. "Lynn complimented your work, and that makes me proud."

"Yeah? I'm a lot faster than Clyde. He's a real retard."

Sheena opened her mouth to say something, but Regan beat her to it.

"What an awful thing to say, Meaghan. Jeez. You know he has problems. Why would you make fun of him?"

There was an edge to Regan's voice that Sheena realized came from past experience.

A look of shock slackened Meaghan's face. "Why are you picking on me?" she asked Regan in a high whine.

"I'm not..." Regan began, but Meaghan had already jumped up from the table and was racing away.

Regan grimaced. "I'm sorry," she said to Sheena.

"I'm not. I'm very happy you said that. Meaghan needs to hear it from others, not just me."

They left the restaurant. While Regan headed back to the Egret Building to continue painting, Sheena headed to the house to work on a revised budget. She'd almost reached the house when her cell phone rang. *Tony*. She clicked on the call.

"Hi, Sweetheart! How are you? What's up?"

"I might ask the same of you," said Tony in a strained voice that alarmed Sheena. "What's going on? Meaghan called in tears to tell me she'd worked for six hours straight and that you and Regan are being mean to her and now you want her to help Regan paint some furniture. What in the hell is that all about? We didn't agree that you'd work her to death."

Sheena headed away from the house to keep Meaghan from hearing her. As she walked down to the bay, she formed her thoughts. She didn't want to start a fight with Tony, but she was mad as hell that Meaghan went crying to him.

"Meaghan worked a double shift at Gracie's to learn the routine. Tomorrow she'll only work the lunch hours so she can sleep in the morning. And, yes, Meaghan, like the rest of us, is going to be busy painting furniture whenever she has free time. Regan spoke to her before I could when she called Clyde a retard. I won't permit that kind of language from our daughter. Got it?"

"Whew! You don't have to be angry with me. I don't talk that way."

"Neither do I. That's why we're all going to have to land on Meaghan when she does."

"Okay, okay. I understand. You've got everything under control. How's everything else going?"

Sheena's anger melted away. "Things are shaping up. We did well at the hotel auction yesterday—won some lamps and artwork. The computer programs are almost done, and we're looking into wiring the family suite building for internet service."

"Glad to hear it. Look, I've got to go. I've got a couple of important meetings."

"Anything I should know about?"

"No," said Tony with an emphasis on the word that made Sheena curious.

They hung up and Sheena went back to the house to deal with her daughter.

CHAPTER THIRTY-SEVEN
REGAN

Regan checked on the men taking the last of the carpets out of the guest rooms and then went to the paint room. As she set to work stirring the paint and then brushing it onto the bedside table, she wondered if she'd been too outspoken with Meaghan. But Meaghan's mean, dismissive remark had brought back unpleasant memories.

Working here at the hotel had made Regan believe she had a lot to contribute. Sheena, especially, seemed grateful for her guidance with the decorating of the guest rooms.

Regan had almost finished with the table when Sheena showed up with Meaghan.

"Okay, we're here to help," said Sheena. She looked around. "When is the rest of the paint going to be delivered?"

"Tomorrow morning. First thing. I just checked," said Regan. "In the meantime, we can work on the headboard here and go on to the next room." She drew a deep breath and turned to her niece. "I'm sorry I snapped at you, Meaghan, but it's important to me that you treat others with respect. I love you and I always will."

Meaghan's cheeks flushed. She glared at Regan. "I get it. Mom and I have already talked about it. I don't need another lecture."

Regan exchanged apologetic glances with Sheena. "Okay. From now on, it's a closed subject." She went to Meaghan to give her a quick hug, but Meaghan turned away.

As Sheena and Meaghan were painting the headboard, Regan brought up the subject of the pictures they'd bought at the auction.

"Is it okay with you if I call Austin Blakely and request a carved sign of a sandpiper?" she asked Sheena.

"Yes, it's a good idea and it shouldn't be that expensive. Besides, I think you should thank him for rescuing you."

"Rescue? What happened?" asked Meaghan.

Sheena told her about the drugging. "Have you ever heard of that happening to someone at your school?"

Meaghan shook her head. "No, but I know about roofies. A girl in the high school claims she was given some at one of the big parties."

"Pretty scary stuff. Another reason parties should be supervised."

Meaghan rolled her eyes.

They were cleaning up the paint supplies for the day when Darcy stormed into the room. "Thanks, Regan! You just ruined my last chance with Brian!"

Regan set down her paint brush. "What do you mean? I have no interest in Brian. I told him so."

"Yeah, I know you don't, but I do. When I tried to apologize to him, he said he didn't want anything more to do with the Sullivan sisters."

Sheena gave Darcy a steady look. "He might have had a very good reason to turn you down. Remember?"

A sigh full of disappointment came from Darcy's lips. "The only guy who's shown any interest in me is Austin Blakely, and I have no interest in him."

"Why?" said Regan. "I'm supposed to call him to talk about another wood carving."

"Oh, he's nice enough, but he's not as handsome as Brian."

Sheena turned to Meaghan. "I hope you never tell me

something like this."

"Dammit, Sheena," said Darcy. "Don't turn this into a big-sister or good-mother moment. Brian hurt my feelings."

"Think how he must feel. You're throwing yourself at him, and Regan is rejecting him. It isn't easy for guys. I know that from listening to Michael."

"Yeah? Michael is a total jerk when it comes to girls," Meaghan commented.

Sheena shot Meagan a silent warning and went over to Darcy. "Come on, everybody! Group hug."

Darcy laughed when Regan and the others surrounded her. "All right. All right. I feel better now."

"Go ahead to the house. I'll finish the cleanup," said Regan. Her mind was whirling. Maybe she'd been too harsh on Brian. Though she still didn't want to date him, she could've said it in a nicer way.

When she arrived at the house, music was blaring and Darcy and Meaghan were dancing in the living room. They waved at her as she passed them to go into the kitchen.

Sheena looked up from the spaghetti sauce she was stirring. "Everything done?"

Regan nodded. "I was wondering where you put the business card for Austin Blakely. I'll go ahead and call him."

Sheena set down her spoon, went over to her paperwork, and handed Regan the card. "Get the best price you can."

Regan gave Sheena a mock salute and went upstairs to her room. She needed privacy to thank the person who'd saved her from a terrible situation.

She shut the door to her room and lowered herself to the bed. Punching in his number, she wondered exactly what to say. *Thanks for saving my virginity? Nooo. He'd think she was lying.*

"Hello?" The voice that answered was almost melodious

with its tenor tone.

"Is this Austin Blakely?"

"Yes, and this is?"

"Regan Sullivan. First of all, I want to thank you very much for your help the other night. I understand you were the one who rescued me."

"No problem, but I must admit you had me worried. I couldn't be sure what it was, but I'm pretty certain you were drugged. Do you know who did it? Was it that guy with you?"

"I don't know. He says it wasn't. He says it may have happened when I carried my drink through the crowd. I guess we'll never know. I'm just glad you were there to help me."

"Me too."

"The other reason I called was to ask you if you could make one more carved wooden sign for us. A sandpiper this time. I've found some prints of them and want to use it as a theme for one of the guest buildings here at the hotel."

"Sounds good. I'm going to visit my grandparents again this weekend. My grandmother is ill, and I need to check on them for my parents. I could meet up with you, take a look at the prints, and try to match the design."

"Really? That would be wonderful," gushed Regan.

"I might even be able to get the heron design done by the time we meet," said Austin.

"Great. Why don't you plan on having lunch at the hotel and then you can see what we're doing?"

"I'd like that very much. The whole idea of renovating a place like that is intriguing to me."

"Good. Give me a call on Saturday and we'll meet." Regan hung up the phone and raced downstairs to tell the others.

The next few days seemed to alternately race by and drag.

Painting furniture and headboards was a tedious process, even with a team of people doing it. Sheena, Darcy, and Meaghan spent as many hours as they could helping her. Gavin's people also pitched in. Regan's supervising ability was put to the test as she guided them in the process. By leaving the finishing touches to Sheena and her, they were able to get a lot of the work done in an orderly fashion. It was amusing, then annoying, when some questioned the technique of making something look old instead of shiny and new.

By Saturday, Regan was ready for some time off. The prospect of talking to someone like Austin about her decorating ideas was appealing. He was an artist who'd understand what she was trying to do little by little.

For the first time in days, she shampooed her hair and blew it dry, letting the long, dark, locks of hair settle around her shoulders instead of being pulled up into a ponytail. She put on her denim skirt and a blouse and dabbed on just a touch of makeup.

When Austin called to tell her he was on his way, Regan decided to meet him outside the restaurant. It seemed more impersonal that way.

As she crossed the hotel grounds, she stopped to look at the pool. The mechanical and fencing repairs and pool-surface painting had been done, and now Brian's men were filling it with water. The heater, thank God, had been replaced earlier by Gavin.

Regan stood a moment and looked around the property. To save money, Brian had suggested power washing the guest room buildings. They looked fresh and clean. The landscaping had been trimmed and weeded, but they couldn't afford to do much planting. Later, when they were renting rooms and bringing in some money, Brian's group would plant more bushes. Still, it looked a lot better.

She moved on, wishing they could afford to do everything they wanted to make things right. But like Sheena kept reminding them, they had to stick to their priorities. And in today's world, it was more important to have internet access than pretty flowers. And if the rooms renovation had to be in three phases, that's what they'd do. And when they met their challenge, then they'd have money to do the special things they all wanted to do.

As she approached the restaurant, she spied a man pacing in front of it. She studied him. His broad shoulders and sturdy body gave her an impression of strength—and safety.

"Austin?"

He looked over at her and grinned. "Hi, Regan. We meet again."

She walked up to him and held out her hand. "I'm glad to finally meet you." His hand felt warm and competent around hers. She remembered he was studying to be a dentist and smiled.

He removed his sunglasses. As he gazed at her, his bright blue eyes sparkled with intelligence and kindness. His hair, she noted, was a rich, chocolate brown. He was good-looking—with regular features—but not a surfer type like Brian. Between his build, his size, his friendliness, Regan thought of him as a teddy bear.

"Come have a taste of Gracie's cooking. It's fabulous," said Regan, leading him toward the door.

They went inside and found an empty table on the patio, under the shade of an umbrella.

Austin helped her into her seat and then sat opposite her. "Old Florida décor. I noticed the beadboard inside. Love stuff like that."

"Have you always worked with wood? Did you take art courses? How did you end up in dental school?"

Austin laughed. "Okay, one thing at a time. Yes, I've taken art courses and really wanted to be an artist. But my parents convinced me that I had to be practical, to think of raising a family and being able to take care of them. With dentistry, you have to be skilled at working with your hands. I can have the best of both worlds by becoming a dentist and using time off to work on my art projects."

Regan smiled. "That sounds wonderful, well thought out. I'm very interested in decorating. I love working with colors and textures."

Maggie came over to them with glasses of water and menus. "Hi, Regan. Glad to see you."

Regan introduced Austin. "He's the talented guy who is making signs for the buildings."

"Nice. Anything else to drink while you look at the menu?"

Austin shook his head. "Water's fine with me."

"And me," said Regan. She noticed Austin watching Maggie walking away from them and said, "Maggie is one of the people we inherited with the hotel. She and the seven others are interesting people who knew my uncle."

"Nice," said Austin.

After they placed their orders, Regan asked Austin about his grandparents.

A trace of sadness filled his face. "It's hard to see them grow old. They've been a very important part of my life because my parents are gone a lot. Through their travel business, they give tours to Europe and Asia. On many occasions, that left me at home with my grandparents."

"Did you ever get to go on trips with them? That would be cool. I've never really traveled at all."

"As someone who likes art, you'd love to see some of the things I have. Someday I hope you get to go to Florence, Paris, London, and many other places. Traveling to cities like that made up for all the time I was left alone. Even now, my parents are in China with a group."

"No brothers or sisters?" Regan asked.

Austin shook his head. "I guess I was tough enough to bring into the world that they didn't even try again."

Regan laughed with him, but she wondered what it would be like to be an only child. There had been a few moments when she'd wished she were. Especially when Darcy was mean to her.

Meaghan proudly carried their food over to them. Regan introduced her to Austin and then dug into her salad. Austin ate his fried grouper sandwich with such gusto it brought a smile of amusement to her. He was the most natural, most easy-going guy she'd ever met.

They continued chatting as they left the restaurant. She found out Austin's grandmother was dying of cancer.

"She fought it for a while but now she's losing the battle," explained Austin. "My grandfather is beside himself with worry. He hates the idea of being left alone. I told him I'd set up practice somewhere in the area, but that won't happen until a year from June."

"I'm sure he's very grateful that you are taking such an interest in them." She couldn't imagine any grandchildren of her own father being that close to him. Maybe because he was such a hard man to please. He'd made Regan cry plenty of times by not understanding what her learning problems were.

When they reached the Egret Building, Regan showed Austin where they would place his wooden plaque. "The sandpiper plaque will go on the suites building across the way, and the heron sign will go on our house, which is back behind those trees."

"Very nice. I'll do my best," said Austin with sweet sincerity.

"And now we'll take a look at the furniture. I'm using a whole new technique to paint it. And then I want to show you the print of the sandpiper. You can take one with you if you want."

"Great."

Regan led him to the paint room and demonstrated how she used chalk paint. Then she led him to a guest room up on the second floor where the prints, lamps, and other decorative items were being stored.

She showed him the prints of the sandpipers. "Looks a little like an Audubon print, doesn't it? Quite formal and detailed. It seemed a little old-fashioned to me which is why I love it with the distressed look of the furniture."

"Yes, I like it too. And it matches the egret print. You got this at a hotel auction?"

Regan beamed at him. "For such a deal."

He laughed. "Good job, Regan."

His words, his smile washed over her in welcoming waves.

CHAPTER THIRTY-EIGHT
SHEENA

Sheena moved briskly down the beach, needing to stretch her sore muscles. Days and days of painting furniture had made the muscles she hadn't used in some time twinge with pain. Michael and Tony were due to arrive the next day, and she wanted to be able to greet them without moaning.

As she walked along, she thought back to the time she and Tony had painted a bedroom in anticipation of Michael's birth. It hardly seemed as if that was almost seventeen years ago. They'd been such babies— she and Tony—full of hope, optimism, and fun. She hoped her time in Florida with him would help to bring back some of those feelings.

The sun felt good on her body. Warmer weather meant her early morning walks were more comfortable. Dressed only in her bathing suit—the one her sisters thought was boring—she lifted her arms and sprinted along the water's edge, momentarily feeling carefree. She slowed and thought of the last couple of months. Three women living with one bathroom was enough to challenge anyone's patience. Although they all tried to be civil about it, quarrels were inevitable. And the tension between Darcy and Regan continued to flare over Brian Harwood's lack of interest. Sheena thought Darcy's stance was foolish but vowed to stay out of their fight. Darcy was one of those people who had to learn things the hard way, and, like a bulldog holding tight to something in its jaws, she would not give up on an idea.

As Sheena turned to head back to the hotel, she saw a small figure in the distance heading her way. She realized it was Meaghan and hurried toward her.

Meaghan came running up to her. "Hi! This is the day we go shopping, right?"

"This is the day we get you another skirt and top to wear in Gracie's. Not exactly what you call shopping."

"While we're out, can't we look at some of the really cool stores?"

"I don't think that's a good idea," said Sheena. "It would only be frustrating because I'm not buying you anything else. We're on a real economy kick down here."

"Mom! I can't go back to school without any new clothes," Meaghan whined.

"At the end of your stay, you can choose one pair of pants and one top. With all that you have at home, that'll be all you need until you come back down here."

Meaghan placed her hands on her hips and gave her a challenging look. "What if I don't want to come back?"

Sheena waved a hand to stop her. "I'm not going there, so don't waste your breath."

Meaghan glared at her. Sheena started walking. Every time Meaghan did something really wonderful—like doing double time at the restaurant because Clyde didn't feel well—she quickly ruined it by reverting back to her whiny self. *Patience!* Sheena told herself.

Meaghan caught up to her. "Maybe we could look for those pants and blouse today?"

"No, I promised Regan and Darcy I'd help them set up a temporary room in the suites building. They insisted on moving out of the house so we can be together as a family. Isn't that nice?"

Meaghan shrugged. "I guess."

Sheena was excited about being a family again. As much as she liked her independence, she was a mom and always would be. And that meant, like a mother hen, she wanted her chicks nearby.

By the time Sheena and Meaghan returned to the house, Regan was up and in the kitchen, sipping coffee.

"Coffee. I need coffee," Darcy said, stumbling into the room. "I stayed up too late reading."

"Good book?" Sheena said.

"The best. I laughed. I cried." Darcy sighed. "I'd love to be able to write one as good someday."

"That day will come," said Sheena. "As soon as we're up and running and on a better schedule, you'll have some time to yourself. I would think this peaceful location by the water would be great for writing."

"From your lips to God's ears," said Darcy, quoting a famous saying.

By the end of the afternoon, Sheena didn't know who was more exhausted. Darcy, Regan, or her. They'd spent the day cleaning one of the suites, changing out furniture, and stocking the kitchenette. New mattresses were delivered for the beds. Towels, sheets, pillows and bedspreads bought from a hotel supplier were on the beds and in the bathrooms. Everything had been purchased with the idea of testing them out for the hotel.

"Wow! I have my own bathroom," said Regan. "I don't want to ever go back to the house."

"Me either. I've got room to spread out," said Darcy.

"Eventually you'll have to move out when we renovate the rooms here," Sheena reminded them. They'd done their best to make the suite livable, but it wasn't up to her standards of clean and fresh.

"Can I come and stay here?" Meaghan said.

Sheena shook her head. "We're going to stay together as a family for the week we're all here."

Meaghan's lips formed a pout.

"You can take showers here," said Darcy. "Right?"

Sheena nodded. "That's fine with me."

Actually, she wouldn't mind a real shower herself.

The next morning, as Sheena and Meaghan drove into Tampa to the airport to pick up Tony and Michael, Sheena's spirits rose. She was excited to see them. And even in the short time since Tony had visited, lots of work had been done on the hotel. She hoped he'd be pleased.

Sheena pulled into the short-term parking garage and, after circling, finally found a space.

"Hurry," said Meaghan, "their plane should be here soon."

Sheena smiled at her enthusiasm. Though Meaghan probably wouldn't admit it, she was anxious to see her brother. While they might quarrel and tease, they really did love one another. They hurried into the building and down to the baggage claim area. The arrival and departure display indicated Tony and Michael's plane had landed a few minutes ago. Meaghan ran over to the escalator to watch people descending and then hurried back to Sheena.

"When are they going to get here?" Meaghan's eyes shone with excitement, reminding Sheena of the times Meaghan couldn't wait for friends to arrive for a birthday party.

"They should be here any moment," Sheena said and looked up to find Tony and Michael...and Rosa and Paul walking toward them.

Sheena hurried over to them. "Oh, my! Rosa and Paul,

what a surprise!" She hugged them both and then turned to Michael. "Have you grown since I've seen you? You seem much taller."

"Aw, Mom. It hasn't been that long," he mumbled, but he hugged her back with surprising strength.

Sheena moved to Tony and wrapped her arms around him. "I'm awfully glad you're here. What a surprise to see all of you."

He beamed at her. "Yep, Mom and Dad wanted to see what we were talking about. I told them I'd put them up in a nearby hotel, that yours wasn't ready for guests."

Sheena turned to her in-laws. "You can share one of our family suites with Regan and Darcy. Unless you'd rather be on your own."

Rosa gave Paul a shy smile. "Actually, we'd like to have some time to ourselves." Her cheeks grew pink. "Sort of a special honeymoon many years too late."

The kids groaned at the wink Rosa gave them. Sheena and Tony exchanged grins. *Wonders never cease*, Sheena thought. *Imagine a honeymoon at their age.*

They all loaded their luggage in the back of the van, and then Sheena headed down the highway to the hotel. She decided not to call her sisters ahead of time. She wanted Rosa and Paul to see how hard they were all working.

"The hotel is very much a work in progress," Sheena explained. She drove along the shoreline to allow everyone to get a good look at the surrounding area.

"Gracie's is a great restaurant, though," Meaghan said. "I should know. I work there."

Through the rearview mirror, Sheena glanced at her mother-in-law, giving her a silent prompt.

"That's wonderful, honey. I'm proud of you," Rosa said with feeling.

"I can't wait to stretch out on the beach," said Michael. "I've been telling the guys all about it."

Sheena drew a breath, and said firmly, "Your beach time will be limited by how much work you get done each day."

"Whaaat! No way!" Michael's incredulous look would be amusing if it wasn't so pitiful. He was as spoiled as Meaghan.

"Our entire family is working together to make this a success for the benefit of everyone," Sheena said. "You included, Michael. You'll be working with Brian on a number of projects or working under Regan's direction. For one thing, we need help hauling stuff around. But there are plenty of other projects for you."

"Not fair," grumped Michael.

Sheena ignored him.

"You're only too happy to drive the car, play sports and everything," said Tony. "Now, Michael, it's your turn to pitch in and help."

Sheena gave Tony a quick smile of thanks for his support.

"Do you like living here?" Paul asked her from the back seat of the van.

"Yes," said Sheena. "We're not into the hot summer yet, but I love being able to get up in the morning and take a walk along the beach. It's very soothing."

"It looks like a lovely beach," said Rosa. She sighed. "I'm tired of northern winters. I guess it's my age showing, but I swear it gets colder and colder."

"Now, honey, you're looking great," said Paul.

Sheena and Tony exchanged amused glances. Maybe this trip would be the honeymoon his parents wanted.

Before she got to the hotel, Sheena slowed the car. "Just a warning. The Salty Key Inn is old Florida style. Not fancy. But it's really growing on us."

As Sheena turned into the parking lot for Gracie's, she

recalled how shocked she and her sisters had been when they first saw the place. Now, with a fresh coat of paint, new plantings around the building, and a better understanding of the style, she thought it looked great.

"Not fancy? Got that right," said Michael. "Jeez, Mom."

Sheena turned to the right, taking them past the suites building, right up to the house.

"This is where we'll be staying," Sheena said to Tony. "All four of us. A real family."

Tony grinned. "Sounds good."

"A pink house? You've got to be kidding," said Michael.

"Very different," commented Rosa diplomatically.

After they sorted through the luggage and the others went into the house, Sheena smiled at her mother-in-law. "Where is Tony putting you up?"

"A nice hotel not far from here. It's called the Don CeSar."

Sheena blinked in surprise.

Rosa placed a hand on Sheena's arm and beamed at her. "He's not paying for it. We are. It's been years since Paul and I have been away, and I told Paul that's where I wanted to stay. Wait until you see the new clothes I bought."

Sheena gave her mother-in-law a quick hug. "Oh, Rosa. I'm pleased for you. I think you'll love it."

"Before we go there, I want to take a look around your hotel. It's been good for all of us to have this change. Tony might not like having you away, but he's become a much better father. And, frankly, it's been eye-opening to the kids. How's Meaghan doing?"

"I think having her here with my sisters has been good for her. It isn't just Mom talking to her. Though Regan and Darcy love her, they don't mind speaking to her about things they don't like."

"That's good. Your mother would approve of their helping

you, don't you think?"

Sheena smiled. "I'm sure she would." She took Rosa's arm. "Living in this house together has been a whole other experience—three women, one outdated bathroom, and a fifties kitchen. But with their moving into one of the suites, my sisters will now have their own bathrooms. Meaghan's already opted to shower there."

"Outdated bathroom? But's that's ironic with Tony being in the plumbing business. Can't he fix it up for you?"

Sheena nodded. "Probably. But I have to wait to see if we meet the challenge before bringing it up."

Before lunchtime, Sheena led Rosa and Paul down to the bay to show them what would someday be a useable dock and water sports area. Tony and the kids tagged along.

As they crossed the lawn to the Egret Building, they passed the pool whose clear water sparkled in the sunshine.

"Can we swim in the pool?" Michael asked.

"Sure," said Sheena. "Why don't you wait until after the tour and lunch, and then you can have the afternoon off. Tomorrow you'll begin to work."

Michael grimaced.

Suddenly a blur of blue attacked them, squawking loudly.

"What in God's name is that?" asked Paul, looking askance at the big bird.

"That is Petey, the peacock that Rocky saved," said Sheena. "He's a nuisance most of the time. But he's all fluttering feathers, no real danger to anyone."

"He's kinda cute, once you get used to him," said Meaghan. "He likes me."

They moved on. A dumpster stood by the entrance to the Egret Building, half-filled with remnants of carpet. "We're pulling apart the guest rooms in this building," Sheena explained. "We hope to have the twenty rooms on the first floor done and ready to rent out by the time the kids come for the summer."

"In the meantime, we're painting furniture," said Meaghan proudly. "I help Regan. We're in charge."

"You're not going to be in charge of me," said Michael, giving her a warning look.

"Nooo," said Sheena. "Regan is."

"What about Darcy? What is she doing?" said Rosa, changing the subject.

"She's been working with the guy setting up a wireless system in the front building. This afternoon, they're going to install a new cash register that will be able to track inventory. It's a big deal because Gracie's is very successful. After you taste the food, you'll understand why."

"Let's hurry up with the tour. I want to eat and then go sit by the pool," said Michael.

"In time, son. In time," Tony cautioned.

Regan was working on a headboard in one of the guest rooms when they found her. She smiled and approached. "I'd give you guys a hug, but as you can see, I'm a mess."

"I like what you're doing with the furniture. It looks wonderful," gushed Rosa. "From what I've seen, it's going to be very nice. Seems like all you girls have worked really hard to get this far this quickly."

Regan and Sheena exchanged knowing smiles. "We have," they said together and laughed. It had been a trying couple of months, living in the house and then working together on the project.

Sheena checked her watch. "After lunch, I'll show you the other rooms. Now, let's go see what Gracie's is all about."

They entered the restaurant to find it humming with

activity. Darcy and Chip were working at the cash register, Lynn, Sally, and Maggie were bustling about. All the tables but one were filled.

Maggie noticed them and hurried over to Sheena. "The table we set aside for you is almost ready. We're waiting for the couple next to it to pay so we can move the tables together."

"Okay, no problem." Sheena was delighted to be able to demonstrate to Tony's parents how successful Gracie's was.

They stepped outside to wait.

"You're even busier than when I was here," said Tony, giving her an encouraging smile.

Sheena's lips curved in response. "Gracie has become known for her good cooking."

From a distance, Brian called to them and waved.

"I'll be right back," said Tony. "I want to ask him about the job I did."

Sheena watched her husband jog to where Brian stood. He seemed different somehow, but she couldn't decide what it was.

Rosa noticed her staring at him. "Has it been hard on you to be apart from your family?"

Sheena hesitated. She had to be honest. "It's been an eye-opening experience for all of us. But the good outweighs the difficulties."

"Are you finding you?"

Sheena's lips twitched with humor. "Let's say I'm emerging."

Rosa chuckled. "Well, then, this has been good."

Grateful she understood, Sheena gave her a quick hug.

"All right," said Michael. "The waitress is waving us inside." He held the door open as a couple emerged, and then Sheena and the others entered.

As soon as they were seated, Gracie came out of the kitchen to greet them. "Welcome. Y'all enjoy."

Sheena introduced everyone to her and after exchanging hellos, Gracie went back to her work.

Lynn hurried over to them with menus. "Good to see you, Sheena. This your family?"

Sheena nodded and made introductions again.

Then, scanning the menus, their conversation revolved around food choices.

Tony entered the restaurant and sat next to Sheena.

Speaking quietly, he said, "Brian wants me to work on another project, and we decided to put Michael to work helping to clear the area down by the dock."

"Sounds good," said Sheena. She was surprised by Tony's willingness to work with Brian. But then she supposed anything was better than hanging around waiting for everyone else to finish work.

After lunch, during which Paul declared it was the best fish sandwich he'd ever had, the group prepared to head over to the suites building.

Clyde waved to them from the patio where he was bussing tables. "Hi! Hi! Hi! It's me! Clyde!"

"Hi, Clyde! It's good to see you busy," said Sheena.

"Yep. I'm busy," Clyde said proudly.

Rosa gave her a questioning look.

"He's one of Gavin's people. A sweet guy and a hard worker."

Rosa nodded. "Interesting group."

"Yes," agreed Sheena. "I still don't know much about them, but I'm hoping as time passes, they'll open up more. They've all been rescued by Gavin."

CHAPTER THIRTY-NINE
SHEENA

As they crossed the lawn, Petey paraded in front of them like a drum major.

"Funny bird," remarked Paul, keeping a good distance away.

Outside the suites building, Sheena halted the group. Knowing Tony's parents would be staying at "the Don," Sheena was a little embarrassed to show them the one suite they had temporarily cleaned up. It was far from ready for guests.

"When you see Regan and Darcy's suite, you can get an idea of what we're trying to do. After their stay, the carpet will be pulled up and new furniture, fixtures and all will be put in."

She led them inside and gave the rooms a critical look. The bones of the building and the design of the rooms were good. The entire building, though, needed a lot of TLC.

"I like the layout of the space." Rosa's face lit with excitement. "Will you be doing long-term rentals?"

"I would hope to," Sheena said. "Apparently, a lot of places in the area have guests who come down for several months at a time."

Rosa winked at Sheena. "We just might be one of your first customers. We'll have to wait and see if Paul likes it here."

Paul looked at Rosa and put his arm around her.

Sheena hid a smile. She'd never seen them this affectionate.

"It's not time to check into the hotel," said Tony to his father. "What would you like to do?"

Paul stretched and yawned. "Actually, I'd like to take a nap. Hardly slept last night."

"Okay, not a problem," said Tony. He turned to Sheena and Rosa. "If you ladies don't mind, I want to meet up with Brian."

Michael said, "I'm heading to the pool."

"Me too," said Meaghan. "C'mon, Michael!"

Tony left to find Brian, and the kids took off for the house.

Sheena, Rosa, and Paul followed behind the kids at a slower pace. Out of the corner of her eye, Sheena studied her in-laws. In their sixties, they moved easily. Paul had had a scare with high blood pressure a couple of years ago, but medicine and a healthy diet seemed to have taken care of that problem. Rosa was obviously a cook who enjoyed good food but she, too, was in good health. Sheena wondered why her own, sweet mother had suffered for much of her life and realized her death had been a factor in making the choice to come to Florida. Life was too short not to take a few chances.

Before Sheena and her in-laws reached the house, Michael and Meaghan emerged in their swimsuits, carrying towels.

"Have fun," Sheena called to them as they raced across the clearing to the pool.

At the house, Sheena made sure that Michael's things were settled in Darcy's old room, and brought a blanket and pillow downstairs for Paul, who was stretching out on the couch.

She looked at her mother-in-law. "Want a cup of coffee or iced tea or something?"

Rosa smiled. "Plain ice water would be nice."

"Sounds good. I'll get one for me, too."

Rosa followed Sheena into the kitchen and stopped. "Oh, my! I haven't seen a kitchen like this in years. Why did Gavin leave it this way?"

Sheena shrugged. "I wonder if this was one of his crazy tests—putting three women in a small house with one bathroom and an outdated kitchen. It would be enough to drive most women crazy."

Rosa laughed. "From what you've told me about him, it sounds possible."

Sheena gazed at her mother-in-law. "In a note he left me, Gavin said I was a lot more like him than I thought. Do you think that's true, Rosa?"

Rosa shook her head. "Not in personality. But, you're smart and determined, like he must have been. And, Sheena, Tony's business would never have functioned as well if you hadn't handled a lot of the business end."

"How is the business? Tony hasn't talked to me about it, and I haven't pushed him."

Rosa accepted a glass of water from her. "Let's go outside where we can talk in private."

Sheena led Rosa to the porch.

Grateful for the shade from the sun and for the light, Sheena took a seat in a chair next to Rosa. A playful breeze kept the air stirring around them.

Sheena took a long sip of cold water and turned to Rosa. "I've missed our chats. Talking on the phone isn't the same."

Rosa reached over and squeezed her hand. "I've missed you too. But I think you're doing the right thing by trying to make this work."

"Thanks. How are things at home—really?"

Sadness filled Rosa's eyes. "Anna and Dave have had some disappointments. Dave was let go from his job. Sales everywhere are down. Even in the eyewear business."

Tony's sister was eight years younger and lacked Tony's outgoing personality, but Sheena had always liked her. Dave more than made up for Anna's quietness and was a good match for her.

"What's Dave doing now? With a baby on the way, he needs a job."

Rosa's eyebrows lifted. "Tony hasn't told you?"

"Told me what?" Sheena shifted in her chair uneasily. Lately, Tony had stopped railing at her about her responsibilities to the family, but he'd kept conversations short, especially when she'd asked him about the business. It had bothered her, but with all the other issues between them, Sheena hadn't confronted him with it.

"Dave is now working for the plumbing business. He's putting together sales material to increase chances of getting some new bids. He's also starting his apprenticeship with Tony and John Larson."

Sheena hid her surprise. "I'm glad John decided to stay with Tony. At one time, he was thinking of leaving."

Rosa nodded thoughtfully. "He seems like a good man— ambitious, but a good co-worker for Tony."

"And how is Anna doing with all this?"

"She's doing well, though I know it's a worry for her. The baby is due in two months, and they're still getting settled into their new house." Rosa sighed. "Nothing ever seems to go smoothly for them. First, the difficulty of getting pregnant, and now this uncertainty."

"I'm sure things will be fine. Dave's a pretty resourceful guy."

"It's good to get away." Rosa's eyes sparkled. "I think Paul is going to have a few surprises while we're here. I got up my courage and went to a new boutique, similar to Victoria's Secret. He's been feeling low about being retired and I plan to convince him we're not that old."

Sheena chuckled and gave her mother-in-law a high five. "Good for you."

Rosa leaned her head back against the chair and closed her eyes. "This warm air feels good."

Sheena glanced out across the lawn to check on Meaghan and Michael and saw them walking away from the pool, toward the road.

"Where are you going?" she called to them.

"The beach!" Meaghan answered, and hurried to catch up to her brother.

Sheena waved and settled back against her chair, letting out a sigh of satisfaction. It was nice to have her children in Florida with her. She hoped it would prove to be a healing time for all of them.

Sheena's eyes fluttered opened. Next to her, Rosa dozed, her mouth open, allowing soft snores to escape.

Sensing movement, Sheena glanced across the lawn. A child, a toddler, was opening the gate to the pool.

Sheena checked the area, but the child was alone.

Before she was even fully awake, Sheena was on her feet and running. She reached the fencing around the pool at the same time the child fell into the pool.

"Hold on! I'm coming!" she said, bursting through the open gate, stumbling past the three lounge chairs Regan had picked up at a sale.

Just as she was about to jump into the pool, she noticed a black, slithering creature swimming in the water.

A snake! A snake! her mind screamed.

The child bobbed helplessly in the water in front of her.

Gasping with terror, Sheena jumped into the pool.

As if in a dream—more like a gut-wrenching nightmare— Sheena snatched the child by the arm and flailed her free arm, splashing crazily to keep the snake away.

Sobbing from fear, she watched the snake swim in agitated circles and then glide up out of the water onto the pool deck in front of the gate.

Sheena pulled the child up onto the steps in the shallow end of the pool and hugged the little girl to her chest. "You're all right, sweetie," she said, keeping a wary eye on the snake.

The little girl began to cry. And when she saw a woman running toward them, the child's cries turned into shrieks. "Mommy! Mommy!"

Sheena stood in her wet clothes, still holding the girl who was now kicking to get down from her.

"Be careful! There's a snake by the gate," Sheena called to the girl's mother.

"Bring Lily out here," said the mother. "I'm afraid of snakes."

Me too! Fear wrapped around Sheena, like the snake itself.

Sheena gulped and headed toward the gate. Shivers that had nothing to do with the water on her skin racked her body.

Move! Move! She silently ordered the snake, unable to step any closer.

Sheena and the snake faced each other. With its cold steady stare, the snake seemed to be challenging Sheena to move.

At the last minute, the snake slithered through a hole in the chain link fence and disappeared in the grass.

Wanting to sob with relief, Sheena moved forward and shakily handed the little girl over to her mother. "I'm sorry this happened, and here on our property."

The mother wrapped her arms around the child and kissed her cheek. Then she turned on Sheena. "She could've drowned. And it would have been all *your* fault. How did Lily get into the pool? The gate shouldn't have been open."

Sheena steadied herself. She remembered seeing the gate shut after Michael and Meaghan had left the pool. "We'll check to make sure there's no defect with the gate, but it was shut. How did your daughter get out here alone? There was no one within sight of her."

"Don't you go blaming me," said the mother. "I was in the restaurant waiting for my check to arrive. That's when I noticed Lily was gone. If the service had been any better, this problem wouldn't have happened."

Sheena's mind filled with all the things she wanted to shout at the woman, but she reined in her anger. "The important thing is your daughter is safe. Right, Lily?"

Lily smiled when Sheena tousled her hair.

Her mother sighed. "She's safe. Thank God. But I'm warning you. If anything had happened to her, your hotel would have been sued for everything you had. Now, I just want to leave."

"Let me help you to your car. Is it parked by the restaurant?" Sheena couldn't wait to get the woman off the property.

"Thank you. I'll make it on my own," the woman said in a haughty manner that irritated Sheena even further.

Sheena stood by as the woman walked away, and then, on legs still shaking from the experience, she followed her at a distance. Only after the woman had buckled Lily into her car seat, had settled behind the wheel of the car, and had driven off, could Sheena draw a sigh of relief.

"What happened to you?" Darcy said, coming out of the restaurant and staring at her.

Sheena looked at her sister and burst into tears. "A baby, a snake, the pool..."

Darcy put an arm around her. "Easy. Take a deep breath and then tell me what happened."

Sheena pulled herself together and was finally able to give Darcy the details. But even as she clung to her, Sheena wished it was Tony comforting her.

"We'd better check the gate," Darcy said, taking Sheena's arm.

"Michael and Meaghan were using the pool before they headed to the beach. We'll have to make sure they understand how important it is to lock it properly."

"More than that, we need a different gate—a heavy one with a special key pass, one that closes quickly and securely. I've seen them at other hotels."

"You're right," said Sheena. "That should fix it." Tears came to her eyes as she recalled her frightening encounter. Her voice quivered, "But what about snakes?"

Chuckling softly, Darcy clapped a hand on Sheena's back. "That's a whole different problem. Maybe that's where Petey comes in."

As if on cue, the peacock crossed the lawn toward them, making his awful sound.

Darcy took Sheena's arm, and ignoring Petey, they walked across the lawn toward the pink house.

Rosa met them halfway and wrapped her arms around Sheena. "My word! You saved that child!"

"God! I was scared," said Sheena. "I'm still shaking." She gave Darcy a smile. "Thank goodness, Darcy came along." Rosa beamed at her. "Thank you, Darcy, dear. Would you like to join us? Paul and I are taking the family out for dinner."

"No, thanks. I appreciate the offer, Rosa, I really do. But I have a date."

"You do?" said Sheena.

"Chip asked me out, and I said yes," Darcy said proudly.

"I thought he had a girlfriend," said Sheena, giving her a steady look.

"It turns out the girl he talks about is his dog—a golden retriever named Lucy. Cute, huh?"

Sheena smiled. "Sounds like the kind of competition any girl would like."

Darcy laughed, but Sheena knew how insecure her sister was.

Later, changed and refreshed, Sheena checked her watch. Where were her children? They'd been at the beach a long time—long enough to get some bad sunburns.

"I'll go check on the kids," Sheena assured her mother-in-law. Paul and Rosa wanted time to stop at the hotel before taking the family out to dinner at a seafood restaurant they'd read about.

As she crossed the hotel grounds, she saw Tony walking toward her. She jogged over to him.

"Where are you going?" Tony asked her.

She explained the situation and said, "Want to join me?"

"Sure. I wanted to talk to you alone anyway, to make sure you were okay with my parents making a surprise visit."

"It's no problem. I love your parents." She gave Tony a wicked grin. "According to your mother, they're going to have a relaxing, fun time. And they deserve it. She's even bought lingerie."

He laughed. "Really? No wonder they wouldn't let me pay for the hotel. I tried."

They crossed the road and walked down the boardwalk more in sync than they'd been in a long time.

Stepping onto the white sand, Sheena cupped a hand over her eyes and scanned the beach. She didn't see either Michael or Meaghan, but a small crowd had gathered farther down the beach.

Tony kept pace with her as she headed toward them, walking briskly. When she saw a kid with reddish hair struggling in the water, Sheena broke into a trot, her mother's instinct on high alert.

Michael broke from the crowd and hurried to them. "Mom! Dad! It's Meaghan! She's caught in a rip tide. I tried to help her, but I couldn't. It was too strong. Now, a man is trying to help her."

"Oh my God!" Sheena clutched her hands together in a silent prayer.

"He has to get her to swim parallel to the shore for her to get out of it," said Tony. He raced to the edge of the water and followed their progress.

Sheena and Michael stood with Tony. Sheena prayed Meaghan, stubborn girl that she was, would listen to the directions the man was apparently trying to give her. Anyone's natural instinct would be to try to come directly to shore.

Meaghan was a good swimmer, but Sheena wondered how long her energy could last. Sheena's mind, like a movie projector, streamed memories of Meaghan from the tiny, squalling baby she'd been to the teenager trying to find her way.

"Please, God, please don't let her drown," Sheena whispered, fighting the urge to race into the water herself to get to her daughter.

Michael put an arm around her. "She'll be okay, Mom. The man is helping her. She's coming closer to the shore."

"Who is he? Do you know?" said Sheena. She'd been so focused on Meaghan she hadn't really studied him.

"He's someone named Sam. Someone who works at the hotel."

"Oh my God! Sam Patterson? He's one of Gavin's people." What a horrible thing it would be if he drowned trying to save her daughter. She turned to her husband, but Tony was racing into the water fully clothed.

And now she could see that Sam had hold of Meaghan and was pulling her toward her father.

Oblivious of her own clothing, she waded into the water to greet them. Tony got there first and hugged their daughter to his chest. Tears streamed down Meaghan's cheeks as she sucked in air in loud gasps, trying to catch her breath.

Sheena turned to Sam and wrapped her arms around his thin body, aware of his heaving chest. "Thank you! Thank you!" she said, and burst into sobs that came from deep inside her.

She watched as Tony had lifted Meaghan in his arms and stumbled to shore with her.

Michael met him and together they set Meaghan on her feet. Sheena hurried to join them. The four of them stood, hugging each other.

Sheena looked around for Sam and waved him over.

"Tony, this is Sam Patterson. He works at the hotel."

"Thank you for saving our daughter," Tony said, pumping Sam's hand up and down as he fought tears of his own. He turned to the crowd around them. "That's enough folks. We need some time alone."

The small crowd dispersed, leaving the five of them alone.

Meaghan looked up at Sam. "I thought I was going to drown but you saved me."

Sam shuffled his feet, and when he lifted his face, tears flooded his eyes. "Thought I was going to lose you. Those rip tides can be tricky."

A cameraman from a television station showed up. "What do we have here? A rescue?"

Sheena nodded and turned to Sam. But Sam was running down the beach away from them.

"It's a private matter," she said firmly, wondering why Sam was on the run.

###

Rosa met them outside the house. "My word! What happened? Sheena, this is the second time today your clothes are soaked. Did you save someone else?"

Tony gave her a quizzical look.

"I'll tell you later," said Sheena, thinking it had been one of the worst days of her life. "Right now, I need to get Meaghan into the tub. She's shaking."

A haunting thought clung to Sheena's mind as she got cleaned up and changed her clothes. Things came in threes. What other horrible thing was about to happen to her?

CHAPTER FORTY
DARCY

Darcy let herself into the suite. It was nice to share the larger space with just one other person. As she walked into her spacious bedroom and closed the door, she wondered why she and Regan hadn't moved away from the house earlier. They'd both chafed being under Sheena's constant supervision.

She heard Regan enter the suite and went to greet her in the living area.

Seeing her, Regan jumped with surprise. "I thought you'd be with Sheena. They're going out to dinner soon."

"Me too." Darcy grinned. "With Chip."

"Oh." Regan's look of surprise gave Darcy a sense of satisfaction.

"I'm meeting Austin. He's finished the carved signs and wants to show them to me." Regan started for her room, stopped, and turned around. "Want to double date?"

Darcy shook her head. "Definitely not." She couldn't compete with Regan, and she knew it.

After Regan left to meet Austin, Darcy paced her bedroom, glancing out at the parking lot behind the building, anxiously waiting for Chip's blue jeep to appear. She'd done her best to look casual, but sexy. She'd noticed the girls at the party at Chip's house all seemed to favor very short skirts and low cut tops or little dresses that barely covered themselves.

She went into her bathroom to reassess herself. Her rebellious red curls floated around her face, accenting the pink flush on her cheeks. Freckles, those dots she hated, spread across her nose and tumbled onto her cheeks here and there, like pesky little ants. But it was her figure she studied. Not quite as tall as Sheena, she had a fullness to her breasts that both her sisters lacked. The bright-colored flowers of the sundress she'd found at Walmart battled with the color of her hair in an intriguing way. She let out a sigh of relief. Her appearance wasn't as dramatic as Regan's, but it would do.

Through the bedroom window, she caught a glimpse of Chip's jeep and went outside to meet him. He got out of the car to greet her.

"Wow, Darcy! You look great!"

She smiled. "Thanks. Where are we going?"

"There's a cool place down the beach. They have good beer and burgers and lots of great food. At nine o'clock the bands come in. Everybody goes there."

"Sounds great," she said, pleased to be on her first real date since coming to Florida.

The Pink Dolphin turned out to be a funky bar right on the beach. A small, concrete-block building painted the appropriate pink held the kitchen, a bar, and several tall bar stools lined up at three long tables that could accommodate eight seats on either side of them. Outside, smaller tables sat on a number of wooden decks that surrounded the building. Roofs extended over some of them; others were open to nature. Beyond the decking, a volleyball court stood empty on the beach, unused now in the dark.

Chip waved to a few people as he ushered Darcy to an

empty table near the beach. Tall patio fixtures standing between tables offered heat as well as dim light. The effect was cozy, intimate.

They'd no sooner taken seats when two girls came over to their table.

"Where's Mel?" One of them demanded. "I thought you two had made up."

Chip shook his head. "It's over between us."

"That's not what she thinks." A tall girl with short, dark hair swayed on her feet and glared at Darcy. "I don't know who you are, but you look like Raggedy Ann with those curls and that awful dress."

Darcy inhaled a sharp breath and stared at the girl's glassy eyes.

The short girl with her tugged on her friend's arms. "Come on, Tricia. You're drunk."

As she led Tricia away, the girl turned back and mouthed, "I'm sorry," to Chip.

"Who is this Tricia person?" said Darcy. Her anger was fueled by humiliation. "And maybe you'd better tell me about Mel."

"Melody Sweeney is my ex. She and I broke up right after my roommate's party. Tricia is a friend of hers."

"Why'd you break up with Mel?" Darcy stared into Chip's eyes. She guessed any girl would be upset to lose a good-looking, hard-working guy like Chip.

"It was for a lot of personal reasons. I don't want to get into it now."

"Okay, let's forget it happened." But she decided as soon as she got home, she was going to burn the dress.

They were sipping beer and sharing wings and fries when Darcy heard a familiar voice. "Hey, Chip! What are you and Darcy doing here?"

She looked up and froze, even as heat shot through her body. Brian Harwood approached the table.

"Hey, man! Sit down," said Chip. "The band's about to start playing."

Brian gave her a questioning look.

Darcy waved him to an empty chair at their table.

He sat down, and at his signal, a waitress approached. "What'll you have, handsome?"

"An IPA for me, and refresh whatever these two are having."

The waitress took off, leaving Darcy to face Brian with nothing to say. She still hadn't fully apologized for making such a fool of herself over him. Thankfully, Chip started talking to Brian about the Tampa Bay Rays baseball team, which allowed her to sit back in her chair and listen.

The dating situation was crazy. Her one real interest lay in Brian who had sworn off the Sullivan sisters. She was pleased to be with Chip, but she knew Regan was the one who was dying to date him. All she needed at the moment was for Regan and Austin to show up.

CHAPTER FORTY-ONE
REGAN

Austin helped Regan out of his car and took her elbow. "Nice night for a little beach music."

Regan smiled. "I can hear it from here and it sounds good."

They walked through the crowd gathered at the Pink Dolphin and headed out to the deck closest to the beach. Regan liked being with Austin. He already seemed like a wonderful friend.

Regan turned at the sound of someone calling, "Hey, Austin!"

Austin grabbed her arm and tugged her with him. "Chip and Darcy are here."

Regan glanced at Darcy, who looked unhappy at seeing them approach their table.

"Hey, man! I didn't know you were in town. Grab a chair and stay with us. We've got great seats," Chip said to Austin.

As Chip and Regan sat down, a figure walked over to the table.

"Hey, Austin, do you know Brian Harwood? He's doing a lot of work at the Salty Key Inn with these girls."

Austin and Brian shook hands, and then they sat down together.

While a waitress took their orders, Regan exchanged glances with her sister. She was as uncomfortable at the chance meeting as Darcy. Fortunately, the guys were busy talking and didn't notice.

Regan stared out at the beach. The dim lighting from the decks broke through the shadows, exposing the white sand alongside the decks. Beyond, moonlight touched the crests of the waves with golden accents, giving the scene a surreal look. Some people were dancing on the sand in the dark, their bodies little more than black masses moving to the beat of the music.

Chip jumped up. "C'mon, Darcy! Let's dance!"

He led Darcy out onto the sand, leaving Regan to cope with the suspicious looks Austin and Brian were exchanging.

"Want to dance?" Austin asked her.

She shook her head. "Maybe later." She knew, though, if Brian had asked her, she would have said yes, and she hated herself for even thinking that way.

Austin excused himself to talk to a friend who was calling out to him.

Alone with Brian, Regan sipped her beer quietly.

"I was surprised to find you here," said Brian, breaking into their awkwardness. "I thought you weren't interested in dating me or anyone else. Or is it just me you don't want to see."

Regan swallowed hard. Seeing him here, handsome as ever in a golf shirt and shorts that accentuated his trim build, he looked downright delicious. "I've been too busy to think about a social life."

"Hmmm," he said, staring into her face, reading the feelings she tried to hide. "For your information, I'm not a playboy. I thought you were a better judge of character than that."

Regan didn't know what to say. She knew she'd treated him badly.

When Austin returned to the table, he glanced from Regan to Brian and back again.

"Hey! Everything all right?"

Regan sighed. "If you don't mind, I'm not feeling well. I think I'm just overtired, but I'd like to go home."

"All right." Austin's disappointment was obvious, but he helped Regan to her feet. "I know how hard you've been working on getting that furniture painted."

As Regan turned to leave, she saw Brian shaking his head at her.

CHAPTER FORTY-TWO
SHEENA

Throughout dinner, Sheena kept touching her daughter—a tap on the shoulder, a pat on the back. Having thought she might lose her, she needed to be reassured that Meaghan was safe beside her.

Tony noticed and gave her a knowing look. He'd been as shaken as she by the almost-drowning. Even Michael was gentle in talking with his sister. Though they'd all been scared witless, losing Meaghan had brought them together in a way that hadn't seemed possible earlier.

The feeling persisted long after they'd dropped Rosa and Paul off at their hotel. Sheena was happy that her sisters had temporarily moved out of the house. It gave her family more opportunity to continue this closeness.

Tony pulled the van up to the house and parked it. "Okay, we're home. Time to settle down for the evening. Tomorrow is a busy day for all of us."

"What's on TV?" Michael said.

"Nothing. We don't have one," said Sheena. "But we do have Wi-Fi. Darcy put that in a few days ago."

"I'm going up to my room," announced Michael.

"Me, too," said Meaghan.

"Okay, we'll come say goodnight in a bit," Sheena said, recognizing they were as emotionally drained as she.

"Let's sit outside for a while," said Tony. "I'm enjoying this warm weather."

She collapsed into one of the chairs and let out a trembling sigh. "What a day!"

"I know," said Tony. "We came close to losing Meaghan. We'll have to make sure both kids understand about rip tides and any other dangers of swimming in the Gulf."

"I agree. I'm very glad Sam was there to help her."

"What's up with his running away?" said Tony. "Do you think there's a reason he doesn't want to be known? What do you know about Gavin's people anyway?"

"Not a lot," Sheena admitted. "I'm trying to find out about them without probing too much. I don't believe Gavin would have them at the hotel if they were dangerous."

Tony shook his head. "This whole thing of you and your sisters inheriting a hotel with challenges like this is one of the craziest things I've ever heard. Are you going to stick it out?"

"Yes," said Sheena quietly. "Want to tell me what's going on with the plumbing business? Your mother mentioned that Dave was doing some marketing for you."

"He said he'd help with that if we trained him. He lost his job unexpectedly, and he's scared to go back into sales. With internet sales dominating every field, selling on the road has become unpredictable."

"How do you feel about having your brother-in-law come into the business? You've sometimes had disagreements with him in the past."

"I like it. He and John get along and it takes a lot of the burden off me." Tony gave her an apologetic look. "All those years you wanted me to let go of some of those weekends? You were right. It feels good."

Sheena clasped his hand. "Now, more than ever, I want our family to be together. In a matter of weeks, the kids will come for the summer. Will you try to spend as much time here as you can?"

Tony nodded. "And maybe I can help with some of the work here. Brian has even offered me a job, but I told him I couldn't give up my business in Boston. It wouldn't be fair to you or the kids to just walk away. He understands."

Though Sheena remained quiet, her mind spun with ideas.

Tony squeezed her hand. "It's my creation, like this hotel may be yours. I can't and won't walk away from it."

The excitement that had captured her at the thought of Tony living and working here evaporated. How could she ask Tony to give up the very idea of owning a business when she knew she, herself, would not.

Tony continued to hold her hand as they stared out into the night, listening to the sound of frogs as they remained lost in thoughts of their own.

When she and Tony went inside, Sheena tiptoed upstairs to check on the kids.

She opened the door to Meaghan's room and peeked inside. Meaghan was curled up in a fetal position, sound asleep. Sheena's heart went out to her. It had been such a scary afternoon for them all, but Meaghan had really believed she was going to die.

On tiptoes, Sheena approached her and stared down at her daughter. The gold necklace Sheena had given her was around Meaghan's neck. One hand clasped the shell. Filled with gratitude, Sheena looked up at the ceiling and whispered, "Thank you." No child should die before a parent. She'd known of a woman who'd lost a son to cancer. It had destroyed her.

Sheena leaned over and kissed Meaghan's cheek. "Love you," she whispered, feeling the sting of tears.

Quietly, she left the room and opened the door to Michael's

bedroom. He was sprawled across the bed at an angle, seemingly filling every inch of it. Gazing at him, she realized how close he was to being a man. She hoped staying and working in Florida would help him become the best person he could be.

Hoping not to disturb him, Sheena blew him a kiss and backed out of the room.

Downstairs, she found Tony sitting on the couch. As she walked toward him, he looked up at her with a devilish grin. "Kids settled for the night?"

She smiled and nodded. "After the day they've had, they are both sound asleep."

"Good." He patted the cushion next to him. "Come here."

Sheena's pulse sprinted with pleasure. She lowered herself next to Tony and leaned against his sturdy chest. As his strong arms wrapped around her, she inhaled the spicy aftershave he wore and exhaled a long breath of deep satisfaction.

"I've missed you, Sheena," he whispered in her ear.

She gazed up at him.

His lips captured hers, testing, probing.

Her mouth opened to his and the feel of his tongue thrusting against hers sent a frisson of anticipation through her. She gave in to her body's demands, allowing Tony to demonstrate exactly how much he'd missed her.

Later, lying next to him, she looked at the satisfied smile on his face and chuckled softly to herself. She felt eighteen again. They'd made love with the same intense abandonment they'd experienced at the beginning of their relationship. And God! It felt great!

The alarm on her cell phone drew Sheena from a languid sleep. She groaned softly and rolled over, bumping into Tony.

His eyes flashed open. Seeing her, he smiled.

"Time for a quickie?"

Sheena reached for him and hugged him close before pulling away. "Hold on! Meaghan's calling me."

Tony groaned and moved away to allow to her rise from the bed. "Guess I'd better plan a trip or two down here without the kids, huh?"

She laughed. "It would be easier."

Meaghan appeared at their bedroom doorway. "The sunburn on my back hurts. Can you put some lotion on it?"

"Sure, hon. Are you able to go to work today?"

Meaghan nodded. "Yeah, they're counting on me."

Sheena smiled. "I'm really proud of all the work you're doing, Meaghan. It means a lot to all of us."

A shy smile, one that Sheena remembered from a few years ago, crept across Meaghan's pink face. For a moment, Sheena's breath caught at the beauty of it.

CHAPTER FORTY-THREE
DARCY

Darcy awoke and tiptoed into the kitchen of the suite to get a cup of coffee. She was still frustrated by the events of last night. The date with Chip had gone from good to bad to downright awful. Coffee would, she hoped, improve her temperament.

She fixed an individual cup of coffee in the new machine they'd bought for the suite and sank down into a chair at the table. Bleary-eyed, she stared out at the expanse of lawn in front of the room and took several sips of the hot liquid, attempting to pull herself together. When she'd showed up at the Pink Dolphin, Regan's appearance had ruined her chances to speak privately to Brian.

"You're up early!" came a cheerful voice behind her.

Darcy turned to find Regan dressed for the day in her painting clothes. "You're awful happy," she said, warning herself to be careful. It wasn't Regan's fault Brian was besotted with her. And it wasn't Regan's fault that Chip had more or less dumped her to talk to his old girlfriend.

Regan came over to the table and took a seat opposite Darcy. "Sorry I couldn't stay last night. The band was good. Did you do a lot of dancing?"

Darcy shook her head. "Chip's old girlfriend showed up. Turns out she's not an ex, after all. They got back together last night."

"Oh no! Where did that leave you? With Brian?"

"No, Brian left right after you did. That left me with a creep I never want to see again."

Regan rose and gave her a quick hug. "Oh, Darcy, I'm sorry. We really haven't had much luck dating, have we?"

"Nope. How did it go with you and Austin?"

"Austin Blakely is one of the nicest guys I've ever met," said Regan. "But I think of him as only a friend."

"He's not my type either," said Darcy. "I want someone a little more exciting, you know?"

During the moment of silence that followed, Sheena came into their suite. "Can I grab a cup of coffee? I need to tell you what happened last evening."

Sheena fixed herself a cup of coffee and took a seat at the table. "It's about Meaghan."

"What's going on?" Darcy asked, alarmed by the way Sheena's eyes had filled.

Sheena drew a deep breath and told them about the rip tide and how Meaghan had been saved by Sam. "I thought we were going to lose her, but Sam stayed right with her, forcing her to swim in the proper direction. And then, when a cameraman showed up, he took off."

"Oh my God! I'm so glad he was there," said Darcy, feeling sick at the thought of what might have happened. "Sam doesn't strike me as the heroic type. He's thin and very quiet. And it takes a lot of strength to do what he did for Meaghan. I wonder what his story is."

"Thank God he managed to save her," said Regan. "You must have been frantic, Sheena, watching the whole thing."

"Yes, I was. I never want to feel that way again. Sam was a true hero. I intend to find out more about him, see if there's anything we can do for him," said Sheena. "You two can help me. Gavin's people are very secretive, but maybe we can piece together what little bits we can learn about them."

"Good idea," said Darcy. "But I don't want anything to do with Rocky. He gives me the creeps."

"Grace says he's harmless, and I believe her," said Sheena. "Especially after getting to know his brother and realizing how Gavin trusted them both."

"Is Meaghan working this morning?" asked Regan, a worried look on her face.

Sheena nodded. "Both she and Michael have sunburns, but she insisted on going into work. I'm very proud of her for that."

A sigh escaped Darcy. "Sometimes I wonder if we're crazy to keep going on this project. Nothing is the way I thought it would be. Look at us. We're living here in this suite or in that tiny house, working our butts off, and with no real income to speak of. It spells crazy with a capital C to me."

"And the dating scene is dismal," said Regan.

"Yeah, a complete washout," added Darcy.

"Do you want to walk away?" Sheena asked, distress written on her face.

Darcy and Regan looked at each other and shook their heads.

"Okay," said Sheena. "Time for a heart-to-heart talk. First of all, we knew this was a risky situation. We, of course, didn't know the sad state of affairs we'd find when we got here. But you both have been working hard, doing wonderful things to make this challenge work. We can't give up—not now when we're getting close to the time we could be ready for paying guests."

Sheena studied Regan and then turned the full force of her gaze onto Darcy. "Time to pull on your big-girl panties and get a grip. We're moving forward, ladies."

Darcy collapsed against the back of her chair, feeling as if she'd been physically shaken. Surprisingly, she was not offended by Sheena's big sister tactic. She'd needed to hear those words.

Filled with a new energy, she straightened. "You're right, Sheena. It's been a disappointing time, but I guess we'd better keep going."

Sheena rose and gave them each a hug. "We'll talk later, after my family leaves. Until then, keep on keepin' on."

After Sheena left, Darcy's cell phone beeped for a text message. Darcy read it and gasped. "Oh no! Alex and Nicole want to book some rooms here next week. What am I going to say to them? You know how snobby Alex is."

"Tell them we're undergoing a renovation and if they'd like to visit in the fall we'll make special arrangements for them," said Regan.

"Guess I'd better go get dressed and get busy," said Darcy. "No way do I want them down here. Not yet."

Darcy heard Regan's laughter behind her, but she kept running toward her room.

CHAPTER FORTY-FOUR
SHEENA

Sheena left Darcy and Regan with fresh determination to complete the challenge that Gavin had dumped on them. She didn't blame her sisters for their disappointment, but she couldn't let them slow down. They were too close to winning. Except for Meaghan's mishap, things were going fairly well.

She hurried over to Gracie's. Tony and Michael had headed to the restaurant earlier, and she hoped to catch up with them. Michael was supposed to help clear the back area by the bay, but with his sunburn, he was hoping to work for Regan instead.

The restaurant was crowded when Sheena walked in. She waved to Lynn and Maggie and joined Tony and Michael at a small table.

"Michael will be working with Regan today. Brian will have him help out tomorrow," said Tony.

Michael grimaced. "How long do I have to work for her? It's kind of sissy stuff."

"Stay with her until she says she doesn't need you. She and a crew have been working really hard to get all the furniture painted. Now, some of them are starting to get the walls painted and the floors prepped for new carpeting. It will take a couple of weeks."

"Some vacation," complained Michael.

Maggie approached the table. "What can I get you, Sheena?"

"The pancakes were great," offered Michael.

Sheena smiled and turned to Maggie. "I think I'll have my usual—two scrambled eggs, wheat toast and honey."

"Coming right up." Maggie poured her a cup of coffee and moved away.

"Brian's going to pick me up in a few minutes," said Tony, getting to his feet. He leaned over and gave her a kiss. "See you later."

Regan entered the restaurant and came over to their table. "Mind if I sit down?"

"Not at all. I just ordered, and Michael is waiting to work with you."

Regan smiled at him. "Lots of things to do. You ready?"

Michael shrugged. "I guess."

When Maggie returned with Sheena's order, Regan declined to order. "I had a light breakfast earlier." She motioned Michael to his feet. "We'll see you later."

Watching them walk away, Sheena noticed how Michael towered over her sister. Though he looked like an adult, he was still a kid who had a lot to learn about many things.

Her thoughts drifted to Uncle Gavin. He'd wanted this challenge to be a life lesson for her and her sisters. She had a feeling he'd be pleased that her family was participating. As for life lessons, she was learning a whole bunch of them. Independence gave her a freedom she'd never known. And working together with her sisters was giving them all an opportunity to settle old resentments and work on their insecurities.

Meaghan came over to clear the table.

Seeing her, Sheena swallowed hard at what might have been. "Doing okay?"

Meaghan nodded. "My shift is almost over. Then I'm going to veg out."

"Okay. See you later." Sheena rose and went into the kitchen to find Sam.

Gracie waved and came right over to her. "Heard Sam is some kind of hero."

"Yes!" said Sheena. "He saved Meaghan's life."

"Yep, that's what Meaghan said." Gracie laid a hand on Sheena's shoulder and gave her an unwavering stare. "Sam's a real good guy."

"What's his story? He ran away when a cameraman showed up."

"Not mine to tell," said Gracie. "He's upstairs in his room. You can ask him yourself."

Sheena left the kitchen and climbed the stairs to the second floor. The eight guest rooms upstairs lined the hallway, four on each side. All doors but one were closed tight. Sheena went to the one that was partially open and gently knocked.

"Yeah?"

"Sam, it's me. Sheena. I want to thank you again for all you did for us."

He opened the door.

Sheena faced the man she'd once likened to Ichabod Crane and gazed into his kind, brown eyes. "Tony and I will always be grateful to you for saving Meaghan. I noticed your reaction to the cameraman. I don't know why you ran, but I want to assure you that if there's anything Tony and I can do for you, anything at all, we will."

"Come on in," said Sam. He opened the door, crossed the room, and sat down on the edge of his bed. "Have a seat." He indicated the overstuffed chair sitting in the corner of the room. On a nearby table, a Bible lay open.

"You might as well know. I served a couple years in prison for a murder I didn't commit. It was a horrible experience—one that everyone imagines. The cops had me guilty without even following through on leads. Gavin paid a lawyer to help clear me. New DNA tests and new witnesses proved it couldn't be me, but I'd already paid a horrible price by losing my freedom. I have never really gotten over it. I don't want anything to do with publicity of any kind. I need to live the rest of my life peacefully. Understand? There are still some who don't believe the results of a new trial."

Sheena felt as if cold water was running through her veins. "That's awful! I'm truly sorry that happened to you. And, Sam, like I said, if we can help you in any way we will. You are a hero to me. Not only for saving Meaghan's life but for being the kind of man you are. Gavin knew that, and now, I do too."

Tears threatened, but Sheena blinked them away. She knew instinctively that Sam would not like them.

Rising to her feet, Sheena gave him a quick hug and left the room without looking back. Talk about a life lesson, she thought. Sam had demonstrated a quiet strength she could never emulate.

Back at the house, Sheena sat at the kitchen table and went to work on estimates for carpeting. Next week, she and Regan were going to view samples at one of the hotel suppliers. The square yardage for the twenty rooms and eight suites seemed huge. But she went ahead and figured in the additional yardage for the twenty rooms on the second floor. She hoped they could work out a deal to put that carpet on hold.

Numbers, numbers. It all added up quickly.

Meaghan walked into the kitchen and plopped down into the chair opposite Sheena. "Hi, what's up?" Sheena said, noting her daughter's glum expression.

"I just got a text from Lauren. She's unfriending me on all the sites."

"I guess you're upset by that, huh?" Sheena said, quietly stating the obvious. She waited for Meaghan to speak.

Meaghan's eyes filled with tears. "She's mean. She's telling everyone you and Dad are divorcing and he's going out of business."

"Really? I wonder where she got those ideas," Sheena said calmly, though anger pulsed through her. Lauren's mother was a gossip queen. No doubt, her daughter, Lauren, was following in her footsteps.

Meaghan shrugged. "I dunno. Maybe I told her I was worried you were getting a divorce."

"You know that Dad and I are not getting a divorce. Right?"

Meaghan nodded.

"And what about Dad's business?"

"I've never said a word about his business. Honest."

Sheena got up and put her arm around Meaghan. "You know, when I moved here, I hoped we'd all learn something from it—something that would be helpful to us. What have you learned from this experience?"

Meaghan bit her lip. "I've learned that it hurts when people are mean. I don't want to be friends with Lauren. She's mean. And now I know she tells lies."

"I think you've made a good decision. There are many good people in the world. And, Meaghan, there are other girls in your class who are better friends than Lauren. I'm sorry if she hurt your feelings. I really am."

Meaghan gazed up at her. "Is Dad's business failing?"

Sheena drew a deep breath, searching for the right words. "It's going through a difficult time, but we've gone through worse and survived. It's not for you to worry about, sweetie."

"Good. I'm going to tell Lauren I don't care if she unfriends me because I hate her!"

"Whoa!" said Sheena. "Don't become mean yourself.

Remember why you came to Florida. You are a much better person because of it, someone I like and respect."

"Mom?" Meaghan threw her arms around her. "I love you."

"And I love you, Meaghan Eileen Morelli," Sheena said, forcing the words out through a throat choked with emotion.

Late morning, Tony called her on her cell. "Want to meet for lunch? Brian is meeting with someone regarding a bid on a project and I'm free."

"Great! Shall we meet at Gracie's?"

"No, I want to go off property. See a few other places."

"Okay, meet me at the house and we'll take off. I'll let the others know." Meaghan had left to go find Regan and her brother.

Sheena made phone calls to her sisters and then happily raced upstairs to freshen up. After their lovemaking, the idea of a real date with Tony was exciting. Besides, she wanted to talk to him about his business.

Tony arrived. Realizing they were alone, he grinned. "Want to skip lunch?"

She laughed. "Sorry, I never know when someone will show up. Besides, I'm starving."

"Me, too," he said, laughing with her.

They got in the van and took off down the street, with Tony driving. "I wanted to get a good look around the area," he said. "Brian told me there's a great little bar down the road called Jimmy's. Have you heard of it?"

Sheena shook her head. "I rarely get off the property. That's why Blackie Gatto wanted me to see the restaurant where he took me."

Tony glanced at her with a sheepish grin. "Sorry I got a little out of control with him. You haven't gone out with him again, have you?"

"No," teased Sheena, arching her eyebrow at him. "He hasn't asked me."

"But..."

"But if he did and it was important, I might meet him...for coffee," said Sheena. She couldn't help being flattered that Tony was jealous of another man's interest in her. She knew then how much he loved her, how much he'd missed her.

Jimmy's was larger than Sheena had imagined and was more like a regular restaurant than a bar. But it appeared they had a good selection of wines and beers, along with a normal selection of liquor.

They were shown to a table by a window.

Perusing the menu, Sheena checked to see if any of the items on the list might be something they could use at Gracie's or in another restaurant in the future. They'd talked about putting up a refreshment bar by the pool sometime.

After considering a number of choices, she decided on a shrimp salad because it reminded her of her favorite lobster rolls in Maine.

Sheena glanced out the window. The fronds of a palm tree swayed in the sea breeze like a friendly hello, and bougainvillea brightened the landscaping with their colorful red and pink flowers. She couldn't hide her pleasure; she'd grown to love the tropical feel and look.

Tony smiled at her. "Nice, huh?"

"Yes. And nice that we can be together like this." The smile left her face. "Meaghan was upset this morning when she received a message from Lauren unfriending her. Apparently, Lauren has told everyone we're getting a divorce and you're going out of business."

"Lauren? That little brat," growled Tony. "What did you say to Meaghan?"

"She knows we're not getting a divorce and I told her we'd gone through hard times in business before and we'd do it again. But, Tony, how bad are things with you and the business?"

The waitress appeared with their food, making it impossible for Tony to respond.

They took a moment to enjoy their food. Sheena's shrimp was tossed with a lemony mayonnaise dressing, bits of celery and, surprisingly, capers.

Tony had ordered the sausage and onion sandwich, along with a draft beer. He took a couple of bites of his sandwich and sipped his beer. Then he wiped his mouth and faced her.

She looked at his worried expression and set down her fork.

"What is it, Tony?"

"The business isn't doing well. That's why I brought Dave in. John wants to buy into it. He thinks between Dave and him, they can make a go of it. But I'm not sure."

Sheena felt her jaw grow slack. "And were you going to discuss this with me? I'm your partner too. Remember?"

Tony let out a derisive snort. "You *were* my partner. You gave that up when you decided you had your own business to run. God knew, none of us had any idea what the real state of affairs was here, but it's yours."

To give herself time to think, Sheena took a swallow of water and fought back the urge to cry. "Tony, you can't mean that you would make a huge decision like this without discussing it with me. Maybe our marriage isn't on as solid a footing as I thought."

"Look, let's not fight about it," said Tony, setting down the beer mug he'd just lifted. "The whole situation is up in the air.

I'm not sure what to do. I need to talk to a financial guy about it."

"Do you want to talk to Blackie Gatto? He's really good."

Tony's lips thinned. "No, Sheena, I don't. He's the guy who almost kissed you the last time we met."

"Is everything okay here?" the waitress asked. "More water for you, Miss? More beer?"

Tony waved her away. "We're fine, thanks."

Sheena stared at him. She wasn't sure they were fine at all.

CHAPTER FORTY-FIVE
REGAN

Regan stood by as one of Brian's men showed Michael how to handle the long-handled floor scraper he'd been given. The concrete floors of the rooms needed to be cleaned of all carpeting and padding remnants that had been left behind.

"No problem," said Michael. "This will be easy."

"Remember, we don't want to chip the concrete," warned the man doing the demonstration. "Start here and I'll catch up with you later."

He nodded to Regan and left the room.

"Okay, Michael, you know where to find me at the end of the hall. See you later." Regan gave him a little wave and left.

As she walked back to the paint room, she thought of how much Michael had changed. He'd been such a sweet little boy. Now, he'd become a mouthy know-it-all. But then, she recalled how difficult teen years had been for her and decided he was merely typical of guys that age.

Regan was deep into her painting when Meaghan appeared. "Hi, sweetie! You here to watch or help?"

"I'll help for a while. I wanted someone to talk to. Lauren, who used to be my best friend, just dumped me."

Regan gave Meaghan a hug. "Sorry, sweetie. I remember days like that."

"You do? I thought you were the most popular girl in your class."

Regan shook her head. "Far from it. Grab a paintbrush and

I'll tell you all about your aunt who was the class dummy."

It was amusing to Regan to see how fast Meaghan found a brush and started painting.

"What happened to you?" Meaghan said.

As Regan recounted some of her story, she felt some of the old pain slip away. Coming to Florida was turning out to be a wonderful thing for her emotionally. Uncle Gavin had wanted each of them to experience life lessons, and she was learning a lot—not only about herself but about her sisters. Funny how you could be in the same family and not even know them. She'd had no idea that Sheena hadn't wanted to get married so soon, or that Darcy had always felt abandoned by Sheena when she left.

Later, Regan walked down the hallway to see if Michael was ready for a break. As she passed each room, she grew more concerned. None of the rooms had been touched. She entered the room where Michael had first set to work and stopped in surprise.

Michael was sitting on the floor playing a game on his phone.

"What are you doing?" she asked.

Michael glanced up at her with a startled expression.

"Why haven't you done the other rooms?" Regan asked.

"I finished this room and was waiting for you to tell me what to do next," he answered with a smirk.

Regan's temper exploded. "You knew you were to go on to the next room, Michael. I made sure you understood that."

"Yeah? Well, Mom lied to me. This was supposed to be a vacation."

"I see," Regan said, placing her hands on her hips. "She didn't lie to me when she said you needed to understand how hard everyone else works to make sure you have the things you need, the things you want. Now, you need to get to work in the next room."

"Sheesh! Get upset about it," mumbled Michael.

Regan walked away before it became a verbal battle neither of them could win. But she vowed she'd never have kids of her own. Cute little babies turned into teenagers.

CHAPTER FORTY-SIX
SHEENA

Let's finish our lunch and get out of here," said Tony. "I promised my mother we'd stop by the hotel sometime today to see how they're doing."

"Okay." Sheena decided not to ruin their time together by arguing over his business. In a few days, her family would leave to go back to Boston.

After they'd finished eating and were waiting for the check, Tony called his mother. "How are you? Sheena and I thought we'd stop by."

He listened and then he burst out laughing. "Here, tell Sheena what you just told me." Tony handed the phone to her.

Curious, Sheena said, "Hi, Rosa. What's up?"

"I'm not sure what is so funny. I just told Tony that he'd interrupted our 'nooner' but that we were fine."

"Nooner? Really?" Sheena clamped down on the inside of her cheeks to keep from shrieking with laughter.

"You know, our little noon-time nap before we go out," said Rosa.

"Oh, yes," Sheena managed to say without laughing. "Well, if you like we can stop by later."

"Why don't you make it tomorrow, dear," said Rosa. "We have plans for this afternoon and this evening."

Sheena clicked off the call and burst out laughing. "The nooner your mother is talking about is a nap. And, no, they don't want us to stop by. They're apparently busy this afternoon and evening."

"All right," said Tony. He sounded disappointed.

"You know, maybe they like getting away from us for a while," Sheena said.

Tony nodded thoughtfully. "Maybe you're right. We've lived next door to each other all these years. It can't have been any easier for them than it has been for us, though we've had it pretty good."

"Yes, they've been very good to us," said Sheena. "In all truth, it's been great for me to be away. I'm sure they're feeling the same."

"I guess so," said Tony. "Mom not wanting to see us. That's a first."

"Well, let's get back to our family. I want to make sure Meaghan is all right, and we need to check on Michael. He doesn't know how lucky he is to have a family like ours." She shook her head. "And this idea of not working? Where does that come from? We've both worked hard all our lives."

"To make matters worse, he's with friends who have a lot more money. He thinks he should have whatever they have."

"For better or worse, we're what he has," said Sheena. She studied Tony, unable to hide her unease. "We will make it, won't we?"

Tony merely squeezed her hand.

The next afternoon, alone in the house, Sheena picked up her phone to call Rosa. Before she could punch in the phone number, her cell rang. She checked it. *Rosa.*

"Hey, there! I was about to call you. What's up?"

"I just wanted to check in. It's been such an enjoyable visit, and we've been busy. I haven't had time to chat."

"What have you been doing?" asked Sheena. Rosa's voice

was bubbling with excitement.

"Looking at places to buy. Paul has an old schoolmate who lives in the area in a great, older community. After playing a round of golf with him, Paul wants to consider it. I couldn't be happier about it."

"Nice," said Sheena, feeling as if the wind had been knocked out of her. Paul and Rosa owned the house Sheena and Tony had been renting for years.

"It's just a thought at this point," said Rosa, reassuring her. "But a happy one."

Sheena was pleased for her in-laws but she worried about the future. It all seemed very uncertain.

On this, the last night of her family's visit, Sheena insisted on cooking dinner for them. She had only hours, not days, with them and she wanted, no, needed the illusion that the family would stay strong even after they returned to Boston, leaving her behind.

Rather than do the traditional Italian meals she'd come to rely on at home, she'd chosen to do something with fish and fresh fruit and other reminders of the Florida setting.

The kitchen table was set for four. Regan and Darcy had opted out of the meal. Though it was crowded at the small table, it suited Sheena's plan for a cozy gathering. At each place, she'd left a gift, like she'd done when she'd left Boston for Florida. This time, the gifts were four different, simple shells—reminders of the beach and being together.

As her family dug into the food, Sheena studied them. Meaghan's fairer skin still had a light pink coating on pale tan. Michael's tan accented the color of his brown eyes, giving them a deeper depth that was intriguing. And Tony? He was even more handsome now that the sun and the vacation from the daily grind of his business had smoothed his skin, making him look younger than his years.

He caught her studying him and smiled. For the last couple of days, he'd been eager to prove to her that somehow they'd make it through the trials ahead of them, both in their marriage and with his business.

"I'm going to miss everyone." Sheena sighed and then forced a smile. "But in just a matter of weeks, you kids will be back here for the summer."

"Yeah, and by then Brian said I can help him fix up the dock, both here at the hotel and behind the bar. He's thinking of setting up a boat rental business and he wants me to run it," said Michael. There was a new pride in his voice that Sheena liked. After making sure that Michael did his fair share for Regan, Brian had taken on Michael, showing him things he could do around the hotel. A male bond had quickly formed between them, mellowing Michael's attitude.

"Brian is into so many businesses, I can't keep count," Sheena said. "But he's good at whatever he does. I'm glad you stepped up and did some good work for him, Michael."

She turned to Meaghan. "This summer are you going to work at Gracie's?"

"Yes!" Wearing a new pair of pants and a cotton top that Sheena had promised her, Meaghan stood up and twirled around for them. "I want to be able to save money for school clothes. It's really true that I can go to school down here next Fall?"

Sheena and Tony exchanged glances.

"We're still working on that," said Tony. Though it was Meaghan herself who had asked him about it, he wasn't happy with the idea.

"Everybody ready for dessert?" asked Sheena.

She smiled when all three heads nodded enthusiastically.

"Okay, Meaghan, you can clear."

While Meaghan carried dishes to the sink, Sheena cut the pineapple upside-down cake in slices and served them.

"You really are a good cook," Tony said. "We've missed your cooking. Right, kids?"

"And?" Sheena waited for a response.

"And you, too, of course," said Tony.

"Really, Mom, you too," Michael said.

"Enough to answer the phone when I call?" Sheena didn't want to go through another couple of months of not hearing from her children or talking to them on a regular basis.

"Okaaay," said Meaghan. "I promise."

"Good. Now, does anyone want to go for a walk on the beach? It's pleasant outside."

Michael shook his head. "Not me. I'm going up to my room to listen to music."

"I'm going to try on my new clothes again," said Meaghan.

Sheena shrugged. "Okay. How about you, Tony?"

"You're on. I've heard we got another cold spell in Boston. It's going to feel nice to take one last warm walk here."

Tony and Sheena left the house and headed toward the beach.

CHAPTER FORTY-SEVEN
SHEENA

As Sheena and Tony headed for the beach, the sky was heightening in color in anticipation of a nice sunset. Clouds floated above them like dollops of whipped cream. Sheena knew from past experience that soon they would be tipped in red and orange from the setting sun.

Sheena held Tony's hand as they made their way down the boardwalk to the sand. She'd miss him more than she could say.

They took off their sandals and stood on the white sand together.

A peace came over her. The sound of the waves embracing the shore and shyly racing away in a constant rhythm was soothing. And with Tony beside her, she closed her eyes, enjoying the magical moment of a peaceful surrounding while her heart filled with love.

"Somehow, we'll make things work," Tony said softly.

She opened her eyes and faced him.

He drew her into his arms and lowered his lips to hers.

She responded, not caring who saw. This was her man, and for better or worse, she loved him.

When they broke apart, she took his hand. "Shall we walk down the beach?"

They strolled hand in hand, watching as the sun began its descent below the horizon.

"Stop," Sheena said to Tony. "Let's stand here and look for

the green flash."

"Green flash. What are you talking about?" said Tony.

Sheena explained that she'd been told that at the very moment the sun dips behind the horizon, you can sometimes see a green flash. It's become sort of a game for people on the coast to look for it."

They watched in comfortable silence as the sun slipped lower and lower, an orange orb in a darkening sky.

When at last it was gone, leaving an empty space behind, Sheena and Tony headed back to the hotel.

They'd just reached the boardwalk and slipped on their sandals when they heard a loud explosion. And then a fireball burst above the hotel like misplaced fireworks.

"Oh my God!" Sheena cried. "What's that?"

Tony grabbed her hand and they ran together toward the hotel.

Gavin's people were standing in a group outside of Gracie's, murmuring and milling about. Then, as a group, they began running toward the back of the lot.

"What is it? What is it?" Sheena cried, racing to catch up to them.

"It's the house. It's on fire," said Gracie, hurrying to catch up to Sam and Rocky who were leading the pack of people.

Sheena turned to look for Tony, but he was racing to the head of the group.

"My God! My God! My children!" screamed Sheena. She saw Regan and Darcy ahead of her. "Darcy! Help me!" she cried.

Darcy turned around and ran back to her. "C'mon! Let's go!" She grabbed Sheena's arm and sprinted forward.

Darcy's longer legs and better shape made it easier to bypass the others. By the time they made it to the house, Sheena was gasping so hard for air, she felt dizzy. And when she saw flames shooting out of the kitchen windows on the first floor, her legs wobbled.

Regan sprinted over to them and caught Sheena in her arms as she was about to fall to the ground.

"Meaghan! Michael!" Sheena cried, sobbing hysterically as she clung to her sisters.

"Tony's trying to get them out," Darcy said. "You two stay here. I'm going to see if I can help him."

"Oh God! Oh God! I'm going to lose them all," moaned Sheena, unable to tear her gaze away from the yellow and orange flames that licked the night air like the tongue of a fire-eating dragon.

Sirens wailed behind them and then a number of vehicles, lights flashing, raced down the driveway.

"Help is here," Regan said to her. "And look, Meaghan and Tony are coming out of the house."

"Michael! Where's my baby boy!" Sheena screamed. "Michael! Michael!" She ran to Tony and grabbed his arm.

"Where's Michael?"

"He's inside, upstairs. Come with me."

They ran around to the side of the house. Michael stood by the window.

Sheena howled. "Jump, Michael! Jump!"

"Stand back!" he shouted. She could see now that he had a chair in his hands. He swung the chair against the window, splintering wood and glass.

"Hurry!" Tony shouted.

Crying hysterically, Meaghan grabbed onto Sheena. Regan and Darcy stood behind them, clinging to each other, as helpless as Sheena.

Michael climbed onto the window ledge and teetered uncertainly. Then, with a bellow, he leaped from it onto the soft grass.

He landed with a thud that rocked the ground near Sheena and lay on the ground groaning.

Sheena ran over to him and threw her arms around him. "Thank God! Thank God!" She knelt on the ground, hugging him to her, afraid to let go.

"Mom," said Michael, gently pushing her away. "Let me up. I just got the wind knocked out of me."

Tony helped her to her feet and turned to Michael. "Are you all right? Do you hurt anywhere?" He held out a hand to him.

Michael grabbed hold of it and got his feet. "I'm okay, except for this. I cut it on the glass." He held out his left hand. Though it was bleeding, Sheena could see that it wasn't serious.

Laughing hysterically with relief, Sheena wrapped her arms around him. "That, we can live with."

Crying softly, Regan and Darcy hugged Michael, then did the same to her, Tony, and Meaghan.

Sheena had been too busy concentrating on Michael to focus on the firemen who were working diligently to put out the fire. But as she gazed at the house, seeing for the first time all the damage that had been done to it, she doubted anyone could ever live there again.

"What happened?" she asked one of the firemen standing by.

"Can't be sure. Looks like it started in the kitchen. Maybe with the stove."

Once the fire was out and the fire chief and others had inspected the house and made sure it was safe enough, they allowed Sheena to go inside to retrieve what she could.

Holding one of the firemen's flashlights, Sheena stepped cautiously through the doorway. Downstairs the kitchen and adjacent living area were gone. But the stairs leading upstairs were intact.

She climbed the stairs, testing each step carefully. The acrid odor of smoke and fire and water turned her stomach.

At the top of the stairs, she entered her bedroom. Her purse was still sitting on top of the bureau where she'd left it. It was soaking wet. She grabbed it. After opening one of the bureau drawers, she let out a sigh of relief. Her computer downstairs was gone, but her external hard drive, which she updated constantly and kept in that drawer had survived. She checked her closet. Her clothes had survived the flames, but looking at the pasty ash that covered them, she wondered if they'd ever come clean.

Sheena did a quick check of the rooms the kids had used. They'd kept their phones with them, but the computer they shared was soaked. Their clothes were a mess.

Tony joined her. "Hey, hon! C'mon, we've got to get out of here."

Together they gathered what items of clothing they could and made their way out of the house.

Outside, with her family gathered around her, she turned to her sisters, "All in all, not too bad, considering our children are safe," she said and burst into tears. She'd been terribly frightened. She didn't know how she could live without her family.

"Why don't you all stay in the suite tonight?" Regan said. "Darcy and I will find someplace else to stay."

Sheena turned to Tony.

He shook his head. "No. We'll go to a motel nearby. The stench of smoke is too much a reminder of what we almost lost."

Tears filled his eyes.

Sheena wrapped an arm around him and leaned into him, as emotionally upset as he.

#

The next morning, Sheena got up early and dressed in the clothes she'd worn the night before.

Tony stirred and gave her a questioning look.

"Try to get some more sleep," she whispered. "I'm going to talk to my sisters. I'm done with this project. I've almost lost Meaghan twice and Michael once. And you've never been happy with my decision."

"Wait! Don't you even want to talk about it?" said Tony, rising up on his elbow.

Sheena shook her head. "No, we don't need to talk about it. I know I'm doing what's best for my family. My sisters will have to understand."

Sheena left the motel and decided to walk down the beach, allowing Tony and the kids to have the van. She made her way onto the beach and walked along the sand toward the Salty Key Inn.

The rising sun spread fingers of orange and red through the gray clouds that hovered on the horizon, reminding Sheena of her horror at seeing flames light up and then destroy her home.

She'd hardly slept during the night, and then only after she'd made her decision about her future. She knew she'd miss Florida and the project she and her sisters had worked so hard to complete. But she decided life was too short and her family too precious to keep fighting for a cause she might never win.

Normally the sound of the waves soothed her. But on this early morning, the wind seemed to sense her turmoil and whipped the water into frothy waves that smacked the shore like an angry hand.

She'd wanted to find herself. In many ways, she had. But

she felt like a tightrope walker who'd only crossed the high wire halfway and was trying to catch her balance in the middle.

She paused and watched the seagulls, hoping for strength to do what she must. She'd been very optimistic about finding herself, building a friendship with her sisters, and securing a future for her family. She'd persevered even when Tony told her it was a selfish move. And when the kids had rebelled, becoming even more self-centered, more upset with her departure, she'd told herself they'd get over it. Now, with Tony's business in such bad shape and possibly no secure home with their in-laws in the future, she had a bigger battle in Boston.

She continued her walk along the shore, chasing the sandpipers away with heavy steps.

When she caught sight of the Salty Key Inn with its crazy blue building, she stopped. And though she tried to pull herself together, tears streamed down her cheeks. Damn! The hotel could be a wonderful place; she knew it in her heart.

She climbed onto the boardwalk and walked toward Gracie's. It was early yet, but as she approached the building, she could hear the sounds of activity in the kitchen and realized life for Gavin and his people would go on—with or without her. Gavin certainly would have made sure of that.

She bypassed the restaurant and crossed the grounds to the suites building.

Knowing she was making the right choice, she pounded on the door to Darcy and Regan's suite and waited for a reply.

Regan answered the door sleepily. "Sheena? What's wrong?"

"I need a good strong cup of coffee and then I need to talk to you and Darcy."

"Come on in. I'll get Darcy up." Regan frowned at her. "Are

you okay? Are the kids okay?"

"Just get Darcy," Sheena answered, unwilling to go through the whole speech twice.

Moments later, Darcy and Regan stumbled into the room, both still in tank tops over sleep shorts. They walked up to the kitchen counter and stared at her sleepily.

Sheena fixed each of them a cup of coffee at the machine, taking deep sips of her own while she waited for each cup to fill.

Darcy accepted a cup of coffee from Sheena. "What's going on?"

"We'd better sit down," said Sheena. "All of us."

They each grabbed a chair at the table and sat.

Sheena took a steadying breath, telling herself not to cry. "My family is flying out to Boston this afternoon and I'm going with them. I've tried my best to make this challenge work. I haven't minded the hard work, the uncertainty, the living conditions. None of it. But I can't let my family be hurt physically or emotionally by what I'm doing. I'm done with this project. Now and forever."

"What about us?" Regan said. "I've put everything into this project—all so the three of us could have a chance for a better life." Tears filled her eyes. "And you're going to take this away from us, just like that?"

Darcy slammed her hand on the table. "You've got to be shitting me! After all your big pep talk last week, you're doing this to us?"

There was a rattling sound at the door, and then Tony burst into the suite.

"She's not going anywhere," Tony said.

Sheena and her sisters stared at him in surprise.

Tony held up a finger of warning. "I heard what you said, Regan, and I'm here to tell you and Darcy that I'm not going to allow Sheena to give up. The kids and I just talked about it, and we voted unanimously for Sheena to stay. This is what she wanted. The kids will come for the summer and stay for school. And I will be here any way I can, as often as I can. God knows I may end up with no business at all. I'm trying to work something out, but who knows?"

"You'd do that for me? For us?" Sheena scrambled to her feet, ran over to Tony and threw her arms around him. Tears blurred her vision.

"Damn right," Tony said and grinned at her and then her sisters. "I've seen what all of you have done to make this hotel project work. And now, you'll need more help than ever getting rid of that house, building something better." He winked at them. "You might even need a plumber."

"Hooray!" Regan shouted. She hurried over to him.

Darcy followed her.

"You're the best brother-in-law ever," gushed Regan, giving him a hug.

"She might be right," Darcy said, grinning at him before breaking down and giving him a hug.

Sheena wrapped her arms tighter around Tony. "He's the best husband I could ever have."

"The only one you'll ever have, I hope," amended Tony. "Love you, sweetheart."

Suddenly, Sheena was laughing and crying at the same time. She'd been so scared, so down. Now, she couldn't contain the happiness that bubbled out of her.

She turned to her sisters.

Regan and Darcy wrapped their arms around her. They stood, hugging each other, closer than they'd ever been.

The last few months had been one hell of a ride, but Sheena knew it was just the beginning.

Thank you for reading *Finding Me*. If you enjoyed this book, please help other readers discover it by leaving a review on Amazon, Goodreads, or your favorite site. It's such a nice thing to do.

Enjoy an excerpt from my book, *Finding My Way* - A Salty Key Inn Book, Book 2 in the Salty Key Inn series.

CHAPTER ONE
DARCY

Darcy Sullivan crossed the lawn of the Salty Key Inn in Sunset Beach on the west coast of Florida, her thoughts still on the challenge her Uncle Gavin had given her and her two sisters. They'd each been left a one-third share of the hotel—a share that might or might not mean a large amount of money in the future. Right now, it meant nothing but a ton of work and a lot of uncertainty.

Darcy couldn't take her mind off the special message Uncle Gavin had written at the end of his letter to her. *Darcy, you are not who we think you are.*

"What in the hell does that mean?" Darcy mumbled to herself. Uncle Gavin Sullivan, or the Big G, as he sometimes called himself, had been a mystery to her and her sisters. Even though they were related, he hadn't been much of a presence in her life. She had a vague memory of a big man with a big voice, but her father never got along with this brother, and she'd rarely seen Gavin. That's why his crazy scheme for them to renovate the hotel in a year's time in exchange for a lot of money was so weird.

You are not who we think you are. Whoa! She, more than her sisters had her shit together. Didn't she? Her older sister, Sheena, was still making her way through motherhood with a family who'd all but taken away her true identity. And her younger sister, Regan, the family beauty, was learning she was a lot smarter than she'd always thought. As for herself, Darcy intended to see this project through, get the money, and take off for exciting destinations.

Sheena strode across the hotel property toward Darcy with confident steps that swung her auburn hair back and forth above her shoulders. The young mother of two teenagers, she was still an attractive woman...and still the so-called "perfect one" in the family.

"Darcy! You're just the person I want to see!" said Sheena. "I've made an appointment for you to meet with a reporter from the local newspaper. They're going to run a story on the Salty Key Inn and what we're trying to do here. Nick Howard is the reporter's name. I told him you'd call to confirm a meeting as soon as possible."

Darcy rolled her eyes. *What was it about big sisters that made them so damn bossy?*

"Okaaay, I'll do it."

As she said the words, Darcy felt a shiver cross her shoulders like a long-legged spider. Ever since she was a kid, her secret desire was to become either a newspaper reporter or the author of the world's favorite novel. She'd ended up doing computer programming because that's where the money was. But, now, the idea of traveling while writing the perfect novel was pretty compelling.

Darcy eagerly accepted a piece of paper with Nick's name and phone number. Somehow she'd have to put a positive spin on the situation she and her sisters found themselves in. Darcy had thought she'd be rich and sitting on the beach sipping margaritas. What a bad joke!

Inside her office, Darcy punched in the number for the newspaper reporter.

"Hello?" said a deep, rich voice that reminded Darcy of the heavy-set actor whose well-known bass voice made even television commercials seem sexy.

Darcy explained who she was, and they quickly agreed to meet for lunch outside Gracie's at the hotel.

As she hung up the phone, Darcy wondered about the man behind the voice. The dating scene in Florida hadn't worked well for her. She'd made a fool of herself over Brian Harwood, the guy next door, and her one other date had been a flop. If this Nick Howard looked anything like his voice sounded, she was a goner.

For the rest of the morning, the issues of installing a wireless system in the two guest rooms buildings took over Darcy's attention. As tight as their budget was, all three sisters had agreed in today's world, having WiFi was essential. With the help of Chip Carson, a young guy eager to do the work for a reasonable price, they were making good progress.

Just before noon, Darcy left her office in the main hotel and restaurant building fronting the road and hurried across the grounds of the hotel to the suite where she and Regan were temporarily staying. She wanted to freshen up before her luncheon appointment with Nick.

Before she reached the suites building, she stopped and stared at what once had been a small, pink-clapboard house. It was where Uncle Gavin had intended for her to live with her two sisters for an entire year. After a terrible fire, the house was now being torn down. The insurance adjuster had called it a liability. She and her sisters were grateful the cost of rebuilding would not come from their skimpy budget, but from the fire insurance settlement and any extra funds needed from Uncle Gavin's estate. But it did mean a possible loss of revenue. They wouldn't be able to rent out the rooms they were staying in until it was done.

Darcy hurried along to the suites building and into her room.

As Darcy was washing up, she heard Regan enter the suite, and cross the hall into Darcy's bathroom.

Wearing cut-off jeans and an old T-shirt spotted with blue paint, Regan looked as beautiful as ever with her long, dark hair and eyes of violet-blue. Some people said she was a Liz Taylor look-alike.

"Hey! What are you doing? You're all dressed up," said Regan, giving her a good, hard look.

"I'm meeting a reporter for lunch. Sheena made arrangements for me to do an interview for a newspaper article on us and the Salty Key Inn."

Regan smiled. "Nice. A good way for us to get started on our advertising program."

Darcy nodded, but inside she was thinking it might be a good way for her to start being a creative writer not only for the hotel project but for the novel she wanted to write.

After checking herself in the mirror, Darcy ran a hand through her red curls and brushed off an imaginary spot on her simple dark-green sleeveless dress. "Guess I'm as ready as I ever will be." It seemed so easy for her sisters to look put together while she had to really work at it.

Once more, Darcy hurried across the hotel grounds.

A blur of blue feathers headed toward her.

"No, Petey! Go away!" Darcy cried. She pretended to

charge the peacock that ruled the area.

When the big bird realized that Darcy was serious, he strutted away, dragging his tail feathers behind him.

As Darcy approached the restaurant, her steps slowed. Standing outside the entrance was a tall, broad-shouldered, heavy-set man with white hair and a white beard that contrasted with his tanned skin. *Was this Nick Howard?*

Darcy waited for others to show up, and when they didn't, she approached the man.

"Nick?"

He bobbed his head and grinned at her. "Darcy?"

Darcy held out her hand. "For a minute I didn't know whether to call you St. Nick or Ernest Hemingway."

His laughter was hearty, almost a ho-ho-ho as if he practiced it at Christmastime.

Delighted, Darcy chuckled.

Nick ended his handshake and, with twinkling eyes, said, "I like a woman with a good sense of humor. How old are you, Darcy?"

"Twenty-six," she replied, wondering if he was trying to hit on her. The idea both amused and worried her. "Shall we go inside?"

He patted his stomach. "Definitely. I have to confess I've heard of Gracie's. It has a very good reputation in these parts. I sometimes do restaurant reviews for the paper, so let's not tell anyone who I am or why I'm here. Okay?"

"Sure," she said.

They entered Gracie's, the hotel restaurant which was run by Gracie Rogers and the rest of the group everyone called Gavin's people. Gavin had helped eight people from his life—giving them a place to live for free in exchange for what they could do working at the hotel. Darcy and her sisters had continued this arrangement when they inherited them, along with the hotel.

Lynn Michaels waved to her as they entered the restaurant and came right over to them.

"Good afternoon." She led them to a table out on the patio under an umbrella.

Maggie O'Neill hurried over to their table.

"Good afternoon, Darcy." She smiled at Darcy and then turned her attention to Nick.

"Can I get you anything to drink besides water?"

Nick glanced at Darcy. "How's the iced lemonade?"

"Delicious. But I'm having bubbling water. Would you like some of that?"

"Sure," said Nick. He accepted a menu from Maggie and began studying it.

After Maggie left them, Darcy said, "Because we just serve breakfast and lunch, we haven't applied for a wine or beer license. But we may in the future."

Nick nodded. "I see. The menu looks pretty impressive. There are several things I'd love to try." He frowned when his cell phone buzzed, but he lifted it out of his blue-plaid shirt pocket.

Darcy watched him as he studied a message and then typed a rapid reply.

"Sorry about that." Nick gave her a chagrinned look as he slipped the phone back into the shirt pocket. "It was my wife, checking on me to make sure I'm sticking to the diet she put me on."

At the guilty expression that crossed his face, Darcy hid a laugh.

He leaned across the table and whispered, "You won't tell on me if I order something not on her list, will you?"

Darcy's couldn't help laughing now. "No, I promise. You give the restaurant a good rating, and I'll keep your secret."

"Deal," he said, straightening with a smile. "It's hell being married to someone who wants to take care of you all the time. But I love her."

After a few more moments of studying the menu, Nick set it down.

Maggie noticed and hurried over to the table. "Are we ready to order?"

Darcy smiled. "I'll have my usual. Chicken salad."

Nick glanced at Darcy and then smiled up at Maggie. "Thought I'd sample a couple of things. Chicken wings, grouper sandwich, and tomato salad."

Maggie's eyes widened, but she maintained a smile.

After she left, Darcy shook a finger at Nick playfully. "Can't wait to read your review."

They laughed together and then Nick grew serious. "Tell me about the hotel. I see you've put in some work on it already. Some years ago, it was one of the best family places around with its great location and beach access. I understand your uncle left it to you and your sisters."

Darcy nodded and found herself telling Nick about the surprises, the disappointments, and the determination of all the sisters to meet the challenge.

While she was talking, their food came. Between bites, she continued speaking.

Nick listened intently, even when smacking his lips with pleasure over the food.

Darcy suddenly realized how long she'd been talking and stopped. She felt her cheeks grow hot. "I didn't mean to rattle on and on."

Nick studied her. "Have you ever thought of writing? You have such a natural way of telling a story."

Darcy blinked in surprise. "Actually, I have. As a kid, I wanted to be a newspaper reporter, and then later I thought

I'd like to try my hand at writing a novel. But, so far, I haven't had the time to do either."

Nick leaned forward. "How would you like to be the restaurant reviewer for the *West Coast News*? I'd help you, of course, but it would get my wife off my back."

Darcy laughed and sat back in her chair to study him. "You're serious?"

He nodded. "And who knows? Maybe later, you could work your way into a weekly column of some kind. I like you, Darcy. We could use someone like you at the paper."

A rush of excitement filled Darcy. She could see herself on a tropical island, swinging back and forth in a hammock, plotting out her prizewinning novel.

"Okay, I'll do it." As she spoke, she recalled the creepy feeling she'd had saying those very words earlier. Maybe this was all part of a bigger plan, she thought, suddenly nervous.

"All right," said Nick. "What would you say about your meal?"

Darcy took a deep breath, conjuring up the best words she could use. "My chicken salad was tasty, with exotic additions of melon and ginger, topped with crisply browned almond slices, and flavored with a lemony dressing."

Nick grinned. "I knew it." He reached across the table and offered his hand. "You're hired."

She accepted his hand and gave it a firm shake. "I'll take the job. How much do I get paid?"

He laughed. "In addition to free food?"

"Oh, I get it," said Darcy. "Even so, I'll do it. But, Nick, I want that newspaper column."

"Good. We'll talk about that in a couple of months." He smiled. "Now, let's order dessert. The food here is dynamite."

As she waited for Nick to finish tasting the Key Lime Pie and the Orange Chocolate Cake, Darcy studied him. He seemed to be such a happy, pleasant guy. Maybe, she thought, that's what I've been missing. Her recent dates had seemed so uptight. Sheena had told her to relax, that she'd find someone someday. Maybe with her new part-time position at the paper, she'd stop worrying about the future and take each day as it came—with or without a boyfriend.

After paying for the meal, Nick smiled at her. "Ready to give me a tour of the property?"

"Yes, but only if you understand we're still very much in the renovation process. If things go well with it, then after the first of the year, we'll be adding a lot more upgrades to the rooms and other facilities."

"Gotcha. Let's do it." Nick stood and helped her out of her chair.

As Darcy showed Nick the property, including the dock area and the pool, she described plans for how they intended to add to them. And when she took him inside the Egret guest rooms building to where a bedroom was being completed, a real sense of pride filled her. The painted furniture, sitting atop a sand-colored commercial rug, looked wonderful. Shabby chic is how Regan described the stressed finish of the wooden pieces.

"Very nice job," said Nick to Regan, after Darcy made the introductions. "You have a real good eye for this."

Darcy smiled at the happy expression that crossed Regan's face. Of them all, Regan was the one who was happiest about their effort to meet Uncle Gavin's challenge. She was already a much different person, with a lot more self-confidence.

They left the building and headed toward the parking lot by Gracie's.

Sheena emerged from the restaurant, saw them, and

waved. Crossing the lawn toward them, Darcy studied her sister. Sheena had fought her family to participate in this challenge of Gavin's. Darcy was glad she had. Smart and willing to work the numbers, Sheena was a great asset, even if she was a bit bossy.

"Nice to meet you, Nick," Sheena was saying. "I hope you give us a lot of good publicity."

Nick grinned. "Believe me, I will. And I'm giving Gracie's a five-star rating for the best place around for lunch." He clapped a hand on Darcy's back. "And Dee Summers, here, is going to help me do restaurant reviews."

Sheena and Darcy exchanged questioning looks.

"Dee Summers?" said Darcy.

Nick let out a belly laugh. "That's going to be your name at the paper. You can't do reviews under your own name. And I have a special column idea in mind."

"What are you talking about?" asked Sheena.

"Like Nick says, I'm going to be helping him with some restaurant reviews. And then, I might get my own weekly newspaper column." Darcy couldn't hide the wonder in her voice. It was a dream come true. Well, maybe not the one she wanted, but it was a beginning.

Sheena gave her a thoughtful nod. "Good for you, Darcy."

After she walked away, Darcy looked over at Nick. "I think I will call you St. Nick. I feel as if I've just opened a Christmas package."

He grinned. "Okay, Dee. See you around."

\# \# \#

About the Author

Judith Keim enjoyed her childhood and young-adult years in Elmira, New York, and now makes her home in Boise, Idaho, with her husband and their two dachshunds, Winston and Wally, and other members of her family.

While growing up, she was drawn to the idea of writing stories from a young age. Books were always present, being read, ready to go back to the library, or about to be discovered. All in her family shared information from the books in general conversation, giving them a wealth of knowledge and vivid imaginations.

A hybrid author who both has a publisher and self-publishes, Ms. Keim writes heart-warming novels about women who face unexpected challenges, meet them with strength, and find love and happiness along the way. Her best-selling books are based, in part, on many of the places she's lived or visited and on the interesting people she's met, creating believable characters and realistic settings her many loyal readers love. Ms. Keim loves to hear from her readers and appreciates their enthusiasm for her stories.

"I hope you've enjoyed this book. If you have, please help other readers discover it by leaving a review on Amazon,

Goodreads, or the site of your choice. And please check out my other books:

The Hartwell Women Series
The Beach House Hotel Series
The Fat Fridays Group
The Salty Key Inn Series
Seashell Cottage Books
Chandler Hill Inn Series
Desert Sage Inn Series

ALL THE BOOKS ARE NOW AVAILABLE IN AUDIO on Audible and iTunes! So fun to have these characters come alive!"

Ms. Keim can be reached at **www.judithkeim.com**

And to like her author page on Facebook and keep up with the news, go to: **https://bit.ly/3acs5Qc**

To receive notices about new books, follow her on Book Bub - **http://bit.ly/2pZBDXq**

And here's a link to where you can sign up for her periodic newsletter! **http://bit.ly/2OQsb7s**

She is also on Twitter @judithkeim, LinkedIn, and Goodreads. Come say hello!

Acknowledgements

I wish to thank Lynn Mapp for her wise input on plotting. As always, I thank my husband, Peter, for his editorial assistance and knowledge of the hotel business. His willingness to answer big questions and little as I'm typing away is invaluable in making the story and situation real. Also, thanks to those in the RWA chapter here in Boise for their support. No one can understand the ups and downs of the writing world like other writers.

Made in United States
North Haven, CT
01 October 2022